Praise for Derek Raymond's
Factory Series

"No one claiming interest in literature truly written from the edge of human experience, no one wondering at the limits of the crime novel and of literature itself, can overlook these extraordinary books."
—**JAMES SALLIS**

"A pioneer of British noir ... No one has come near to matching his style or overwhelming sense of madness... he does not strive for accuracy, but achieves an emotional truth all his own."
—*THE TIMES* (LONDON)

"The beautiful, ruthless simplicity of the Factory novels is that Raymond rewrites the basic ethos of the classic detective novel."
—**CHARLES TAYLOR,** *THE NATION*

"A sulphurous mixture of ferocious violence and high-flown philosophy."
—*PROSPECT*

"A mixture of thin-lipped Chandleresque backchat and of idioms more icily subversive."
—*OBSERVER*

"Hellishly bleak and moving."
—*NEW STATESMAN*

"He writes beautifully, and his sincerity cannot be faulted."
—*EVENING STANDARD*

"Raw-edged, strong and disturbing stuff."
—*THE SCOTSMAN*

D1250361

DEREK RAYMOND was the pseudonym of British writer Robert "Robin" Cook, who was born in London in 1931. The son of a textile magnate, he dropped out of Eton and rejected a life of privilege for a life of adventure. He traveled the world, living in Paris at the Beat Hotel and on New York's seedy Lower East Side, smuggled artworks into Amsterdam, and spent time in a Spanish prison for publicly making fun of Franco. Finally, he landed back in London, working in the lower echelons of the Kray Brothers' crime syndicate laundering money, organizing illegal gambling, and setting up insurance scams. He eventually took to writing—first as a pornographer, but then as an increasingly serious novelist, writing about the desperate characters and experiences he'd known in London's underground. His work culminated in the Factory novels, landmarks that have led many to consider him the founding father of British noir. He died in London in 1993.

The Devil's Home on Leave

Derek Raymond

MELVILLEHOUSE
BROOKLYN, NEW YORK

MELVILLE
INTERNATIONAL
CRIME

For Peter and Honor Mochan

The Devil's Home on Leave

First published in 1985 in Great Britain by Secker & Warburg

© 1984 Estate of Robin William Arthur Cook

This edition published by arrangement with Serpent's Tail

First Melville House printing: September 2011

Melville House Publishing

145 Plymouth Street

Brooklyn, NY 11201

www.mhpbooks.com

ISBN: 978-1-935554-58-5

Printed in the United States of America

1 2 3 4 5 6 7 8 9 10

Library of Congress Control Number: 2011932388

'Les mois d'avril sont meurtriers.'

1

I knocked at a second-floor flat in a dreary house, one of two hundred in a dreary Catford street.

After a while I heard steps the other side of the door. 'McGruder?'

'Who's that?' said a man's voice. 'Who wants him?'

'I do,' I said. 'Open up. Police.'

2

Later, I knew the following. At half past seven on the cold, sunny evening of Wednesday, April 13th, Billy McGruder went up to a passer-by in Hammersmith.

'Excuse me, mate. You know a pub called the Nine Foot Drop?'

'The Drop? Sure. You cross over the Broadway here, go up King Street, turn out of Ravenscourt Road into Tofton Avenue and it's on the right. Ten-minute walk. You can't miss it – great barracks of a place.'

'Thanks.'

When McGruder got in there everything had gone fine – sweet as a nut. The solid man in his blue blazer was there all right, scanning newcomers through a mirror that covered the entrance. His back turned to Billy, he shifted on his stool at the bar to show that he had seen him and Billy, standing next to him for a moment to order, got a sweet cider and carried it over to the table that had been agreed on. Once Billy was settled, the man in the blazer – villain's scar across his left ear – nodded across the bar at a man sitting alone at a table under a window with a raincoat over his shoulders.

This man was ageless and thin, with the bright, uneasy face of a stoat. His pale eyes blinked under colourless lashes, never still in his head which jerked on its thin neck, the prominent Adam's apple throbbing nervously up at his chin. At times the man's shoulders twitched under the mac with the quick gestures of a bird undecided whether to stay or fly with the fine-honed instinct of the weak, forever attuned to danger. He looked smart in a way to suit his thinness; he wore high, expensive boots, brown and polished bright – ninety quid's worth easy – and a corduroy cap, clipper style, at an angle half to the back, half to the side of his head, favouring his lifeless, gingery hair. A third of a pint of beer stood in front of him, a mess of foam trailing down the inside of the glass. Billy pushed his cider away; he hardly ever drank. He lit a cigarette, drew on it three times and put it out. He didn't smoke; it was just the sign that he had understood all right who the target was.

Billy was very careful to be precise about the agreed signs. There was money in this job, fifteen hundred pounds; so naturally he didn't want to make a mess of it.

He didn't look near the target again. He knew who it was now, and that was enough. Indeed, Billy seldom looked directly at anyone; when he did, it meant that it was already too late for the person.

After a little while, the stout young man got up to go. In doing so, he left two keys on a ring behind him on the bar.

'Night, Tony.'

'*Night*, squire! *Night*, Merrill!'

If Tony Williams, the governor, who was standing behind his bar looking benevolent and polishing a glass, noticed that the keys had been left there he gave no sign of it – and when Billy, getting up to go to the gents, swept them casually into his pocket as he went by, the governor happened to have his back turned. No one else at the bar remarked on the incident, even if they noticed it. It didn't pay to notice things in the Nine Foot Drop.

When Billy got to the gents, pungent with the smell of disinfectant, he went on past the splashback into the single cubicle and locked the door. He took the keys out of one pocket, a pair of thin gloves out of another, and put the gloves on. He rubbed the keys thoroughly and looked at the paper tag attached to the ring. He memorized the car registration number, tore the tag off, shredded it, dropped the pieces into the bowl and pulled the chain. He didn't bother checking his other gear. He'd done all that before leaving for this rendezvous; he had everything he needed with him in a briefcase which he never lost sight of. He had it with him now.

He went back to the bar, strolled to a window, and looked out to check that the car whose plates corresponded to the number he had memorized was parked outside. In the bar everything was as it had been, except that someone else had taken the solid man's place at the Kronenbourg pump. The target was still sitting at his table all right, Billy saw, and that was going to be just too bad for the target. Women in the place looked at Billy admiringly, taking him for the spruce young businessman with the executive briefcase that he appeared to be. They couldn't know that within less than an hour he would be stripped naked, carefully removing and preparing everything that he had in his case. They couldn't know what he had in it.

Billy wondered if after all his man was waiting for somebody real; it could complicate matters if he were. Billy had been told definitely that he wouldn't be — that a moody meet had been arranged for the target where the other man wouldn't show. But you never knew. Using the mirrors, therefore, Billy watched while the target picked up his glass and turned it, as if undecided whether to have another. He went on watching until the target made up its mind, drained the glass suddenly and stood up.

3

Someone once asked me why I ever became a copper, never mind why I stayed on for fifteen years. I told him about the woman I found one night on the M1. It was early days. I was just a uniformed constable then, working out of Watford on patrol car duty. My place was next to the driver; the CID man was in the back. It was dreadful weather in late autumn. The rain was pissing down on a north wind, and we were cruising up to the Bedford turn-off, the end of our stretch, well below the legal limit because the motorway was flooded in places.

Then I saw what looked like a bundle of rags over on the hard shoulder. 'Jam them on,' I said to the driver. 'Go on, hard.'

I realized it was a woman as we pulled over and stopped. I checked the time – it was midnight – got out into the rain and was immediately soaked. I knelt down by her and got my torch out of my back pocket; she looked about sixty. Her brown coat was sodden with rain and she was bleeding heavily from her stomach, though the blood was constantly being washed away by the rain. Her face was grey, and her legs and arms were sprawled out as she had fallen.

The detective rolled down his window and shouted: 'What is it?'

'It's a body, you fool,' I said. 'Get the surgeon on the radio, an ambulance. Do it fast.'

'Who're you giving orders to?' he yelled furiously. 'You want to get your knees brown, son!'

I ignored him. Soon the driver joined me, the rain pelting on his cap, and he bent over her too. He listened to her heart for a minute, took her pulse and stood up. 'I don't think she'll be needing the ambulance,' he said, rubbing his clean-shaven jaw in a judicious way.

'Well, she won't if it doesn't hurry,' I said.

He looked at me. 'You want to watch your tone.'

I said: 'Just get that ambulance up here.'

He was glad enough to get back to the car and inside out of the rain with the plainclothes man; that showed. I watched them fiddling with the radio in the lit interior of the car until I got fed up and went over. 'Well?'

'They're trying to get the doctor,' said the CID man, 'but he's busy giving some drunk an alcohol test.' He added, looking at her from the car window: 'Thrown out of a motor, was she?'

'Well, what do you think?'

'What I think is, we'll never find out who did it,' he said. Passing traffic drowned out some of what he said. Standing in the rain I shouted: 'I want to try and save her life!' I went back to her. She was still alive, just. I turned her until she was face up to me, then put my arms under her broken shoulders. Her face was streaked with mud. There was gravel in her grey hair and a raw wound in her scalp where her head had smashed down on the tarmac when she was thrown out of the car.

She looked at me blindly out of half-closed eyes. 'Katie?' she whispered. 'Katie, is that you, dear?' She gazed past me, her eyes darkening, her life slipping apologetically away past me out of the torchlight − out into the perimeter of endless rain beyond the squad car's headlights. I took each of her arms gently in my fingers and they stirred; but when I did the same to her legs nothing happened at all. I told the others in the car this and went back to her. Presently the CID man shouted: 'Doctor reckons her back's broken, and the ambulance'll be about half an hour!'

'But that's too long!' I yelled back. 'Too fucking long! Tell them it's got to come quicker than that − it's got to!'

'They say they're short of crews!'

'They'll be short of another crew when I've done with them!'

I shouted. A forty-ton truck thrashed past us northwards and drowned out my words. Now the rain came down on us in white towers, great lances of water, hissing through hair, up sleeves, soaking everyone, flooding everything. I was crying with frustration as I knelt over her, but the rain skimmed the tears off my face. We waited and waited, well past the half hour, and no ambulance came. We had the first-aid kit in the car but were afraid to use it; she was so badly injured that we didn't know where to start. We had her covered up as best we could with whatever we could find; she died in my arms, and just before she went, which she did suddenly, one hand crept up and she died feeling at the buttons on my tunic and asking in a whisper for Katie. That was her daughter, we found out later, who lived in Wales. Meanwhile the night trucks pounded away towards Newcastle in great showers and sheets of rain, shrouding all of us.

Of course she had been murdered. She was a Mrs Mayhew, sixty-two, a widow living on her pension at Dungeness Road, Watford, out by the entrance to the M1. When we got to her house it had been ransacked; the robbers might have got seventy quid's worth of gear, plus maybe a tenner that the neighbours said she kept by her for shopping. What these maniacs couldn't take they had smashed; they had also shat on her living room floor. Outside you could see where she had been dragged through the mud and into their car, to be hurled out of it as it bombed away north.

Nobody was ever caught for her, and Mrs Mayhew made four lines in the *Watford Observer*.

But that's why, when they started Unexplained Deaths, or A14, I was one of the first to join; and that's why I stayed on as a copper, just when I was thinking it was a dog's life and had considered jacking it in.

Mrs Mayhew, I saw on her papers, had a pretty Christian name. I remember it:

Jonquil.

4

I work on the second floor of the Factory when I'm in. Everything has to have an official name in the police, and my room is Room 205. The listed name of the Factory is Poland Street police station, London W1, but it'll never shake off the name of the Factory. The name sticks to the men and women who work there, also to the people who get worked over there, downstairs. I don't go in to the Factory much. If you're with A14 you work your cases on your own. We're too undermanned to do otherwise, and we work only on cases where the victims have been written off upstairs as unimportant, not pressworthy, not well connected and not big crime. I don't do much interviewing in 205. I do all that in my own way, catching the man I want to see on his manor – as often as not at his own place; if not, it might be in his local boozer or else through a grass. Most of the work we get is passed to us from Serious Crimes at the Yard, and the man I generally find myself dealing with there is Charlie Bowman, a cheeky chief inspector of thirty-three with not much on top of his head nor a lot inside it in my opinion, apart from ruthlessness, ambition and drive. To me, Bowman's the other kind of copper, and he's only just got back to work again after a rest. The story officially is that he had an ulcer; the unofficial story is that his wife freaked him out with the habit she had of pushing all four buttons on his quartz watch – which he never took off for the occasion – each time he was coming up to orgasm, making it bleep. I don't believe either version. I think Charlie's real problem is that he never gets that step up to detective-superintendent that he expects each time the promotions come through.

I'd also better mention that I'm just a detective-sergeant and certain to remain one. I reckon I'm a sergeant only because I could hardly have managed otherwise, but they could have left me a constable for all I cared. Bowman doesn't like that. It makes him uneasy that he's nearly ten years younger than I am, and so much higher in rank. He's rightly got the impression that I don't care about rank, and that irks him. We quarrel when we meet, which luckily isn't that often. He enjoys reminding me: 'The one sure way of denying yourself promotion, sergeant – and you're getting no younger – is your bloody insolence.'

But I'm not insolent, I'm just impatient. My trouble is, I can't stand fools. Justice is what I bother about – not rank. I watch men like Charlie Bowman operating and I think Christ, does anyone really expect to get justice that way?

I admit that with my attitude, it really is a good thing I'm just a sergeant. It certainly suits me being low down the ladder, and it's a relief not being interested in promotion – that way I can stay on in A14 which is the lowest budgeted department in the police service, and what I like best about my work is that I can get on with it, as a rule, almost entirely on my own, without a load of keen idiots tripping all over my feet. Yes, I'm happy to work at Unexplained Deaths, though naturally I go through the motions of complaining about it just like everyone else.

5

On the morning of April 14th I was in Room 205 finishing my report on a suicide when Bowman came in. Except that I had a personal problem that I wanted to think about, I was not as sorry to see him as I usually am. I was bored with the report; they're really just bureaucracy for the file. Any clerk could write them himself from my notes, and a computer in turn could do away with the clerk. But if you work for the State, you've always got to make room for the clerks. I also, as I often did in the morning, hated my room with its sickly green paint, its radiator that only worked full blast or not at all, its old police posters that no one renewed, and the plastic tulips I had bought now that Brenda, the WPC who used to bring me real ones sometimes and give me a look or two, had gone off and got married.

I had a paper with me and was looking at the lead story which was to do with the defence minister (yet again) when Bowman arrived. He belched, parked his big behind on the edge of my desk, spread his fat thighs apart and farted.

'Well, I've got one for you.' He snorted into a paper handkerchief and wiped his nose.

'Where?'

'Over at Rotherhithe; he's stapled up in five Waitrose plastic bags. You can come down with me right now. I'm pushed for time, but I've just got enough to give you a lift and I've got a car waiting.'

'Who was he?'

'Nobody knows. Usual A14 stuff. All we know is, he was murdered.'

'That's deduction for you.'

'Now don't ride me,' said Bowman. 'Not today.' He added: 'Nor any day.' He blew his nose again; the noise rocketed off the concrete walls.

'You have a look at his jaws?' I said. 'His teeth?'

'Couldn't. The killer knocked them out and threw them away. Now then, don't fuck me about, sergeant, I've got a big bank job on. It'll be in all the linens.'

'Your cases always are.'

'Look,' said Bowman, 'just pick up your bra and brolly and let's get over there.'

'Your temper's improving to the point of no return,' I said, standing up. 'You undone any of these bags yourself?'

'Two,' he said. He added sarcastically: 'To see what was in them, you know.'

'And what did you find first?'

'His head. I told you his teeth were missing.'

We went out through the main door of the Factory and got into the car. As we drove fast down Gower Street Bowman remarked: 'Yes, this is a tasty one.'

It wasn't raining for once; there was some weak sunshine about, although cloud the colour of a bank manager's suit was scudding over Waterloo Bridge.

Bowman said: 'The forensic mob have been over and looked at it and put everything back again for you to see. But they reckon it's going to take the lab a while to get any real report out on it. All they can say right now is that it was a male, white, probably in his late forties.'

'Why couldn't they tell more than that?' I said. 'Like how he was killed, for instance?'

'The killer didn't seem to want to make things easy,' said Bowman.

'But the head, the trunk.'

'It was all boiled,' said Bowman, 'and let's go easy talking about it, shall we, especially in a moving car, it makes me want to throw up, and I've seen most things. That's why there are no prints, the skin has been boiled off his fingers – he's been altogether boiled, cooked up, see?'

'No traces of blood around? Nothing spilled at all?'

'No. What I think is, there was more than one individual involved, and that they killed him, bled him into something, boiled the blood away with the rest, butchered him and cooked him.'

'No clothing? No object the victim had dropped? Nothing?'

'Well, they didn't find anything,' said Bowman. 'And of course no clothing. They must have stripped him, bundled his clothes up and destroyed all that later.' He added: 'They're fucking cannibals, these people, the sick bastards.'

'Methodical, though,' I said. 'Professional.'

'Well, I agree it isn't the work of a nut,' said Bowman, 'at least, not in the ordinary sense. Too neat, too careful – yes, OK, professional. Just the five bags of gear, grey, pinkish a little here and there.' He thought for a moment and added: 'You know, like pig's trotters. Or veal.'

'Smelling?'

'No, not yet. Good point,' he added grudgingly, 'especially stapled up in plastic like that, you'd have thought it would've. Also, there was still a faint smell of cooking. So that's why they think he was done in the warehouse, and in the last twelve to eighteen hours.'

'Yes,' I said, 'particularly since the weather's warm.' I thought for a minute. 'Well, I don't know, early to say. But Rotherhithe, the professionalism, etcetera – it sounds like good old gangland again to me. Who reported it?'

'The caretaker. He's waiting for you. He found the bags when he was doing his rounds and prodded one. He didn't kind of like the look of them somehow, so he called us in.'

'That was discerning of him,' I said. 'Plenty of people these days would have just dumped them out with the garbage without even looking inside.'

'That's what the killer ought to have done, I reckon,' said Bowman. 'Why he left them sitting up there in an orderly row like that I do not know.'

'Maybe whoever it was didn't want to take the risk of carrying them out in case there was a stray squad car about and anyway, they probably thought they wouldn't be found for weeks.' I added: 'Oh, so the bags were in an orderly row, were they?'

'What are you on about?'

'Nothing,' I said. 'Anyway, it's a good thing the bags were left. If none of these people ever made mistakes our solution rate would look even worse than it does.'

'Speak for yourself,' said Bowman. We were stopped in heavy traffic. Bowman sat forward and said to the driver: 'Don't just sit in this like a berk, constable. Get your arse in first gear and put your siren on, that's what the fucking thing's for.' The driver obeyed, his ears and the back of his neck turning a dull red.

'When I think of the booming recruiting figures for the Met,' I said, 'I think of people like you, and how you deserve a medal for them.'

'Now look,' said Bowman furiously, 'you may never rise above the rank of sergeant at A14, but you could always go back down to constable; I could fix it easy. I could put you back on the beat – how about Brixton?'

'I might see you there if you don't get your brains in straight from time to time,' I said. 'I know a cafe in Brixton Road where they do a plain copper a really nice egg and chips and a good pot of tea for a quid.'

'Don't take the piss,' Bowman shouted, 'they're waiting for me over at that bank. If I'm late I'll get a roasting from the Commissioner.' He blew out through his lips with exasperation, looked at his watch and rubbed his fingers down his face. 'I've got something else on besides this bank business.'

'Yes, the bank sounds more like the Fraud Squad to me.'

'Yes,' said Bowman, 'but Alfie Verlander over there can't crack the man and that's why he sent for me; Alfie and I are old mates.'

I knew that, and a sinister pair they made, too, playing snooker together on Saturday nights. 'What's this other thing?' I said.

'You been reading about the Russians lately?'

'I'm always reading about the Russians,' I said, 'but I'm too busy ever to bother with them; I leave all that to the Branch.'

'I can't tell you everything,' said Bowman, 'except that this one really is dodgy.'

'You'll be telling me next that it's to do with this commotion I read about over at the ministry of defence.'

Bowman turned and poked me in the chest with a stubby finger. 'You forget I spoke to you, sergeant, do you understand?'

'Yes, I understand,' I said, 'I understand I'm just to let you know if I hear anything.'

'You just might,' he said. 'Meantime, get on with your plastic bags.' He added: 'Christ, what a bleeding miracle; we're here.'

6

Where I go, the ghosts go. I go where the evil is. I was walking across the street with Bowman. Six months ago I had my worst case to date. Serious Crimes was over-extended and I was helping Bowman out. I had to arrest Fred Paolacci in his council flat in Hanwell, dressed up in the blood of three women. First he had gone round to the next housing estate to see to his ex-wife because she wouldn't let him screw her; he ripped her up the stomach with a butcher's knife and stuck his cock in her entrails. Next he went round to his new bird, a black prostitute who wouldn't marry him, and saw to her the same way. Then he went back to his wife's place with the knife and waited until his ten-year-old daughter came in from school.

'I don't want you to see your mother the way she is just now,' he explained to her as the child ran up the stairs with her satchel on her shoulder and calling to her mother – he made the point to me later how happy she looked, running up the stairs. Well, they went into the flat together, and then the kid got a look at her mother, one leg in a boot sticking out through the bedroom doorway and blood everywhere. The child started to scream, and when he couldn't stop her he opened her up ('but only a little way, not like the others') and raped her.

'I really came that time,' he said, 'the others was really just like wanking.' He admitted everything, except raping his daughter, straight away. But after I had patiently proved it to him, the traces of his semen that had been found in the child's body and the rest of it, he dropped the eager, honour-bright way he had been staring into my face while he answered my questions; his face went dark and he nodded and looked away and said: 'Oh well, that's it, then.

Yes, I feel easier admitting it, really – it was out of order, that was.'
He added accurately: 'Bloody women.'

I got hold of a man who had seen him walking in the street out
there that evening, covered in blood. His conversation with Fred
was casual:

'Hurt yourself, Fred?'

'That's right,' he said, 'cut myself on a fucking knife, just going
down to the doctor's.'

'OK, well, see you over at the Cricketers later for a pint.'

The fact that Paolacci could coldly lie about what he had done
made him fit to plead. My witness had never thought to come
forward with what he had seen; I had to find him. 'Well, I thought
that was the end of it,' he said indignantly, 'once you'd got him.
Lord, do I have to go to court? The wife and I are booked on this
package holiday to Mallorca.'

Some people.

Attractive-looking bloke, Fred. Dark-haired, regular features,
neat dresser. Italian father, British mother, thirty-eight, worked on
the assembly line at Ford's. None of his mates on the shop floor
had a word to say against him.

'Fred Paolacci? Lovely feller! Buy you a pint any day, lend you
a few bob if you was short till the end of the week – I can't believe
it. You sure you haven't got the wrong man?'

The wrong man! I see him now as I saw him the day we were
in the police van on our way to court, biting his nails to hide a sly
dark smile, his eyes far off and vicious. On the way he asked me if
I thought he would ever be forgiven.

'Only by Lord Longford,' I said. I added: 'What do you mean by
forgiveness, anyway? Where did you get a word like that, Fred?'

He thought about it. 'I don't rightly know,' he said in the end.
'Can't remember.' Must've read it in the *Mirror*.' As we took him
away he looked back into his flat, leaning away from the cuffs and
said: 'One last look at my tools. The tools of a man who's finished
die with him. You can always tell a man who's finished by looking

at his spanners; spanners know when a man's not coming back.'

All the police do is remove the bodies from a scene; it isn't our job to clean up. That's down to the council or the incoming tenant; we're too busy.

Anyway, nobody did clean up; that was why, when two squatters, a girl and a feller, broke into the flat, the girl had a heart attack.

'Teach the bastards to respect council property,' Bowman said when I told him about it.

7

But I could really have done without the plastic bags just then. As I mentioned, I was distracted by a matter in my personal life, and I wanted time to reflect on it. The day before I had been to see my ex-wife at the place she has lived in for a long time now, and always will live. Going down there in the car I found myself, I don't know why, remembering how, while we were courting, we went down to Petticoat Lane market one Sunday, and bought a decorated plate there.

Edie always had to masturbate before she could make love. She used to do it in the bed, on her knees, her thighs straddled across my face while I watched her fingers racing away in the blonde fur of her vagina with patient, concentrated fury. Her eyes were far away, and she kept her lower lip trapped in her teeth so hard that, at her climax, she sometimes bit it till it bled. It turned me on hard. Yet I married the wrong woman. The woman I should have married went off with another man, who beat her up. I always knew there was something wrong with Edie really; but what got me about her was, she had the most beautiful breasts I have ever seen – calm, swollen and white, the nipples a dark red and stiff as castles.

The place wasn't guarded, not even by walls. It was for people who didn't know any more where places meant, outside their minds, or how to get there; inside their minds it was always hell. I drove through the gates and across broad iron grids like the ones farmers and rich country people put down to keep their cattle in, went through a park and drove up to a big, old building in brick the colour of a burned-out fire. There was a half-tended lawn in front, and you wouldn't believe you were only twelve miles from

Hyde Park Corner. Birds sang in the beech and plane trees, the boughs tumbled in the wind just as if they surrounded an ordinary house; I could even hear a transistor going somewhere. On the lawn, old nurses who ought to have retired years ago walked about in their white caps and blue and scarlet cloaks because the breeze was cold, looking after their charges who hopped, skipped, screamed, ran or strolled under the yews and oaks making compulsive or vague gestures, looking down at the ground.

I found Edie in the day room; it was dirty in there and the place smelled funny – well, it smelled of shit. When I came in and said hello, Edie, she snatched her hands out of the pockets of her tear-proof dress, looked at them and shouted at her hands: 'Why are all the Royal Family in my garden? I thought I'd killed the whole lot of them with these!'

'She's been very aggressive all day,' said the male nurse in charge, a new young one I didn't know.

'She senses when I'm coming somehow,' I said, 'and it makes her like that.' I noticed how grey her hair was turning, though she was only thirty-six. It was matted and dirty as well, and I saw how she was reducing to skin and bone because they couldn't get her to eat – not that that surprised me, the crap they gave them. As usual she was far too intense, racing along the tracks of her fantasies. She looked straight through us; human beings, to her, were as flat as the court cards in the pack she had let fall on the floor.

'Yes, what are these kings doing here?' she shouted. 'How dare they be in my garden? Look at Lord Wentworth there! Bold as brass, if you please!'

I followed her gaze to an old man sitting on a bench outside the barred window. He was playing with his healthy, fresh pink cock and shouting grimly: 'Tuppenny nuts! Tuppenny nuts!' His face wore an expression that was tearing him to pieces.

'Valuing the last of his spoons, I see,' said Edie. 'He won't last long.'

The male nurse turned to me and said: 'She should have been

sedated at three, but I didn't want to put her down until after you'd
been.'

'Yes,' I said, 'thanks.'

'I think she's better off when she's catatonic,' said the nurse, 'she
seems to suffer less then, though how can you really tell?' He
walked away to deal with a male patient who was pissing against a
wall on the far side of the room. Others sitting on wooden chairs
sang, knitted their fingers together or sat stonily wrapped up in
their world; some wept, some prayed, at grips with their terror,
rocking to and fro.

Edie's hands shot out and wrenched at my coat pocket. 'Give me
a cigarette!' she screamed. 'Go on, give me one, or else I'll set the
whole fucking palace alight!'

I stepped out of her way and said to distract her: 'What colour
are those spoons they have, Edie?'

'Electro-plate,' she said instantly, without looking at me. 'No,
that's wrong – they're base metal, repainted to look like gold; these
people are so pretentious! Wentworth?' Her raucous voice rose. 'It's
not even an old title. Mind,' she added, 'I fancy him, the lucky
bastard.'

I noticed how bad her language had got; Edie used hardly ever
to swear. I watched the terrible violence rising in her. In its way it
was worse than the kind I spend my time dealing with; I felt
horror, watching a human being I had known so intimately out of
control, no longer human and racking herself to pieces. Oh God,
why don't they stop it, I thought, stop it? Why don't they give her
the last quarter twist and let her leave?

'What else do you see, Edie?' I said.

'Further down the rose garden, there's that greedy old Queen
Mary talking to George the Third.' She peered out of the barred
window, her yellow face seamed with rage. 'They're talking about
money,' she snapped. 'They're related, of course, but only on the
distaff side and that doesn't count with royals, Mother says.'

Oh, didn't I remember how middle-class Edie had been – the

hiccough politely hidden behind the hand after a thin lunch, the distasteful use of the word toilet, the sitting room at Blackheath, the best china picked up as seconds in an Oxford Street sale. How, when we first met, she used to remove my hand from under her unfashionable skirt with surprising strength so as to plunge into labyrinths of meaningless genealogy, until it turned out that she was related through her mother to King Clovis of France.

But her father was a tradesman in the fruit business, and cruel to his children; he and I never got on. 'Edie marrying a copper,' I heard him say to his wife on the eve of our marriage, 'what's the future for our girl in that?'

Edie had lost her thread. 'The writing on the wall,' she was muttering. 'King, king, king, king. The writing, the writing on the wall, the one with the – with the urine on it. There!' she giggled bitterly. 'I've said it, haven't I?'

'I've brought you these,' I said. I had packed up some biscuits and toffees in a parcel. She used to like things like that; yes, in the old days, Edie had a sweet tooth.

She took the parcel without looking at me and let it fall on the floor.

'Oh, come,' said the nurse, 'now that's a pity, Edie.'

'Don't patronize me,' she sneered, looking past us.

'I've never seen her so not on my wavelength,' I said. 'She's worse.'

'Worse?' he said with bright guilt. 'What, Edie? Why, she's fine; she's got a long, long way to go yet!' It was what he had to say.

'I know,' I said, 'but don't come the acid with me, friend.'

Edie's brow creased with fury, her look much farther off than the cement corner with the puddle of piss in it that she was gazing into. 'Why don't they show her the kind door?' I said to the nurse. 'Why imprison her?'

'You should know,' said the male nurse tartly, 'you're in the business yourself.'

'You knew I was a copper?'

'She keeps saying so.'

'How do you stand this, day after day?'

'The way you stand your job.'

'These vulgar Hanoverians,' said Edie. 'They call themselves Windsor these days, but that's a blag; they're all Germans. What I don't understand is, why they all join the navy. Why the navy? Why not the NAAFI?' She burst out laughing and added triumphantly: 'Anyway, I don't fucking care. I'm a baroness in my own right. Plantagenet.'

A haggard man who had wet the pants of his old suit started chasing an elderly visitor, who came out of charity and whom I had seen on other visits, for his cigarettes. They ran up and down the yard several times; at last the patient got the visitor cornered. They stood glaring at each other, the visitor out of fright.

'Help!' shouted the visitor in a high, feeble voice. 'Help!'

'It's funny how they can always tell when you're patronizing them,' muttered the nurse. 'I warned Mr Hodgkin last time not to come in here again. Wait a minute, I'll just see to it.' He went off down the day room, his nylon jacket rustling.

'I don't care how many affairs they have,' said Edie viciously. 'These German kings, they breed like rabbits. They're outsiders! Rabbits!' She started to scream, dribbling down her rubber bib.

The male nurse, who had ushered the visitor out, heard the noise and rejoined me, shaking his head. He ignored Edie. 'They're all disturbed on this wing,' he said. 'You just can't condescend the way Mr Hodgkin does. They spot it every time.' Edie had her back turned to us again. Suddenly she farted. '*Fuck!*' she said. She added, tight-lipped: 'There! That wasn't a ladylike thing to do.'

I said to myself – wait for me in hell, I'll come to you.

Edie shouted: 'The next time I do that I'm going to explode! Do you hear me? Explode! When I get where I'm going I'll take you all with me – every copper in the world! There'll be millions of us, with bombs and candles! We'll go downstairs into the dark, down into the last inch of hell and get my baby back! I'll drag her out!' She wasn't looking at us but through the window, banging her clenched hands on the bars and screaming: 'Dahlia! Your father strangled you with his bare hands! Big, white, peaceful hands! He pushed you, Dahlia! When he's looking at you he smells of shit – that's right, his eyes smell of shit! That's why I never look at him!'

'I'd better do something about her,' said the nurse. He went off.

'Edie,' I said. 'Edie.' She didn't answer, or even move; I might as well not have been there. She stood with her right fist raised, suddenly arrested as she was about to strike the bars again. 'Prime bines,' she muttered, 'prime bines!' Her figure stood firmly in black shoes splayed well apart, statue to a terrible energy. The nurse came back carrying a needle and an ampoule, a syringe in a tray. He sterilized the needle, screwed it to the syringe, charged it, and with one practised hand whipped Edie's clothes up over her head.

'They're going to introduce me to it now all right,' said Edie slyly from under her skirt. She chuckled with satisfaction as the nurse caught her round the middle. There were excreta on her dead white buttocks. The nurse chose his moment, swabbed a place on her flesh; then the needle plunged brightly in. 'There we are,' said the nurse. He dropped the syringe back in the tray and looked at his watch. He brushed her skirt down straight like a perfunctory husband.

'That's why the bastard copper used my hands,' said Edie slowly. Her voice dripped with malice. 'He used my hands to kill my little girl.' I realized I had begun to cry. 'He was too cunning to leave any clues,' she said. 'I'm faint,' she added, sitting down suddenly on the day bed. A middle-aged woman opposite, engaged in destroying the pieces of a jigsaw puzzle, watched every move Edie made, laughing like a hyena; a single incisor jutted greyly out of the side of her mouth like a broken slate.

'That's enough of that, Mrs Singlestick,' the nurse said.

Edie had turned on her side, facing the wall. 'Everything backfires on you,' she mumbled, 'especially little motionless faces.'

'What was that you gave her?' I said.

'Evipan. She'll sleep now.' He looked at me, then put his hand on my shoulder. 'Look, if I were you I'd leave.'

So I left Edie, surrounded by toffees and broken biscuit which had fallen out of the packet when she dropped it and which the other patients already had an eye on.

I went back to London. I thought, what's the point of going to see her any more? She doesn't know me.

She murdered our daughter back in 1979. Her name was Dahlia, after Edie's favourite flower. Edie pushed her under a bus, like that, in the street, because the child had picked up a bar of chocolate as they went past the shelves in the supermarket and hidden it, and there had been a stupid row with the manageress. Dahlia was nine.

I choked on my grief behind the windscreen as soon as I was alone, a vague face among other faces in other cars in the heavy traffic.

Oh, Edie, Edie, are you the same woman who, when you conceived Dahlia, looked up at me from the bed with your ultra-marine eyes that were always too dark and murmured, stroking my face: 'I know I'm moving with a new life now; I must sleep.'

Oh, sleep, Edie, sleep.

And let our cry come unto Thee.

8

When I had finished my report on the suicide I pushed it away and picked up a copy of the *Recorder* that I had brought in with me. On page 3 there was a report on the Police Special Powers Act, which had just been thrown out of Parliament after its first reading. The headline ran: Proposed Bill Rejected – Unreasonable, Unworkable and Dangerous.

Well, yes, it had been thrown out, but I reckoned not for long; it would be back, perhaps in a different form, perhaps looking more innocuous – not tomorrow, possibly not even the day after, but doubtless the day after that. It would look, on the surface, like a good strong bill to protect the public, particularly against acts of terrorism; but I was sure that, just as in its rejected prototype, there would be vague elements in it; there would be bad law. The bill as proposed would, for instance, have enabled me to arrest a man without a warrant and hold him in police custody for a period not exceeding seven days. It would have enabled me to cull the most private facts of a suspect's existence without his knowledge, taking my time while he was held downstairs in the cells. He would, meanwhile, have had no contact whatever with the outside world, not even with a solicitor, and seven days in police custody, subject to close interrogation, can seem a very long time. If called on to justify my action all I would have to say was: 'I have reason to believe that this individual was in the process of committing, or conspiring to commit, an offence in contravention of the Special Powers Act.' That would have been sufficient. It was a formula that a police officer could have stretched to include anybody.

It was what I thought of as banana laws – the law of a society in the process of breaking down. Once properly tightened up, it would have meant that I could stop and arrest a man in the street simply because I didn't like the look on his face, or the way his pockets bulged. It would have synchronized nicely with the plastic ID cards that every citizen would be required to carry by then, and before long we would have turned the country into a birdcage.

I asked myself whether this was the type of law I would ever want to enforce. If it ever passed onto the statute book we would effectively be released from any serious accountability to the public. Populations don't like it; I remembered what had happened, in a film I had seen, to the police in Budapest in 1956 when the public had got hold of them during the brief insurrection under Imre Nagy. Infuriated, the people tore them apart with their bare hands.

Bowman and I had discussed some of these implications on a slack day some weeks previously.

'This new legislation's going to be the making of us,' he said complacently, going to sit on the corner of my desk, 'if it goes through OK.'

'No, you're wrong, Charlie.'

'What do you mean, wrong? And don't call me Charlie.'

'I work it out that you're wrong, chief inspector – we're here to protect the public, not treat everyone like villains.'

'Look, why don't you take a stroll down Railton Road,' he scoffed, 'or run down to Peckham on a Saturday night? Refresh your memory. And get stuffed.'

'It'd be too much power,' I said. 'It would only make people really loathe us – I don't like it.'

'What I don't like,' said Bowman, turning red, 'is low-ranking police officers who think they've got brains.'

'Higher-ranking ones without any are even worse.'

'Listen, you don't understand the first thing about any of this,' said Bowman, his pig's eyes glittering with rage, 'it's way above your head. And talking of heads I could thump you on yours and what's more, one of these days I'm going to.'

'Well, get fit first,' I said. 'Look at you, the sweat you're in just sitting there, you wouldn't last a round.'

He licked his lips. 'You're a right comedian, you are,' he said. 'Christ, why is it I always have to get tangled up with you?'

'One, it's fate,' I said. 'Second, and this is more practical, you reckon that unless a case makes headlines it isn't good enough for you. Your ego's almost as swollen as your liver, so you work on the lines that if a murder's just dull and obscure, it's simply crap that you can leave to people like me.'

'You'd better watch your tongue,' said Bowman. 'You really had.'

'No chance,' I said, 'and don't yield to your lousy judgement and get me fired, otherwise you might find yourself having to sweep the shit up all by yourself instead of having A14 to do it for you.'

'Listen,' said Bowman, 'don't you care about your bleeding pension? They still pay something out, you know, even down on Unexplained Deaths.'

'The way the world's going now,' I said, 'none of us are going to live long enough to collect it — and if you think these powers would have changed that tendency then all I can say is, get a new battery, Charlie, your bulb's gone out.'

'Look, darling,' said Bowman, 'if I hear one more word out of you about these powers you'll be in trouble, a lot of trouble, see?'

'No,' I said, 'I've been thinking a lot about it, I wouldn't like them. What? Pick a man up because I don't like the look of him? Hold him for up to seven days without a warrant? Turn his place over just because I feel like it? Check him out on the police computer and find out when was the last time he changed his knickers? That's not police work, it's just idleness. It's also bloody frightening if you're on the wrong end of it, as any refugee from Eastern Europe could tell you. If I've got reason to suspect a man I'll go and see him, question him, try and trap him, see if I've got grounds to make an arrest. But just questions, understand? I don't arrest the man first, and then break him down under these proposed powers just because he happens to have shown up on some fucking computer, do you get the difference?'

'But Parliament will have decided these powers!' Bowman shouted. 'It'll all have been voted! It'll all be democratic!'

'Democratic my arsehole,' I said. 'MPs, a load of smooth talkers, some of them no better than they should be. Look, Charlie, haven't you any imagination at all? Don't you understand what this act would mean for a man? Terrorism, that's one thing. But those powers could be bent to fit nearly anybody! You could be pulling a geezer under them because he'd done three months for tea-leafing fifteen years ago if you liked! You could have him banged up at the Factory for a week if you wanted, and we all know what that means. He can't ring a lawyer. He can't get bail. Christ, if you think that's democratic, Charlie, then I just give up.'

'Well, it'll be the law if it goes through, sergeant,' said Bowman stubbornly, 'and that's what you and I are here to uphold.' He added: 'I can't wait, myself. This act'll improve our solution rate no end, which is very largely what it's for.'

'Yes, I'm interested in the solution rate all right,' I said, 'only I want our cases solved correctly. Frightening a man with these powers into admitting to something he hasn't done, that's not what I call solved, see?'

'No,' said Bowman, 'I don't see. I'll tell you the only thing I can see is that you're getting dangerously close to taking a political view on this, and politics is none of your business, sergeant. Parliament votes a law; it goes on the statute book; our job is just to enforce it.'

'Oh, you're just being simplistic,' I said, 'let it go, you're a hundred years behind.'

'I'm better than you,' he said, 'letting your poor, weak, silly brains get befuddled from reading too many newspapers.'

'I know we're both here to enforce the law,' I said, 'what matters to me is, what law? I'm not going to just go striding along life's path enforcing any old law. The difference between us is that I try and analyse the law I enforce, whereas you just blindly carry it out.

And I'll go further, Charlie; I sometimes think that the reason you carry out the law as it stands without asking yourself questions is that you find promotion comes easier that way.'

'Fuck you!' he roared.

'Also,' I said, 'it's less wear and tear on the brain. The more you've got a blank cheque, the less you'll have to worry about, you're covered.'

He closed his fists and stood up; I thought he was going to have a go. Instead he said ominously: 'Is there anything else you'd like to say, sergeant? Come on. Why not take this conversation a step further? Why not come straight out and say I'm bent; or that I'm not carrying my duties out correctly? Because then we could get everything between us sorted out – we could repeat this talk in front of a third officer, and then we could all three go up and see the superintendent. What do you say?'

'Don't bludgeon me,' I said. 'I'm not saying you're bent. I haven't used the word; I'm just pointing out your failure to think. I was just putting another point of view to you. I'm not trying to prove anything, I was trying to get you to understand something.'

'Well, don't bother,' said Bowman. He looked satisfied and stood for a moment rubbing his right fist in his open left hand. He shrugged. 'Anyway,' he added, 'if you will stay a sergeant you'll always get the shitty end of the stick.'

'Maybe,' I said, 'but I think that's the end where the truth is.'

I got up and left.

9

The old grain warehouse was in New Dock Road, and the caretaker was waiting for us. He looked cretinous, and smelled of last night's beer. 'What you want, gents,' he said eagerly, 'is the big granary on the second floor up there. That's where it was done, that's where the bags are.'

'You're a ghoul,' said Bowman, 'shut your gob.'

Two photographers snapped us as we got to the door and a reporter stepped up, a young man. '*Daily Recorder*,' he said. 'I wonder if you could—'

'No I couldn't,' said Bowman.

I turned to the reporter and said: 'You want to come up? OK, up you come, then.'

'You don't want him hanging around,' said Bowman.

'I'll play this my way,' I said. 'It's my case, and you're in a hurry.'

He gave me one look, one of the straight kind, turned and got into the back of the Rover. It took off in a puff of rubber fury.

'OK,' I said to the reporter, 'come on.'

I go where the ghosts are, I go where the evil is. I had that phrase going round in my mind. I started upstairs with the young man behind me. I called back to the caretaker: 'You needn't wait. I know where to find you if I want you. You've made a statement, haven't you?' It was plain to me that what he wanted was to make it all over again, which invariably, in my experience, meant he had nothing to say. People with something to say, you had to prise and tease it out of them.

'Well, I wouldn't go up there again anyhow,' the caretaker called back angrily, 'not for a million quid, mate.' No, I thought, but you'd hang about by the door to see if there was anything tasty, and hope you'd maybe get your boat in the linens.

'Shut the street door after you,' I shouted down to him, 'and shut it tight.' When I heard him do that I turned to the reporter on the stairs and said: 'You sure you want to do this? It isn't going to be easy.'

He said yes. I looked him over for a moment. 'All right,' I said, 'let's get on with it then.' We walked up to the second floor and pushed the heavy door open. The water and electricity in the building were off, but there was the daylight to see by. There were the bags all right, standing neatly against the far wall. I smelled dust and plank flooring, also a trace of something else – cooking? corruption? – in that immense space. Far off the city traffic growled, and a tug moaned on the river; I opened the blank doorway that side, above the rusted hoist, and looked down into the Thames which surged along twenty feet from the place. Then I crossed to the bags and looked down at the cheerful logo on them. That was where the smell came from all right. That was less cheerful. The only difference from the original find was that the forensic people hadn't restapled the bags. One gaped open, and I could see the cooked, grey flesh inside.

I found I was thinking as the killer. I thought: *I'm mad. Yes, but we've all got to try and look normal.* That made him a professional for me – because of that psychopath's carapace that stood for reason. I found I had already decided, assumed anyway, that he must have had help. OK, with or without help, I've killed a man, bled him, cooked him and stapled him up in five shopping bags. The staples were a weird touch; someone must actually have had a stapler on him – it was that well planned. Also the weapon, of course. Now, we don't know what that is yet, not till I get something from the lab. Never mind. Look normal, but not be normal, that's me. Kill in cold blood, but then be sure that there is no blood. I looked round the whole floor space looking for a mark, looking for anything, though I knew it was pointless; if there'd been anything found, the forensic people would have told us. All right. So the body must have been held over something like a tub – maybe even one of the pans they afterwards cooked him in, a tub standing on a plastic sheet no doubt, and drained. One of the individuals held and positioned him while the other slit his throat. OK, then they boiled the blood away in the pans with the rest of it. Yes, Bowman was surely right there. Where did they get the water to cook him in? No water on in the building, heavy and difficult to bring enough of it with you, five, ten gallons. Don't be silly; it's dark, it must have been, and there's the river twenty feet away. That's where they got the water. Right, once there's not a drop of anything left in him, now you can start. Disembowel him – all that, the lights and the rest of the shit, into one pan. Cook it clean – no need to leave a smell straight off. Any mess, it's all on the plastic sheet. Then the butchery. Joint him – a good knife and a sharpener, also a hammer to smash the bones so it'll all go into the pans. Sharpen the knife and cut the spine through at the vertebrae in two or three places. Take the head off, the feet and the hands. Especially the head and the hands. Knock the teeth out, too; there's your hammer, whip through the jaw with your knife and knock them out. Then stand around while it all cooks – what a tea party! Heat to cook him on? Easy! Why not good old camping gas? Little cooker, flat, something you could just stick in the motor, and two or three bottles of gas – what could be more innocent than that? A picnic! A midnight picnic! Of course, with no stains or marks anywhere around, it could have been done somewhere else, but I'll bet it wasn't, this is the ideal spot. The whole area's run down, shut up, deserted, abandoned, nothing but those high-rise blocks two hundred yards away on the land side. The caretaker never goes round at night, I'll bet; he's too frightened and he's a boozer. Smell? Smell of cooking meat? OK, some lorry-driver's back home late and got his old woman to fix him a big tasty meal, what's peculiar about that? Nothing. Lights on in this place? No, no lights. All done by torchlight. Very neat, very professional, so far – *only there must have been two of them*. One to pick the victim up and bring him here, the other to set the cooker and the rest of the gear up. Less risk that way because it would have looked funny if the law had stopped the car with the killer and the victim in it for a bald tyre or a u/s exhaust and noted, one, that the victim didn't look happy and then, two, opened the boot and found it crammed with plastic sheeting, saucepans, cooker and gas bottles, a hammer, a butcher's knife and a sharpener. But if you split it so that the killer with the victim has the unobtrusive stuff in his car – the knife, the weapon – and the other bloke has the rest of it in his car, that doubles your chances. All right, then, well, it's a set of assumptions, but you've got to start somewhere. OK, then? OK, now. What about afterwards? He's cooked. He's into his five bags and stapled up. Well, afterwards, you've only got three problems. You've got the dead man's clothing and belongings, you've got the plastic sheet looking like a butcher's apron, and the used water in the pans. Also, the pans themselves have got to go – those, the cooker and the gas-bottle. Well, OK, for my money it all went in the river with solid weights on it. Rivers wash clean and wash fast. They aren't kind to clothes either – clothes soon look old in a river. And who's going to look twice at a washed-up piece of plastic sheet anyway? Or at the remains of clothing, articles turning up at different places if they turn up at all? If there were identifying marks on any of it, you can bet they were removed before they went into the drink. Find the gear? Us? Talk about looking for a needle in a haystack! You should see what turns up when the tide runs out – anything from a Victorian halfpenny to a French letter. And the river so handy! That's why they picked the place, I tell you everything went straight down into the mud. No future in looking for it. No point getting the frogmen out. Better tackle it from a different angle.

OK, what angle? Well, I'm still putting myself in the killer's place, trying to imagine him, trying to get a picture. Talk about cool! Standing around with the other bloke (I'm supposing) waiting for the meat to be cooked. I'm taking my time. All my time. I'm careful. Very methodical, professional. All right. Well, if I am a professional, then, no matter why this man was done, I did it for money. Professionals don't kill in hot blood. So I killed this man for someone – and that means a contract, so we're back to villains again, hard villains.

Still, the killer did bungle, after all – he left the bags. Why? Did he think that if he threw them in the river they might surface too soon? That some of the, well, the contents might be found bobbing around by the river police? Did he calculate that it was safer to leave the bags here? Maybe. But maybe there was another element involved. Egoism. That was where plenty of killers came unstuck. I'm so cool, you wouldn't believe. I'm orderly, too; always method in my madness! Anyway, you'll never catch me, you berks, and meanwhile, look at the way I've stood these bags along this wall for you to find! Yes, that was what struck me right off when Bowman fed me into this. Orderly. A trademark. *I did this*, like painters used to sign in Latin under a picture when they finished it; I read about that somewhere. Well, killer, that was a bad mistake you made, leaving the bags here, and I'm going to nail you because of it.

Next, what sort of a villain? Villains often kill the way they learned in a trade – chemists, doctors and mortuary assistants. But that's delicate murder. At this level, killing isn't. Even so, what sort of past? What trade can a villain have learned who coolly cooks a man away to the point where he can't be identified? A cook? A butcher? A cook–butcher hit man? There can't be many of them about. And he's *orderly*. Cool.

Anyway, all right then, after I've killed him what do I do? How do I use up the time while I'm waiting for him to come to the boil? How do I react? Go over? Shake hands with the mate? – Well done, John, nice one! Have a cup of tea? Do I help clear up the mess, or do I just let John get on with that? I expect I do let him. I expect I always like to be in control though. No matter what, you can bet the killer watched everything the mate did; made sure it was done dead right. Did John start clearing up straight away? Or did they both linger over it – nice deserted spot, plenty of time. Bags of it. Yes, shopping bags. Maybe they got going after half an hour or so, after a sit-down. Had a soothing smoke. I know I'd have

needed one. No sign of any ash or butts, though. I wonder –
maybe I'm a non-smoker, non-drinker, tidy in my habits. Nothing
slovenly about me, mate! Clean knickers three times a week and a
bath Fridays! Look at the lovely neat way those bags are stood up!
Wouldn't his mum have been proud of him!

Yes, it's good, it's professional, it really is, and that's what narrows
the field. Let's go a bit on that, then. I kill. It's my job. A job like
any other job – no more to it than clearing a drain. And there's
money in it! Yes, money! No villain's a charitable organization.
Still, like all hard work it can be fun! Let's make it fun; clean,
orderly fun! Sick bastard. Sick, sick, right through to the back of
his rotten brain.

Now then. Where did I learn to kill so quick and so neat, have
no fear of death and the mess that goes with it? On the streets?
Could well be – in fact, almost certainly must have been. Middle-
class killers are fastidious. Poison's their favourite, or drugs; they
don't like getting themselves dirty. But a street killer doesn't give a
fuck about that. He likely started getting to know death as a kid.
But where? Assuming I'm British (which of course I may not be,
but assuming it), where do I learn to regard killing and death as
normal, almost everyday events? Where on British territory?
London? Hardly, though of course it's possible, particularly round
here. Or you've got Liverpool, Manchester, Glasgow, Newcastle
even – they're all hard places. But where's the hardest place of all,
just as an assumption? Well, there's, yes, there's Belfast! And orderly.
Didn't you say the bags were *orderly*? All stood inside their police
chalk marks, all lined up? Trained. Why yes, of course – surely it
must have taken a trained man to do this lot. A trained man with
a killer's instinct, trained to kill as well as ready to kill, and for
money. Money, because no two men would take risks like this if
there were no money in it. They must have been working for
someone who wanted to make the man in the bags unidentifiable.
Train where, though? We've no national service now. But we've
got, of course what we have got, is an army. An *army*. The army

takes the best now. Killed, bled, fast-cooked, cook away the prints, the face, boil the blood away, destroy the teeth, clear up, no mess – yes, that could sound right. Carry on, corporal! *Corporal?*

Now wait. Wait. A name there somewhere.

Behind me the reporter coughed and I spun round; I had completely forgotten him. 'Well,' he said, 'what do you think?'

'What I think,' I said, 'is that the devil's home on leave.'

'What does that mean?'

'It means there's a maniac on the manor. What's your name?'

'Cryer.' I watched while he made himself look at the bags, come closer up. 'Tom Cryer,' he said, 'that's me. I used to get teased about it at school.'

'I expect you gave as good as you got.' I had started to reopen the bags, kneeling over them as I spoke. Behind me Cryer said: 'Do you have to do that? They've already been opened once. Do you have to do it again? Why?'

'I don't know,' I said slowly, 'but I have to. I'm no ghoul, but I have to do things my way, get my ideas, reach my conclusions my own way.' Behind me I heard Cryer gulp, keeping his stomach in his mouth with his hand as I undid the bags. I pretended not to notice. I thought he was OK the way he stood his ground – a bright youth turning into a man, the romantic idea of being a crime reporter becoming grisly reality.

'Don't you sometimes wonder why you do this job?' I said.

'The public has a right to the facts,' he muttered.

'By Christ,' I said, 'I'm really surprised. You're the first man from a national daily in a long time I've heard say that. Mostly they just think about the scoop.' I had the first two bags open now, and had my hands into the contents. 'Look out,' I said. 'It does smell when you get it out.'

'What are you going to do?'

'I'm going to put him together as much as possible the way he was.' I let the boiled dollops of flesh and bone tumble out of the limp plastic, and opened the other bags. I found Bowman's, the one with the head in it. Grey flesh and a few skeins of colourless hair clung to it. I squatted on the floor with it and turned it round and over; the features wobbled unrecognizably on the bone structure. The skin of the face had boiled off: the eyes were cooked blank. The lower jaw was in another bag. There were no teeth in either jaw, so there was no point in looking for dental records. The teeth themselves were nowhere to be found. I turned the skull face-down and said to Cryer: 'You see that hole in the occiput? That's the wound that killed him. What do you think of it?'

'There's no exit wound.'

'That's right. If it had been a bullet at close range, it would have had to come out somewhere, and it would have been found.'

'It looks exactly like a bullet wound all the same.'

'I know it does,' I said. 'It isn't, but you can bet that whatever it was there was plenty of power behind it. Something sharp went wham, straight into his brain; he can't have known a thing.'

'Why do you keep saying *him*? Couldn't it have been a woman?'

'No, you can see it was a man from the shape of the pelvis.'

'I couldn't have told.'

'That's practice,' I said, 'and reading. I do a lot of that when I have time – pathologists' textbooks, biographies. I'm a man troubled by meanings, and look where it's got me – being here, doing this. Still, I won't settle for anything less than the exact truth. Some of my colleagues think I'm just awkward on purpose, but what it really is – I seldom agree with my colleagues because too often their reasoning is based on the results they expect, and as such is generally ill-found. Excuse me for talking aloud while I work. Too many detectives I know ought to get out of the force altogether, though of course you get the bright ones.'

I finished emptying the bags and laid the contents out. We both bent over what there was. There wasn't much, so it didn't tell us much. The blind flesh on the fingers was no help, just as Bowman had said it wouldn't be. The knuckles and finger ends had popped out through the skin.

'How will you ever find out who he was?' Cryer said. He doubled up suddenly; I saw he was going to vomit by the grey sweat on his face.

'Do it anywhere in the corner there,' I said.

He was horribly sick. When it was over he said: 'Sorry. Had a big lunch today, early.'

'With the mob from the news-desk?'

'No, with my girl. Today's her twenty-second birthday.'

I looked at what lay on the floor, the smashed legs that I had fitted to the severed knees, the elbows, wrists, shoulder-blades and hands. I said: 'Well, mind you look after her.'

'I do my best,' he said, 'but women are so confident.'

'They are till something happens to them.'

'I have to do my job,' he said, 'that's the trouble. I can't be everywhere. I won't let her get on a tube train by herself now, not after six at night. I lecture her till she starts yelling at me, but it's her I'm thinking of.'

'You lecture her,' I said. 'She might end up being glad of it.'

He got out a packet of Kleenex and wiped his face. Now that he had reacted, he was calmer over what was on the floor. He repeated: 'Do you think you will find out who he was?'

'Oh yes.'

'How?'

'It's simpler than you might think,' I said, 'the murderer's going to give me a hand. In fact, he's started to already. The fact he's left no trace, that's a trace in itself. Second, he wasn't alone; there were certainly at least two of them. Thirdly, the job was so well done that I'm certain it was done for money, and that probably means that the victim wasn't just anybody. Therefore, I start looking for anybody who was somebody and who's gone missing. They soon show up – by their absence, if you see what I mean.'

'Are you suggesting it was villains?'

'You bet I am,' I said. 'Look at it. The only other possibility is that it was a nut, but I don't buy it – it feels like a contract to me.

And when it comes to a contract, who are among the first people to get hit?'

'A grass?'

'Dead right,' I said. 'My guess at the moment is that this wretched individual was most likely a grass, and a big-time one, too. There aren't that many of them – that's why, if I'm correct, I'm certain to find out who he was. And the moment I know that, and as soon as I find out what the weapon was that killed him, I shall start getting an idea of who to get after – though, mind, I've got the shadow of an idea already.'

'What can I print?' he said.

'After what you've just been through? Anything you like.'

'You could get in bother, giving me a free hand like that.'

'Yes,' I said, 'and I could get out of it too. I run my cases my way – that's one great advantage of working on your own. And if the folk upstairs don't like it they can fire me. They probably would've already, except that I'm not that easy to replace.'

'Well, I want to feature it.'

'Go on,' I said, 'I'm all for it. Print what you like; who knows, you might turn up something. Someone, somewhere, several people, they know whose body this is – and knowledge, that's money, and aren't we all into that? So offer a reward – say in the region of five long ones. But go easy on the contract angle; I'm not that far on yet – this is all theory so far. By the way,' I added, 'do you happen to know anything of what's going on over at the ministry of defence?'

We were walking downstairs by this time. There was a uniformed copper posted in the street, and I asked him to get through for a vehicle to collect what was upstairs and take it to the morgue.

'Well,' said Cryer, 'there's some almighty mess stewing away there somewhere. We keep trying to get an interview – nothing doing.'

'All right,' I said, 'but let me know anything you pick up.'

I looked around me in the street. After what I had been looking at, it was good to be outdoors again. It was a clear evening, with a red cloud like something mad out of a stripper's hat drifting above the Thames. 'That looks a fair old pub on the corner opposite,' I said to Cryer, 'let's go and have a drink there. You've certainly earned one.'

He said he didn't feel like it, but I insisted, and he looked better when we had settled down in there. It was clean, it was normal, and the real wooden tables smelled of polish; it was one of those pubs you just come across where straightforward people are having a drink after a day's work. It made me feel better just to sit and watch them play darts. It made me feel as if I had been let out of hell.

I got him a large scotch and watched while he drank it. 'How are you feeling now?'

'I'm fine again. But I've got to admit, I've never seen anything like that before.'

'I'm not surprised.'

'I'm four years out of university,' said Cryer. 'It's time I grew up.' He looked at his watch. 'I'm just going to phone the paper.'

'Take your time,' I said. 'Ease down.'

He was gone a while. When he came back he said: 'Well, they've cleared the front page for it.'

'I should think so,' I said. 'Well done.'

'Why well done? It's a story any paper would put on page one.'

'Yes, but you had to get it,' I said. 'That's why well done.'

'That's the job, getting it.'

'How long have you been with the *Recorder*?'

'Eighteen months.'

'If you're still the way you are now in five years' time,' I said, 'you might go a long way. You stood up well to what we saw just now; I can think of older men who would have run for it, freaked out.'

'I can't do that,' he said seriously. 'Angela and I need the money too badly and there are three million folk on the dole. I'm from the Midlands and I'm a working-class lad – not that I insist on that. But it's like my dad says – us gets in there and us keeps trying.'

'Drink up,' I said. 'Fancy a nibble? It says they do a snack.'

'It's too soon, I'd spew it up.'

'Put the worst of it out of your mind,' I said, 'and drink, it'll do you good. I'll get us a lift back.'

'I live right out at Wembley.'

'Doesn't matter,' I said, 'I know a minicab firm that owes me so many favours, a fiver'd take you to the moon and all the way back to your front door.'

I rang for the car and as we were leaving Cryer said to me: 'You know that business you were on about before, what you were asking about, the defence ministry?'

'Yes, I've been asked to keep an eye out.'

'Well, I don't know, but do you remember reading not long ago that we expelled a whole mob of Russians from their place over there at Highgate?'

'That trade delegation of theirs?'

'That's the place. Well, it's only a rumour, and don't quote me because I could get in diabolical bother, and besides, it's probably not even true.' He hesitated. 'I'm sticking my neck out here. I asked a few questions and told my boss on the paper, and he told me to forget the answers.'

'I'll be careful,' I said. 'Don't think I'll name you anywhere, I won't.'

'Well,' said Cryer, 'here goes then, for what it's worth. It seems possible that whatever's stewing over at the ministry and the expulsion of these Soviets may be connected. It's one of those rumours that just won't keep quiet in Fleet Street, and you know what that can mean.'

I did know what it could mean. But I didn't much like the idea of what it was I didn't know.

10

There used to be dignity in life; I used to see it all round me when I was young. But now it's gone. People no longer care about each other the way they used to – not the way my old man used to tell me life was when he worked in the Fire Service during the war and the bombing. Then, people who didn't even know each other would go down into the flattened buildings after a raid and shovel to get at the people buried down there as if the victims were their brothers. Even after the war there was still some trust left; it ran on nearly into the Sixties. But now it's all sorry, squire, don't want to know.

It was the afternoon of Hitler's birthday, April 20th, 1979, that Edie pushed our little girl under the bus; and when I went to bed that night at my horrible flat at Earlsfield after leaving Cryer I saw her, as I often do in my dreams, her flushed face flying backwards from me in a great wind as I try to catch her, and then I woke and thought I saw her like a flame on the end of my bed.

I've heard that abroad people believe the British are cold; it isn't true. No bullet can deliver you into an agony like lost love; yet neither can the great power of innocence be put out. Such sweetness can be mishandled and ignored – but Dahlia always gets through when she wants me, calling: 'Daddy? Daddy? Are you all right, Daddy?'

Great living Christ!

Yes, there used to be dignity in life, and I would die if I thought that would bring it back. I often wonder what people think a police officer is and how he thinks, or whether they believe he thinks at all. They just see the helmet, or the warrant card, and trouble. But we take risks. Some of us go into places because we must, whatever's waiting there. I would give my life to have my little girl back again, but all I can do in the anticlimax that life is without her is to do what I believe to be right in the face of evil. So old-fashioned! But I have only dreams and memories of my daughter to fall back on now – dreams where I see her like a bird, flying free and happy in the face of my trouble.

Yes, I used to pick her up and sing to her before I had to leave and report for duty – at Old Street, that was. But I never managed to protect and love her as I should have because I was too anxious for my career. So now I feel the arms of others round me in the place of her arms, and know that, because of my ambition, I went off to work that day and so let Edie kill Dahlia because I was too proud ever to admit to myself that I knew Edie was mad.

11

'Have you got anything?' I said. I was in the morgue.

'Yes. It wasn't easy, though.'

'Police work never is,' I said, 'not if it's done properly.' I was talking to the snide young pathologist I usually got.

We were in the cold room with its tiled walls and smell of formaldehyde.

'You really are an awkward bastard, aren't you?' he said.

'I wouldn't be any good if I wasn't.' I was still thinking how I used to pick Dahlia up and hold her in my left arm while I threw darts at the old cork board Edie and I used to have in the kitchen.

'Another dart! Oh please, Daddy, please!'

She was the life I had made, and I felt her beside me now bright even in the face of her mother's brooding intensity which never frightened her. I felt her with me here in the morgue; I found myself remembering, I don't know why at that moment, how I used to take her to the football matches I played in those days, at weekends, leaving her with the other wives.

But the young doctor had lit a Gauloise: 'We've found it was done with a humane killer,' he said. 'Unusual, that – not the sort of weapon you expect to find used on a person.' He yawned; some of it was fatigue.

'Well, the funny thing about murders is that they are unusual,' I said. He made me angry, because there were times when I wondered why I bothered to clear up shit that always repeated itself, only to be faced with cynicism and remote-control emotion.

'Calm down, sergeant.'

I barely heard him. My daughter was still in my mind. The window was open in the sitting room of our third-floor flat and she was leaning out. I waved at her as I left for work that last time and she waved back and called out: 'Don't be long, Daddy! Come back quick! I love you!'

'And then he was boiled,' the doctor was saying. 'Amazing.'

'Yes,' I said, 'it was thorough, wasn't it?'

'I just don't understand you people,' said the pathologist, 'you're all cold-blooded. To look at you mob, anyone'd think I was talking about the weather.'

'You're just as bad,' I said.

'That comes from seeing too much of it,' he said bitterly.

'Change your job.'

'I'll ignore that,' he said. 'Anyway, I suppose he was a criminal.'

'Yes,' I said, 'and he's made mistakes. We all do it.'

He thought about that. Then he said: 'As a matter of interest, can you make any sense of it yet?'

'I think so,' I said. 'It's early on and I've got some more checking to do. But it won't be a long list, only a few names – perhaps fewer than that. The fact it was done with a humane killer'll be a help.'

'Why?'

'Because it marks the man who did it,' I said. 'When you're as deep into murder as I am, you come to realize that every crime is signed by the pettifogging care of the killer. The more careful he tries to be, often the easier it is to trip the bastard up.'

'We try to take a humane view of murder these days.'

'That's good,' I said, 'I hope you concentrate on the victim, not the killer.'

He coughed.

There were two kinds of humane killer, I mused. There was the old-fashioned type where a thing like a nail was detonated by a small-calibre cartridge, usually a four-ten. But you don't see many of them now. The new kind works with compressed air. It hardly makes a sound; you can buy one easily. No serial number, no record at all. You've just started up in the butchery trade, let's say, and you've got your own cattle out in the country; you want to

45

slaughter your beasts yourself. Any wholesaler that supplies the trade – a high-class ironmonger even – will sell you what you want. No register to sign, no permit required, no one's to know.

'Still, he might as well have used a knife,' the pathologist was saying.

'Well, he might,' I said, 'but not on a contract. You don't want any mess, do you, and you know what a knife death's like. You've seen plenty of them; it's like the day Father papered the parlour. Also, doctor, supposing you were mad – so mad that you enjoyed doing the job with a weapon that you had so carefully worked out to be untraceable in your weird little mind that it made you stick out as neatly as a sore thumb?'

'All right – I'm following you.'

'Yes, well then, that's the signature of the man. And what a signature! It's intended to be anonymous: yet it's completely original! The man's a villain, I'm sure of that. He's a villain because he planned it all out. He planned it out because he was doing it for money. No money, no incentive. No incentive, no planning. But – you have to be mad to take a life for money. A psychopath. All right, then. Now, how many people would you say in this country filled that bill? He's no raving nut like, say, Fred Paolacci; he doesn't go strolling about on the manor with blood all over him. No, no. I bet you wouldn't spot this little monster if he were standing next to you on a Circle Line train. White, neat and prissy – and very tough, very mad.'

The pathologist went to answer a bleeping phone. When he came back he said: 'Multiple car smash on the A4 at Chiswick roundabout, there'll be three to stay.' He looked pointedly at the clock on the wall. 'The ambulance is on its way.'

'That makes a refreshing change,' I said. 'They're usually not that speedy over picking up the dead.'

'I'm going to be busy,' said the pathologist. 'I'm on my own, the chief's on holiday. Two of them are completely jammed together like Siamese twins. Boy and a girl.'

'They may have been in love.'

'Well, they'll always be together now,' said the doctor. 'I won't get them apart. No need for me to detain you, sergeant. Anything else I get, I'll let you have it.'

'I'll take to the streets again, then.'

'Do that,' he said coldly, 'and try and keep better order in them, will you, it'll save me a lot of work.'

12

I went up to Room 205. I hadn't got a pen in there, as usual, so I looked round the open door of Room 206. Nobody was in, so I nicked the pen I saw on the desk. Then I sat down at my own desk and found some paper. I seldom use paper; the sheets I found were turning yellow at the edges. I sat staring at the opposite wall, which was decorated with an ancient poster showing a dog with its teeth bared and a slogan warning the public against rabies. After an hour I tried to write a single name down on my sheet of paper, only to find that my ballpoint had no ink. It didn't matter. I rang downstairs to the basement and asked for a file.

When it came up I spent a long time gazing at an army photograph. The soldier's uniform was beautifully pressed, with knife-edge creases down the sleeves; on the right arm you could see his stripes. After a little reading I understood why he wasn't going to keep those. The face under the red beret stared at me calmly. Young. Peaceful-looking. Friendly.

Balls.

I read carefully through the file, turning back frequently to verify this or that. I began with the man's birth – Coleraine, County Londonderry, 20 March 1950. No parents' address, no next of kin. Joined the forces June 1968. Parachute regiment. There were copies of his army records – training, company commander's assessment, commanding officer's remarks. Defaulter's sheet, crime sheet blank.

Until.

Until I liked it. The more I read, the better I liked it. Under the heading Previous Employment I saw that before joining the army he had worked casually in restaurants after coming to the mainland, first as a butcher's assistant in Birmingham, then later in various West Midlands restaurants as a cook.

Well, well! A butcher's assistant! A cook!

Officers' reports on his early performance in the army – excellent! Weapon training? A Captain Johnson had commented: 'A first-class marksman.' Lieutenant West: 'As a parachutist, this NCO has a natural aptitude. Displays coolness under any conditions.' But his company commander had noted: 'Impressed as I am by his achievements, this soldier is nevertheless a trouble-maker in 2 Company, making no effort to form friendships with the other men. He is uncommunicative and occasionally violent; I have had to discipline him more than once. Overall, I am dubious as to recommending him for promotion.'

And there was a psychiatrist's report: 'This man's aggression is such as to render him unfit for promotion. I recommend further tests.'

But there was no time for that because the unit was posted to Oman, where there was some action. It was of course performance in action that impressed the army, and as a result of it my man soon made corporal. Always a loner, though. And look out you didn't jostle him; he could go off like a bomb. The first really naughty entry in his records told how he had smashed a man in the face with the sharp edge of a mess-tin because he thought he had overheard a soldier passing a remark on his sexual prowess. Result: he was busted and drew nine months' military prison at Shepton Mallet.

I knew Shepton. They were all staff-sergeants there, picked for brute force; they reckoned to break a man's spirit down there in six months.

Not my man's spirit, though. The army had decided to get rid of him when he came out with a dishonourable discharge, but it was in his records, how he had got them to take him back. He agreed to compensate the man he had injured (he had lost the sight of his left eye) out of his pay by royal warrant and then besides, there was his service record. McGruder? Christ, he had done some pretty amazing things. Just a corporal, but if he was sent out to do a job on the enemy with four or five men he'd leave them well back – just use them to cover him *while he did everything that had to be done on his own.*

Those had been his own words at his court-martial, where he conducted his own defence, telling his 'friend', a lieutenant, to fuck off.

I looked at the sheets in front of me, and thought long and hard about that: 'I did what had to be done on my own.'

Yes. And there was always, of course, much later, the case of Wetherby, the supergrass, unsolved and still on file. The choice of weapon used to murder him – a sailmaker's needle through the eye. Another hit job, another unusual weapon.

Next I turned up the transcript of his other trial, where he had been convicted of murdering a fellow corporal, a man called Brownlow. It made horrible reading. I turned back again to study the killer's photograph. Looking at the date on the back, I saw that it had been taken for records on the day he was arrested. Looking at the face, it seemed incredible, what he had done. That often struck me with psychopaths, the difference between the look on the face and what they had done. Take McGruder, now. He looked so calm. Quiet, neat, peaceable, friendly: buy you a drink, mate!

Wrong. He was tried in a civilian court, since the crime had been committed while the unit was based in the UK at a camp outside Chester. The facts weren't in question. Fifteen witnesses testified to his absence at the time the killing was done, at two in the morning; the special investigation branch of the army could take its pick. Well, it had done that, and then turned McGruder over to us. So he stood up in court and conducted his own defence yet again – there were notes in with the transcript as to how he was calm, uninvolved, you would almost say.

That was what the court couldn't swallow – the nonchalant bearing of the prisoner, also the cold-blooded element in the killing itself – done, as it was, in the dark, deliberately, silently, from behind, and with a piano wire, a garrotting.

Ten years, he drew. But he did just seven – a model prisoner.

Then, when he got out, the records went blank.

He disappeared from Britain.

Well worth a visit, that one, I thought. Yes, really worth it, if the man was around.

Worth it on principle. He was still only an idea I had for the plastic bags, but it was his commando-style past, the fact he'd done bird for murder and for attempted murder and above all, his invariably unusual choice of weapon – that was what made his name stick with me. More than that, people like McGruder are worth paying a call on from time to time anyway, if they're around. Casual, like. They're the ones with the violence forever tight inside them. They're the ones, well, you'd be just plain silly not to watch them.

13

I went back to Earlsfield, and in the night I had a rotten dream. A man the colour of death in a white suit came up to me in the West End out of a side street and offered me his love.

I had other problems in the dream. A man had been knocked down by a car at the bottom of Wardour Street and he was screaming where he lay on the tarmac in the night glare.

I had hired a taxi to drive myself; it was one of those old Beardmores they stopped using back in the Fifties. But I was going to cab it, take it to one of those big West End hotels where they scrape the shit off your voice as soon as you speak. The cab had a roof that folded down at the back like a child's pram so that you could look at the park, and I'd rented it from some South London villains. I saw them laughing as I drove it away. The exhaust had gone, I didn't like its clutch and it had helical gears. I didn't like the sound of its motor either, and it was all wrong for the Eighties traffic around me. But I had to pick some strangers up at their hotel; for some reason I was desperate to pick them up. Well, I couldn't find anywhere to park near their Piccadilly hotel, so I parked up on the rank west of Bond Street, and then started out on foot to look for these people among the night crowds eating hamburgers from the fast-food joints off Piccadilly Circus. It was hot and I was sweating; I could smell the meat frying and the spray-on onion. But I couldn't get my bearings because, although I know the whole area like my hand, in the dream the streets kept fanning away into places I'd never seen before. In the end I got sick with anxiety over finding these people and I thought, shit, after all, I'd be better off back on wheels. So I ran back for my old banger where I'd left it, but a cabby told me as I went looking that the law had towed it away and that there was a ton to pay in fines. And all the time it was raining, bloody raining. They say it's bad luck to dream of rain; they say it foretells death when you dream of water.

Next I was going up the path of my parents' house in Welling, like I used to when I was coming back from school, and there I saw my father leaning exhausted against the neighbour's fence, favouring his left side. He still wore the suit he had died in and his trilby hat; the hat had fallen over one ear. He was completely rotten and dead. He smelled, and the places that death had eaten in his face showed through in a way that ought never to be seen. I said: 'Father, dear God, whatever's the matter? What are you doing here?' He couldn't answer at first, and I knew his disease was hurting him. 'I'm lost,' he said, 'I've got lost somehow. It's a bloody disease, this is.' They sometimes take tumours out of them bigger than cricket balls; they took one like that out of him. So he searched my face earnestly for pity, and I went up to him on the path and took him in my arms and comforted him as best I could. But he just sighed and turned into a garden bird; then he put on his old golfing cap. Wings spread out through his coat and he fluttered up into the air, and as he went away I told him I would care for him for ever. But he couldn't speak, only look tenderly at me from the other world. 'Take the rain out of the names on our graves up at the church,' he said gently, 'with your forefinger; you'll be sure to, won't you, son?' Other people watched us from chairs high up on a terrace; they too were dead.

I awoke and lay for a long while in the dark, thinking about what I had dreamed, remembering how my father had been a small-time draper in Welling, and how my mother had had ideas of clothing us above the other children in the street and how he had been hard on my sister and me, moralizing and punishing us, though he nearly broke himself financially, what with his subscription to the golf club and sending us to grammar school.

And yet he hadn't had a bad death in his own home, considering the cancer that ate him away. I was up in Chelsea; I had just got onto the CID when he died. He was found by my sister who was looking after him; he was in his armchair in the sitting room, gazing at his favourite picture, a reproduction oil of a cottage garden that hung over the fireplace. The trouble being in his lungs, his heart had finished by collapsing, the doctor said; he had this terrible cough. Yet only the day before, my sister Julie said, he seemed to have almost mastered it and appeared much better reciting some of Shakespeare's lines out of *Henry V* and standing up from his armchair in his shirt-tails to do it, and delivering himself of a vile great yellow stool on the cushion, of which he was ashamed and shouted for it to be taken away, of course. My sister and the doctor wanted him to go into hospital, but he wouldn't: 'I've paid for my home,' he told her, 'and I'll die in it, my dear girl, as I've lived in it.' He was very fond of Julie; she married a man in the sports gear business and they've done well, with a house out by Oxford on a mortgage. I like to go down there at times; we listen to music in the evenings and get on well together. She used to wash my father at the end and make his bed, and, in caring for him, looked at the penis which had made her for the first time; he used to take the end of it between his old fingers before he got too bad and squash it eagerly, winking at her; it was strange, she said to me after the funeral, how right to the end he still had the lean buttocks and big, heavy prick of a man in his prime. 'Good-looking to the end,' my sister said proudly after the funeral. 'That's what a wartime commission in the army did for him.'

As for my mother, she'd been dead already very many years – of boredom, I think, really.

14

No, I shouldn't have married Edie. Through Dahlia's end, through the loss of her reason, she dealt me a double blow that changed me into a man with a sparse emotional map: much harder, the peaceful places and the civilized building in me had gone, leaving just main roads to a few goals through bleak, mountainous country, roads carried frequently on precipitous lips that I don't care to look over often.

Why can't Edie die? And why do I have to be faced with these plastic bags just now? There are times, I don't know if they come to everyone, when I feel that the future is beyond my strength: too much horror to deal with and no help to turn to. My flaw now is that I feel half a murderer myself because of what Edie did. No wonder I understand murder.

It was different when I was a young police officer, before I married. I remember central London as it was then, before things got so bad: people, tough in adversity, with nothing to offer but the music in them which they played on mouth-organs at street corners or else they just sang.

I felt like a berk amongst them at first, in my uniform with its bright buttons and the helmet over my nose. Still, I began to understand them after a while. I watched them on day-shift and on night-shift, playing to the walls of their inner silence. Most coppers, unfortunately, don't listen; it would make some of them more human if they did.

The office crowds would be leaving for home still, when I came on in the evening, or else making for the pubs. Men trailed their rags, like the sound of an old man sleeping, towards St Martin-in-the-Fields, feeling for money for a bottle; they would sit out and drink it in the dusk, sitting on the benches in Trafalgar Square. Some were mad, some pretended they were, others wished they were. Once your youth has raced away from you, you can see it better when you look back, closing your eyes at night; I still smell the warm summer chestnut leaves in the parks, the hot dust of the pavements on my beat, and the fumes of traffic halted at the top of Sloane Street or Hyde Park – people going to parties by cab moving through Eaton Square in the evening, the windows down at the back, the girls in expensive dresses and the young men, their eyes as red as their overdrafts, toasting passers-by with champagne as they were transported to Belgrave Square. Then there were the street accidents – later the violence in the same warm evenings south of the river, the big bottle-and-razor fights between mods and rockers; maybe the first time you ever had to show courage was walking between them, alone, to stop it. My first inspector was maimed like that, a broken bottle across his right eye; Clarkie, we called him, a straight bloke.

There used to be a man we called Blind Jamie who stood at the corner of Villiers Street in the Strand. Some of them carry white sticks to help trade along, but he really was blind; you could see where he'd been hit in the face by shrapnel at Monte Cassino. When he turned his face up out of the dark to the street lamps, something he did at times to see if his sight might be returning, you could see the shrapnel they couldn't get out shining in his cheeks. He wore a cap to cover his bruised features and sold the fruit his mates brought up for him from Essex and arranged on his barrow: 'It's amazing, you know,' he said to me one evening, 'the way the birds trample on me, literally trample on me for my apples. All the girlies love my apples – best apples in London, I always say; I get all my regulars queuing for them.'

Well, he's dead now, worsted by a block of matter inside him; he died in Guy's Hospital in the public ward, turned on his side towards the wall.

Life seems poorer without men like him, with their courage; I admire courage and self-respect. I've known others freeze to death in the winter; I've found them, covered with snow in a doorway, mistaken for a sack of coke. I've seen them also, clean and ready for a chat in the queue, waiting outside the office in Beechcroft Road to collect their giro from the DHSS.

I got up and tried to read, to shake off my memories and dreams. I picked up a book. But it made no difference; the book lasted far too long, like a government, and was full of stuff that could have been left out – I suppose to make it thicker-looking and more impressive on the shelves.

I dropped it on the floor. I gave up the idea of sleep. Instead I got a can of cold beer out of the fridge and drank it slowly, thinking and looking at the wall. It was ten past three. I thought about my man in the army. I thought about him all the time, no matter what else I was thinking of. I hadn't an address for him yet, but I was sure I'd turn him up all right. I tried hard, but I couldn't think of anyone else who would fit the plastic bags so well. I didn't really need any more files, though I had had some up during the day. I could see all the known villains, big, small, or mediocre; in the dead of night like this I could parade them all before my eyes. *Parade.* It always came back to the army. My instinct, like a compass, kept swinging round to find north no matter what I did, no matter how I argued it. Finally I got up, trod on my beer can and put it in the garbage; then I went and looked out of the window onto Acacia Circus. It was what passes for peaceful in 1984 – that is, quietly threatening. I found myself thinking of when I was small. The second war was just over and my father, who had left the Fire Service to join the Engineers, used to hum a tune that was popular then:

> 'We'll meet again
> Don't know where, don't know when,
> But I know we'll meet again
> Some sunny day...'

It marked your childhood, the war, even though I was only four when it ended. My mother told me I was born during an air raid; it brought me on, she said, the bombs did. I used to listen to them both as they recalled goodbyes in uniform, a hurried kiss in the blackout, the tail-lamp of a taxi disappearing in the dark, a hand waving from a troopship, and then the telegrams ('deeply regret... you'll be glad to know... died like a man').

When the telegram for his brother came my father, who was on leave, said: 'Christ, what else could he have died like?'

My father had become part of a bomb disposal squad for landmines; quite unexpected people did remarkable things then.

Long ago one December night, when I was on the beat in Euston Road with another officer, a woman came up to me in the fog with the glow of King's Cross station behind her and said: 'Could you help me, please?'

'What's the matter?' I said. She was crying. 'Look, cheer up.'

'No, I'm afraid I can't,' she said, 'my heart's broken.' I looked at her and her expression struck me like ice in the stomach.

'His name's Clive Masters,' she said, 'he's shot himself. We'd had a few words and I went out to calm down, and when I came back he'd shot himself. It's just opposite – forty, Argyle Crescent, would you go? I'm afraid I can't. I'm afraid my life's over now.'

'Come on, it's never that bad.'

'Don't you really understand?' she said.

The city roared softly in the night.

My partner and I had separated, but he came up presently and I said look after her while I go and see. The house was all bedsitters and the landlord and I went to the room. The gas fire there was going out because there was no more money in the meter. There was the unmade bed, and there was the body on it – a small body it looked too, with the blood on the bedding and the white unshaven face and a silly two-two pistol on the floor. Well, we got the usual mob round to the place – lab, fingerprints, a detective-inspector. At last a squad car came and I was going to see her into it and carry on with my duty when she looked at me with eyes that I shall always remember, they were so dark blue, and said: 'You'll come with me, won't you?' and the inspector said yes, it was OK. Going back she told me she had wanted to be an actress and I said well, you will be, but she said no, not now, where are we going? I said to the station for a cup of tea, and then we'll put you to bed there. In a cell? she said and I said no, in the duty room. Whereupon she was silent with me in the back except that once she cried out oh, Clive, come back, come back! Then she looked at me again and said, what am I going to do now? What would you do now, if you were me? Well, it was no good, I was young, I didn't know and couldn't tell her, and I still don't know what I would have done if I'd been her. Then we got back to Tottenham Court Road and she went away with the inspector to make a statement and I didn't see her any more.

'Not all fun in this job, is it, sonny?' said the duty sergeant. 'Well, piss off then, you've got a report to make on it; I want it at nine sharp.'

I heard her cry from one of the interrogation rooms: 'Oh, when may I love somebody, please?'

'But that's from Noël Coward!' said a young copper who was standing nearby. '*Private Lives*, that is. Fancy!'

'What do you think you're in?' said the duty sergeant. 'Amateur dramatics or something?'

'That's right!' said the young constable eagerly. 'I'm playing the lead in *The Doll's House* over at Finsbury Park Saturday night at the Grand; it's going to run right over Christmas. Why don't you come and bring the missis, sarge? Tickets are only five bob.' He babbled happily on: 'Now that's really sad, *The Doll's House*. I play the husband, see, and I just can't believe it at the end there, when the girl says she's going to leave me – I've been blind and uncaring all my life, see?'

'That don't surprise me at all,' the sergeant said.

I went down the room to where I couldn't hear them so well, but he followed me and went on: 'Yes, a real tragedy, the lines just speak themselves. Norwegian feller wrote it, geezer called Ibsen. That's right, Norwegian – same as that maniac we caught up north that time who interfered with all those young men and buried them in his garden.'

I was very angry and stood with my back to him thinking of some lines I remembered from Coward myself: 'I'll leave you never, love you for ever.'

Private Lives.

15

For all his supposedly outstanding service record, this man I was getting interested in had killed Corporal Dick Brownlow in a cowardly and brutal manner, garrotting him at two in the morning as he came out of the latrines at Saighton Camp, Chester, where both men were on an unarmed combat course. It was established at the trial that the two had never got on and that my man, while acting-sergeant because most of the course were on weekend leave, had gone out of his way to fuck Brownlow about, because it had been asserted by witnesses that Brownlow had suggested more than once that my bloke was a murdering queer. Various witnesses had proposed a grudge fight. But my man hadn't waited for that; he killed Brownlow stone dead in the dark, took the body to his car, drove to a canal and dumped the body in it. When the SIB came down my bloke denied any involvement, po-faced, even after it became obvious that, apart from motive, he was the only soldier who couldn't establish his whereabouts for two in the morning. Brownlow was done with a piece of piano wire, and a witness from another unit stated that he had seen the suspect taking one out of a piano that was being broken up by four defaulters with a pair of cutters. Two of Brownlow's hairs were also found in the boot of the suspect's car. When they arrested him he just shrugged and went away with them in handcuffs, politely smiling.

Yes, he conducted his own defence, speaking always in a quiet, restrained manner with a trace of Ulster in his speech.

He was as guilty as a man can be. The jury unanimously found him guilty and the judge said: 'Because of your military record I shall mitigate the sentence I would have imposed and send you to prison for ten years, with the recommendation that you do every day of it. Take him down.'

I went out to the news-stand opposite the Factory and bought a *Recorder*. Cryer had done his work well. On page one the headline, *Plastic Bag Nightmare*, marched across the sheet with the stiff majesty of tombstones. It came hard through the print that what Cryer had seen with me in that warehouse had hit him where he lived.

I dialled Cryer. 'They pleased with you over there?'

'Yes.'

'You don't sound too happy.'

'I've been having bad dreams.'

'Yes, the bags were enough to give anyone a jolt,' I said, 'no matter how hard-boiled he thinks he is.'

'Was that meant to be funny?'

'No, I was talking about myself. Now listen. If anyone contacts you over the story, you let me know straight away. It doesn't matter if it sounds far out.'

'Yes, sure. Got any ideas?'

'Just one so far. It's guesswork, but I've got to start somewhere.'

'Anything on the humane killer angle?'

'How the hell did you hear about that?'

'I've got a friend in the lab.'

'You pick useful friends,' I said. 'OK, well, keep in touch.'

Next I rang the internal number upstairs.

'Where have you been, for Christ's sake?' said the voice. 'I've been trying to get hold of you all morning.'

'I was in bed asleep for once.'

'Well, what the hell did you take that baby wonder from *Boy's Own Paper* up there with you for?'

'Because I wanted someone who was prepared to think for himself,' I said, 'not some world-weary hack. I took Cryer up with me because I got the idea he could think, print what he thought,

62

and make a good job of the story. All of which he did.'

'You'd no right whatever to let them offer a five thousand pound reward for information without clearing it with me first - none at all! The whole thing was a carve-up thanks to you. When television and all the rest of the mob got round there everyone had gone, no spokesman, not even a copper on the door – the whole place shut up like a clam and not a plastic bag to be seen!'

'I know,' I said, 'I fixed it like that. I just wanted the one story in the one big circulation daily that every villain reads. That way the hot tip, if there is one, will go to the one man who covered the bags with me. I got the story out where I wanted it out, the way I wanted it out.'

'I don't care what you wanted!'

'Well, that makes it tricky,' I said, 'because it's my case unless you want to take me off it.'

'Don't talk rubbish, sergeant. What I mean is, a man like Bowman wouldn't have handled it like that at all.'

'No,' I said, 'well, our methods are quite different.'

'You've made a completely obscure murder look like a national flap.'

'Who knows but it might turn out to be one?' I said. 'I know the public are pretty jaded, but this is nasty enough to make even them sit up. Besides, slickly done like this was, it could be connected to something else – a well-buried connection. It's unlikely, but it does happen. And another thing – no murder's completely obscure. Luckily. Otherwise, we'd never solve any of them.'

'Are you coming the acid with me, sergeant?'

'I don't frankly know,' I said, with a rare burst of honesty, 'but I have got an idea.'

'What idea?'

'How many people have we got on file, professionals, most like with form, that might use a humane killer on a wet job?'

'Oh yes, that's right,' said the voice, 'I've just read the lab report.

It's those things they use on cows, knackered horses etcetera. They work the same as an air pistol, don't they? You can put them in your pocket. Yes, my daughter-in-law's got one down on her farm in Somerset.'

'That's the gadget. You hold it against a head of some kind, then you pull the trigger and it fires a fucking great nail through your brain.'

'Mind your language, will you, sergeant?' The voice thought for a while and added: 'Still, it's a remarkable choice of weapon, that.'

'It was certainly remarkable for the victim.'

'We don't know who that was yet, do we?'

'Not yet. But we will. I see it as a question of who's vanished. It won't be just anyone. It must be someone who someone else thought it worth spending money on to help the vanishing trick along. I'm having everyone likely checked in a quiet way.'

'Yes, good,' said the voice. 'You're cheeky, sergeant, but you know what you're doing, I'll say that for you.' It added: 'Yes, a humane killer. Stands out, that does. I can't think of a single killing done with one of those, not in my experience. It kind of sticks in your mind.'

'You could certainly say that.'

'Just keep on being funny, sergeant.'

'I'm not being funny.'

'Still, I can't think of anybody,' the voice reflected.

'Well, I've got a feeling I can,' I said. 'I've got a name in my mind that I can't seem to get out again. Now I know it sounds far out, but how about McGruder? You remember – the ex-paratrooper who did bird for murdering a fellow corporal? When he's around they call him Bully on the manor, because that's the way Billy comes out with his accent; he's out of Ulster.'

'Yes, we thought he'd done Wally Wetherby, the supergrass, only the DPP's office decided there wasn't the evidence.'

'Yes, Wetherby,' I said. 'He grassed Darkie Cole over that big bullion job at Heathrow, and then he was in trouble with Pat

Hawes too, down to grassing. Made himself a fortune.'

'That's right,' said the voice. 'We reckoned it was McGruder who came up to Wetherby in that Soho pub there, what's it called, the Norman Arms, that's right, and gave it to him straight through the eye with a sailmaker's needle while they were having a drink at the bar. No, I'm wrong, it wasn't the Norman Arms. It was that other pub in Greek Street, The Case Is Altered. The Norman's in Frith Street, I'm always getting those two streets muddled up, they look almost identical.'

'The case was certainly altered for Wetherby,' I said. 'But not for the killer. The pub was practically empty at the time, it was only ten to six, and no one would identify McGruder. Besides, he had an alibi for the time in question. Five people swore he'd been at their place drinking, and we could not crack it.'

'But I see what you're driving at,' said the voice. 'Four-inch needle – another far-out weapon.'

'That,' I said, 'and his army past. He was a commando really.'

'They should never have let him sign on.'

'He was all right as long as they pointed him in the right direction.'

'A bit too good, I remember from his trial.'

'Yes, and then he was choked at having to do seven like that,' I said. 'It sort of made him moody and liable to go off the rails some more. It's what a lot of bird does to people, though he should have done twenty for Brownlow, and Christ only knows why he didn't.'

'That was his army record,' said the voice. It sighed. 'They certainly taught him to kill all right.'

'Yes, well, after he came out,' I said, 'and did the Wetherby contract for Cole, well then, he just disappeared, and we've had a nice long rest from him this side of the Channel. Still, he must have been doing something, somewhere.'

'I know what you mean,' said the voice. 'I don't see him just gardening.'

'And he does like money,' I said. 'That's another thing came out at his trial. And whoever this man over at Rotherhithe may have been, somebody paid a big whack of it to have him topped, judging by the sweet tidy way it was done.'

'Well, yes, let's say we take an interest in McGruder, just as a start,' said the voice, 'where do you think he might have been for the last few years or so?'

'Hard to say at this stage,' I told him, 'and silly to guess, but why not foreign armies? He's trained, McGruder. He'd do anything for money. What? Kill? Look at his record. Look at Wetherby, if that was McGruder. The man kills, snap, like that; he's a dangerous bastard, he's like a silencer screwed to a pistol. And if he's around, I think he ought to be definitely checked out – nudged on principle.'

'Yes, foreign armies,' mused the voice, 'a mercenary, yes, why not? Plenty of scope for a man like that. No questions asked of a trained man – Africa, the Middle East, Central America – of course, if the money's right.'

'Yes,' I said, 'money. In the transcript of the Brownlow trial it came out that when the SIB went through his pay-book and private bank account he was worth nine thousand quid – not bad for an army corporal.'

'I wonder how he laid hold of all that?'

'I reckon he pulled a job or two when he was on leave,' I said. 'Anyway, what we do know is, he never spent any money if he could help it. He was a man wouldn't give you the skin off his shit – he was noted for it.'

'Yes, all right,' said the voice, 'it could be promising. Any other names occur to you?'

'Yes, three,' I said, 'but the trouble is, they're so obvious that I don't think they fit. They've each of them done a contract, but two of them used a shooter, and the third split the bloke's head open with an axe. They're none of them into anything sophisticated; you'd have to write humane killer down for them in block caps before they even understood what the adjective meant. Also, unlike McGruder, none of them have ever been cooks or butchers' assistants. The only thing they've got in common with McGruder is that they all worked for hard villains. But that's all – otherwise they're all three as thick as planks bolted together. None of them'd ever have had the bottle to take the time that was taken over this job. They'd none of them ever have made corporal in a parachute regiment either. The competition in there, it's ferocious. You know Frank Ballard – that's right, Inspector Ballard who was shot – he was in them. Of course, the man we want could be someone brand new, but I don't think so; villains don't like using people that've just come in from the street. I can pick the others up and have a go if you like, but I don't think it's worth while – not yet anyway. I'd rather start straight off on McGruder.'

'I keep going back to the weapon that was used,' droned the voice. 'Humane killer. No sound. No serial number. Use it and throw it away.'

'Yes, in the river, why not?' I said. 'It was only twenty-odd feet away – that's why I reckon they picked the place. As for who the victim was, I might even know his name by tomorrow; I'm into it hard. I know you don't like what I did about the *Recorder*, but it could be a lot of help.'

'Yes, all right,' said the voice. It added: 'Depending on who the dead man turns out to be, if it was someone important, or even well placed in villains' circles, then the whole of this thing could go off with a big bang.'

'Well, that suits me,' I said, 'because if there are going to be any more headlines in it, it certainly won't be a case for A14 any more; we can hand it back to Serious Crimes. There's the death of what looks like a derelict out at Shepherd's Bush that's just come in, but Sergeant Thompson can't handle it, he's away sick.'

'Never mind that,' said the voice, 'you just concentrate on these bags. And don't worry about the headlines. I'll handle that side of it; you've done more than enough damage.' It added: 'Cooking the man, now. I keep coming back to that too. Cooking. The weapon.

What trademarks!'

'Yes,' I said. 'The older you grow, the madder you get – if you started out mad.'

'McGruder? Mad, do you think?'

'Yes,' I said, 'I do think. Men hate each other. They hit each other. They kill each other. But nobody garrottes a man, like he did that soldier, not for a chance remark. And no one but a downright nut stabs a man through the eye with a needle – not even for money. I'm assuming McGruder did kill Wetherby, of course.' I added: 'Mind, madness can be handy in solving a case. It leaves improbable traces. The harder your man tries to rub out the evidence of his madness, the clearer it becomes. It's like a child wetting its bed. It can dry it right through the night, but the stain's worse still in the morning.'

'Yes, all right,' said the voice. 'Get going with McGruder – we've nothing to lose and we've got to start somewhere.'

'If there is a link it's soon established,' I said, 'one way or the other. If McGruder's not in the country, that's the end of it. But if he is, I'm in favour of a chat with him anyway, no hard feelings. And I think we'll find he is in the country; my instinct is that this killing's got McGruder written all over it; I can't think of anyone else to fit.'

'That's settled, then,' said the voice, 'keep in touch with me over it.' It added: 'God, I remember that Wetherby case now all right. He put nine men in jail, didn't he?' The voice sighed. 'What a waste of a well-nourished little plant Wetherby was!'

'Yes, it must have been very nasty,' I said, 'the two of them side by side in that near-empty bar and then the killer strikes and Wetherby claps his hand to his eye – but it's just a reflex, he's as dead as yesterday, and the killer got away through the back of the boozer and over the wall into that alley there behind the Pillars of Hercules, what's the name of it? You know, where the bookshop is.'

'Yes, and strange,' said the voice, 'how the governor and his barman remembered some things in every detail. Yet could either of them identify the assailant? Or the victim, even? No, they could not.'

'Well, it's not strange really,' I said, 'they'd got their health to consider.'

'Serious Crimes had a dreadful time with that one before we dropped it for lack of evidence,' said the voice. 'I remember all that now. Bowman, wasn't it?'

'Well, if it wasn't,' I said, 'it might well have been.'

'I won't have you criticizing your superior officers, do you understand?'

I said I understood fine, and we rang off.

16

'Billy McGruder?' I said through the door.

'Yes, what is it?'

'It's me. Open up.'

I wouldn't have got onto McGruder that fast if it hadn't been for Cryer over in Fleet Street. He rang me and said: 'I may have got hold of someone down to those bags. He read the story and phoned in.'

'Terrific!' I said. 'Who is it?'

'Bloke from Peckham way; I met him in the Gunners over at Clerkenwell. He wants to meet you – well, that's what he says now, anyway. He wasn't keen at first. What he wanted at first was to do everything through me, cop for the five long ones, and have me pass his information on to you.'

'It doesn't work like that at all,' I said. 'What is he. A grass?'

'That's right. I met him once before, over the Mayfield robbery.'

'Well, there's always a catch over money,' I said, 'if you're a grass. The catch is, he has to talk to the law. He must know that.'

'Well, what I do know,' said Cryer, 'is he's bloody frightened to talk. But the offer of five thousand was too much for him.'

'What's his name?'

'Smitty, they call him. Duck's arse short, fair hair, damaged upper lip, scar across it.'

'I know him, thirty-odd, quite new in the business. OK. Where do I meet him?'

'The Marquis of Darlington, that's his boozer.'

'I know the Marquis,' I said. 'Old Kent Road. And thanks. Nice one, Tom, well done.'

'He says he may have this name for you.'

'I can't wait,' I said, 'and I mean that.'

'I wouldn't bank on it, he's a born liar.'

'What grass isn't?' I said. 'But they're bright enough to know that in their game only the truth pays out. No play, no pay. And don't you worry, I know how to shell a soft-boiled egg.'

'Evening, Smitty.'

'Who are you?' He came on hard, sprawling against the bar like a big man. They always feel they have to do that so as to look less like what they are.

I sat on the stool next to him and ordered us both a pint. Then I slipped out my warrant card so that only he could see it and said: 'This is to introduce us, OK?'

He swallowed. 'Christ,' he muttered, 'you was quick. You get onto me through Cryer?'

'That's right,' I said. 'You must have been expecting me, seeing you're trying to get your foot in with the newspaper world again.'

'Yeah,' he said, 'but you people are always a shock just the same. Anyway, as long as it ain't a John Bull.'

I looked him over. 'You could probably just do with one,' I said thoughtfully. 'It must be coming up to your time to paint a few more walls over at Wandsworth. What was it last time? Ripping off that wholesale bra showroom up in Great Portland Street, wasn't it?'

He choked on his beer; I thought he was going to start crying.

'I'm clean!' he hissed. 'Clean, do you hear?'

'OK,' I said, 'but watch your step and don't give me any shit. Now, what we're here to talk about is someone who went on a macabre shopping spree and left five Waitrose shopping bags at a warehouse in Rotherhithe – what do you know about it?'

'I'll tell you what,' he muttered, 'why don't we go over to that empty table in the corner, casual like?'

We did that. The door of the pub stood open. It was light still for April – an evening of swiftly fading sunshine and a feeling in the air like the threat of a downpour. The place was filling up fast.

'I don't know,' he said when we were settled, 'I can't decide. I don't really want to talk to you – anyway, not in a boozer.'

'It was your choice for the meet, this place,' I said, 'and maybe this will help you make up your mind.' I took out a ton, folded small in twenties, and pushed it to him under the ashtray.

Three dark, heavy men over by the bar were watching us all the time; their clothes were so casual that they glared.

I said to Smitty: 'Set them up again and keep the change.'

He fondled the money away into his hand. When he came back with the round I said: 'All right. I'm busy, what's the score?'

'Are those people really paying out?' he said. 'The five long ones? That's what I want to know first.'

'If you've got the best seat in the theatre,' I said, 'the State'll pay for it.'

'I'm taking a diabolical risk over this, opening my yap at all.'

'Well, we all have to take risks, don't we?' I said. 'That's how we earn our wages.'

'OK, it was Friday the thirteenth, all right,' he said finally. 'I remember that because it's unlucky, ain't it? It was around nine in the evening, and I was down in Hammersmith. I was over there casual, just casual, see, at a pub called the Nine Foot Drop.'

'I know it,' I said, 'Tony Williams's place. It's full of villains, solid with them, even worse than in here.'

'I'm being a right cunt,' he said, looking round him. But he may not have seen the three heavies; they were dead behind him, about eight feet away. He took a big drink of the whisky he was using as a chaser; sweat broke out on his face.

'Look,' I said, 'there's no need to wear your balls out. I'm not interested in what you were doing in Hammersmith; I just know it's not your manor. And you ought to drink less cheap whisky,' I added, 'that brand's playing havoc with your harpsichord.'

'It's all I can afford,' he croaked, 'and the way my nerves are, mate, I need plenty of it.' His eyes kept darting about; they were a deep, liquid colour like a cross-bred rabbit's. 'We're talking too long over this.'

'Choke it all up, then. I'm not stopping you.'

'I've gotter have more money up front. I mean a lot.'

'You've just had a ton,' I said, 'now talk.' He really was a horrible little git. He'd no bottle. He was a piss-artist who sold people down the river; anyone would do if there was a few bob in it for him. Over the stroke he'd pulled at Great Portland Street, he had actually grassed himself as well as the other two men in it with him, hoping to get off by turning evidence. He didn't, though. He went down just the same, and got properly done over in the shit-houses on the twos.

'Well, this geezer,' said Smitty, 'I don't know if you know of him, but he's bad news. And I mean really bad.'

'How bad?' I said. 'Bad enough for his Christian name to be Billy? Or Bully?'

'How the fuck did you know that?'

'It's practice and instinct,' I said. 'When you've had as much to do with murder as I have, some things that look difficult turn out to be really quite easy. Well, go on. He's out of Ulster, place called Coleraine.'

'That's him,' said Smitty. 'Ex-paratrooper.' He was sweating hard now, and it made him smell bad. 'McGruder.' He made a noise like a sob and said: 'You've got to give me some more readies up front. A lot.'

'What do you think we are over at the Factory,' I said, 'millionaires? OK, so you saw McGruder. What else? Anyone with him?'

'I don't know about with him, but there was a villain called Merrill Edwardes standing next to him for a while: fancy dresser, wears a blazer, glasses, about thirty, nice accent, scar on his left ear. They didn't speak, but that don't mean anything, it could've been a meet just the same. Then I saw Edwardes leave something on the bar and McGruder, he picked it up when he went for a slash – I've got an idea it was car keys.'

'Yes, good,' I said, 'I like it. You're doing well, Smitty, keep going. Then what? He talk to anyone at all in the pub?'

The grass trembled. 'No, but he looked hard at a geezer, and that's terrible news, to be looked at by a man like McGruder.'

'Who was he looking at? Come on.'

'It was a grass I know called Jackie Hadrill.'

'You mean the big grass? You don't mean the one that put Pat Hawes away?'

'That's him.'

'Christ, that's worth another ton,' I said, 'only the trouble is, I haven't got it on me.'

The heavies over at the bar were looking at us all the time; one of them was picking his teeth with a match. They were the Grossman brothers over from Plaistow, and they usually went armed. Between them they'd already done forty years in the grey place, and I took a bet with myself that they hadn't finished yet.

'Anyone seen Hadrill around since you saw him?'

'I haven't heard of anyone seeing him.'

'And Edwardes,' I said. A lot was going on in my head now. 'Yes, that name rings a bell too. So you saw Hadrill in the Drop and fancy that, you were probably the last person except the killer to see him alive.' I added: 'And where were you, by the way, for the rest of that night, while we're at it?'

'Christ,' he said, 'I really am going to spew if you go on like that. I was with three mates and a dolly all that night and I can prove it.'

'Lucky for you,' I said, 'with your form. You get your end away?'

'No bleeding chance,' he said. 'We just played cards over at her place and then one of the other geezers took her knickers off after.'

'I'm surprised he could wait that long,' I said, 'the friends you've got. What were you playing? Seven card?'

'Yeah, hi–low, and I lost.'

'Well, I can't hold your hand for you, can I?' I said. 'I should just give up poker if I were you. So you reckon they were car keys, then, the things McGruder picked up?'

'Well, I couldn't swear to it, but I reckon so, yes. Or to a flat.'

'All right. So then Edwardes leaves the pub first, and then after a while McGruder leaves. Then, finally, Hadrill leaves. Is that right?' He nodded and I said: 'And nothing between any of them? Not a word?'

'That's right.'

'You got an address for McGruder at all?'

'Yes, I reckoned that might be a few extra bob – I've got it for you. I've got ways.' He palmed me a scrap of paper which I pocketed fast.

I drained my pint and stood up. 'OK. Well, drop round and see me at the Factory, and when I'm happy with the statement you make, the paper'll pay you off half – the other half on conviction. That's how it's played.' I glanced at the three heavies behind us. 'On second thoughts,' I added, 'I think you'd better come with me if you know what's good for you. You've got the Grossmans dead behind you and they're taking a kind of interest.'

'Leave with you?' he scoffed. 'From here? I wouldn't be seen dead with you anywhere. Ken, Harry and Dave, they're good mates of mine anyway.'

'I didn't know they had any mates,' I said, starting to leave. 'Still, it's up to you.' Afterwards, I regretted that; if I hadn't had so much on my mind I'd have insisted, but we all make mistakes. I looked back from the door in time to see the brothers moving towards Smitty; his mouth was opening, as usual.

The weather had changed. Black clouds had moved in to cover the sky, and it was starting to weep with rain.

17

'You'd better come in.' McGruder smiled, opening the door.

'Thanks,' I said. 'Try keeping me out.' I went in and stood looking about. 'Not bad,' I remarked, 'if you don't mind everything being repro.'

'Well, I don't frankly mind,' he said.

'Then neither do I,' I said, 'so let's make ourselves comfortable, this is going to take a minute or two.'

'Oh yes?' He sat down in a hard little armchair upholstered the colour of milk chocolate. His Ulster accent showed through a little. 'Is it down to the old?'

'No, Billy,' I said, 'this is a brand-new thing.' I went over to the window and looked out. It was four in the afternoon. Opposite, six eleven-floor blocks stood about in the unimaginative attitudes of those who had conceived them, on a piece of waste ground. Far away, across the river to the north, what was left of London these days tried to look cultured and inviting. It failed – anyway, with me.

'You could give a man a turn,' he said behind me, 'coming in like that.'

'Oh, come on,' I said, 'not you. With what you've got on the slate you must be used to it.'

'What's paid for's paid for,' said McGruder. 'Don't let's talk about that.'

'Oh, so you think it's paid for, do you?' I said. 'What does that mean? That you think you can go out and do it some more?'

'Listen, what's this about, exactly?'

'I'll ask the questions, Billy; you just answer them, that way we both know where we are. You been back in Britain long?'

'No.'

'Any identification on you?'

He shook his head: 'I'm not obliged. Anyway not yet, not till the plastic cards come in.'

'You here on a British passport?'

'Of course not. Eire. I work a lot abroad and listen – you are needling me for some reason and getting right up my nose, why are you having a go at me?'

'Because you've got nasty habits,' I said, 'and have been inside for murder, garrotting a man, and I'm checking up on you on principle, and also your face might just be the missing piece in the puzzle of this new thing I'm investigating.'

'I suppose that means you want to have a look round the pad?'

I nodded. 'Yeah, I think so.'

'Well, I hope you've got a W on you.'

'Look,' I said, 'don't be pathetic. Don't start being a know-it-all about the paperwork, or I might just, to cross a few t's, drift back over to the Factory and get one.'

'And what would the charge be?' he asked in his lilting voice.

'It could be murder.'

'You'll be lucky,' he said. He yawned. He was thirty-three and dark-haired, with a small neat head. His white ears curled tightly into his hair; they had no lobes to them. He hardly had any lips either – just a smile like the slit in a pillbox. His gaze cut straight through you.

I said: 'You'll go down really hard with your form if I can fit you to this. You'll never come up again, Billy. This time you won't bounce.'

He didn't seem to care. He was wearing a red wool pullover, tight black slacks and shoes with gilded buckles on them.

'What was the job, then?'

'It was a wet job,' I said, 'at least it was until someone boiled it dry.'

'And you're looking at me?' He laughed. 'You're like one of

those riddles my old grandad used to pull out of a cracker on Christmas Day.'

'Well, I'd watch your tone if I were you,' I said, 'because today isn't Christmas and I've forgotten my funny hat.'

'You people can't take a joke.'

'No, we're serious folk,' I said. 'It can come from looking into some shopping bags.'

There was a silence. At last he said: 'Are you talking about that job at Rotherhithe? You can't be, for Christ's sake! It must have been a nut that did that!'

'You're right,' I said, 'and my job is to put a name to him and do him. He's got to be caught.'

'Yes, Christ! Cooking a feller up, it's dreadful!' said McGruder solemnly. 'It makes you really want to puke, what a sick bastard!'

'You can stuff the morals,' I said. 'Mind if I have a look round here?'

'Well, frankly I'm not keen,' he said. 'I'm one of those people, I'm fussy, I don't care to have my gear messed about. I used to be in the army, and it comes of that I dare say.'

'I dare say too,' I said, 'also from being in the nick a long time. Well? Can I do it? Or do I have to go back to the Factory for the paperwork?'

He shrugged. 'OK. I'm not a man to make difficulties.'

'For someone with your form,' I said, 'it sounds funny to hear you say that.'

He thought that over. 'Look,' he said finally, 'I'll try and be kind about this, but you're beginning to give me a pain. Tell me what you're looking for, and I'll tell you if it's here. Or else, OK, just get on and have a look round.'

I already was.

'I'm not being deliberate,' he said, following me around, 'but that way we'll save each other a load of trouble, and then you can be on your bike.'

'With people like you,' I said, 'my bike has a flat tyre.'

'What are you after, exactly?' he said, leaning against the wall.

'Well, it's not a sailmaker's needle this time round.'

There was another pause, which I spent whipping through his gear.

'I should think it bloody isn't. I'm no sailmaker.'

But it took him quite a while to come up with that one. Then he said: 'What is it you're looking for, then?'

I said: 'If I found a humane killer that would be just right.' I was into the bedroom by this time and had the mattress off on the floor. 'Don't go mad,' I said, 'I'll put it all back again when I've finished and you can sleep tight; I'm not an unfriendly man.'

'You won't find a humane killer or anything else like that here.'

'No, you threw it in the river like a sensible man. How much did you cop for the job, Billy? A grand? Two grand?'

'Listen,' he said, 'what makes you pick on me?'

'Well, let's just start with the fact that you've done seven for murder and you're worth keeping an eye on.'

'You don't even know who the geezer was yet,' he said, 'it says so in the linens.'

'You're wrong there,' I said. 'When did you last see Jackie Hadrill?'

'I've never heard of him.'

'Oh, come on, Billy,' I said, 'even the general public's heard of Jack Hadrill, let alone every villain, and now, you wouldn't believe it, he's gone and disappeared and not a squeak's been heard out of him since the night of April the thirteenth, and where were you that night?'

'I was pissed out of my brain in a pub in Hammersmith.'

'Rare for you; people I've been asking tell me you don't drink. Which pub was it? The Nine Foot Drop?'

'Could have been.'

'I'm asking you was it,' I said. 'Now don't fuck me about, Billy.'

'Yes, it was the Nine Foot Drop,' he said, 'and I was with some mates of mine there.'

'It had better be good,' I said, 'I shall want the names.'

'You can have the names.' He added: 'I reckon there might be plenty of people would have wanted to waste a geezer like that.'

'Who, for instance?'

'I don't know,' he said. 'But you know, grasses, they usually don't last long, do they? But what I still don't get is, why pick on me?'

'There's no secret about that,' I said. 'This is a big city, but I can't think of six villains in it that would have used a humane killer for a topping job. I'll go further. Right now I can only think of one, and you may not believe this but fancy, you're the one.'

'I don't even know yet,' he said, 'as a matter of interest, how you're sure it was Hadrill; I saw on telly how he was all boiled away to a mess.'

'Look,' I said, 'I keep telling people I come across, anybody that'll listen, how stupid killers are. Particularly when they're trying to be extra clever – that's just what drops them in the shit.'

'None of my business,' said McGruder, 'but I think it'd have to be a sight stronger than that.'

'And it is,' I said, 'and it is your business. Because you were seen in the Nine Foot Drop that night. Also there was a man called Edwardes standing next to you for a while at the bar.'

I wished I could find Edwardes; it wasn't for want of looking.

McGruder shrugged. 'Look, I was there on the evening of the thirteenth, there's no secret about it. Tony Williams the governor there put me up – six of us spent all night in his flat upstairs rabbiting and playing cards. So what about it?'

'If it's waterproof,' I said, 'that's all about it, Billy. But I'm gnawing at it, and if it isn't kosher I'll find where the leak is and when I do, it's you that's going to leak, OK?'

'I don't believe anyone saw anything,' said McGruder, 'I reckon it's just a blag.'

'You can believe what you like,' I said, 'if I crack you you'll have all the time in the world to work out where you went wrong. For the time being, I'm working on it, but I find it strange – same pub, same night, you a convicted killer, and Hadrill vanishes. I find the whole thing a great big coincidence, and I believe in them like I believe in Father Christmas, i.e., not at all, get it?'

'What I get,' said McGruder, 'is that the counsel I can afford, he'd rip it all to pieces if you were daft enough to have a go, you've no proof.'

'It's early days,' I said. 'It isn't proof yet, but it could easily be evidence, and you might find it will be by the time I've finished with it.'

'You're trying to fit me up for this, then,' said McGruder in an easy voice. He kept smiling, even though the smile wasn't really wanted just then; he had the look of a man, to me, who knew he was in trouble.

'Yes, I'm going to have a go,' I said. I stood up. 'I'll be in and out, Billy. Bye for now, and happy wanking.'

18

Next morning, Saturday, I had proof that the body in the bags was Jack Hadrill's. His boyfriend, who hadn't been able to get into the Notting Hill pad that he shared with Jack, broke in (he was a tealeaf), and there was a letter on Jack's bed which he finally brought into us after sweating a lot, hoping to do himself some sort of good. The letter was dated the thirteenth and in it Jack said that he was due to go out that evening – he didn't say where – but he wondered if the meet wasn't moody. He added that he'd been offered a deal with a lot of money in it by an anonymous punter. He'd left the flat key under the mat so that the friend could get in anyway, but the latter had been too stupid to look for it there. He was just, I thought when I had had a word with him, one of those people who preferred breaking into a place to using the key.

I had Hadrill's file in my drawer already – mind, I knew enough about him without it. Now there was a funny man. He'd hardly ever done bird – much too sharp – just three months for whizzing a motor when he was a lad. But he was one of those folk with ears so big for hearing what didn't concern him, you wouldn't believe. His mouth in the photograph was correspondingly small, except when you offered it money; then it expanded in an alarming way and a lot of stuff came out of it – big stuff. It was always more than enough to send somebody down for a long while. I hate grasses. I use them because I have to, but I hate them. I had met Hadrill, though he mightn't have remembered because it wasn't my case. He'd done well for himself, he thought; he was smug, frightened, gay and a tiny spender. Now, if he were still alive, he mightn't be sure that he'd done that well. Still, it had been the good life while it lasted – good clothes, food and a bachelor's pad in W11, though he'd kicked off, like plenty of other people, in SE12. I'd seen Jack around on his manor up at the Gate; everybody had. He drank over at the Wild Card Club up by the underground, wore a clipper-style cap which was supposed to make you think he was something out of *The Onedin Line* (he sometimes said he was, after his fourth pint) and tight knee-length boots. He probably went to bed in all that and thought he was a fucking Sturmbannführer every time he had a wet dream.

But he was just a grass, and I considered that other interesting thing about him, that he was gay. A gay grass.

'Well,' I said, 'now we know it was Jack Hadrill. We know it two ways – what I got out of this man Smitty and the note.'

'Yes, when you leave a note like that it makes it almost official. The DPP'll like that,' said the voice.

'Do you remember the last thing Jack did? It made him a lot of taxpayers' money, but it got him in right shtuck as well.'

'That was over Pat Hawes, wasn't it?'

'Yes, we didn't handle it. Too high-powered for us.'

'We didn't handle it, sir.'

'No, that's right, we didn't. Hadrill went to Bowman over it.'

'Chief Inspector Bowman.'

'Yes, Bowman, that's the man, over at Serious Crimes. Jack grassed Hawes over that big wages snatch up north, out York way, and Hawes drew a lot of bird because a security guard was killed and so, what with his form, they threw the book at him, and a good thing too.'

'You think eight years in Parkhurst or Wakefield will improve his morale, sergeant?'

'He never had any. If I'd been Serious Crimes I'd have liked to know more about that business with the guard. He was going off shift; he wasn't even armed, it says in the transcript. Either Hawes was just trigger-happy, or there was more to it, I'd say; I like the second possibility better. Still, having people like Hawes out of circulation does clear the ground for other business. Mopping up the same old thieves and murderers time after time does get monotonous, you feel you're getting nowhere.'

'We're quite the philosopher today, sergeant, aren't we? So you still want to get after McGruder, do you?'

'I've started. I want to get after him even harder now, sir.'

'Good God,' said the voice, 'you finally said it. I know I'm only a deputy commander, but I thought you were never going to.'

I imagined he was trying to be funny.

'Hawes never forgets,' I said, 'people like that never do from their viewpoint, why should they? There's every reason to think he had Hadrill done; he's got plenty of money available even if he is inside. And Hadrill told Serious Crimes a lot about that raid, you'll remember, but neither they nor the DPP's office thought fit to go after it at the time.'

'No, that was killed from on high,' said the voice.

'How high?'

'High enough. What the mind doesn't know, the heart doesn't grieve over, sergeant; you must know that old saying.'

'I know lots of old sayings,' I said. 'One of them is that what's allowed to go cold can be warmed over. I can't remember the exact words.'

'The exact words, *sir*.'

'That's it. I can't remember them.'

'I don t give a damn about your memory. This Hadrill business – I want to be kept informed the whole time.'

'Why?'

'Because that's the way I want it, and that's all you need bother about.'

'Do you know something about it that I don't?'

'I'm not saying that. All I'm saying is, you never know what a case like this can turn into.'

'What I do know,' I said, 'is that if this one gets out of hand it could turn into a bloody nightmare.'

'What I want you to understand, sergeant,' said the voice, 'is that if you disobey my orders it'll turn into a nightmare for you.'

'You don't often give any orders.'

'No, I know. So that when I do, I want them obeyed.'

He rang off on that.

I put down the phone and looked out of the window at the grey clouds, full of rain, bursting on the roof of Marks & Sparks opposite. I had a sudden dreadful feeling, like the man who realizes too late that he shouldn't have overtaken on a double bend and sees the accident racing towards him. A mate of mine, a motorcycle patrolman, was crippled for life that way, chasing a souped-up Cortina full of villains through the lanes round Maidstone one Saturday night. It took him six months to get his memory back; then he described it to me when I went to see him in hospital – how the road was slippery after rain and how his bike hit the front of the oncoming van sideways while he was on the wrong side of the road overtaking two other vehicles and trying to brake from ninety: the disbelief, the impact, the nothing. 'They've rechristened me Mr Multiple Fracture,' he told me, grinning through his smashed teeth. He was retired, of course, and they weren't generous with him because he had been in the wrong and the van driver had been badly injured.

It didn't matter that much; he died in hospital three months later.

Now I wondered if something sudden like that was going to happen to me – even down to being in the wrong as well.

19

'Can we have a truce?' I said to Bowman. 'Now don't lose your wig – I mean just ten minutes' worth.'

'Christ,' he said, 'you must be fucking desperate.'

'Yes, I am,' I said, 'I'm anxious for some information. I want to know everything you can tell me about Pat Hawes and that factory up north, that shoe factory that was robbed. You made that arrest, didn't you?'

'That's right,' said Bowman. 'I don't feel like helping you,' he grumbled, 'I never feel like helping you.'

'This is a truce.'

'Yes, all right. Well, thanks to Jackie Hadrill it was easy, a doddle. Hawes went down hard because he shot that security man. He shot him because the feller caught them at it, and they didn't expect him, see?'

'No,' I said, 'because I suppose they'd had their card marked that it was OK just to go in.'

'Right,' said Bowman, 'Hadrill had marked it for them, so they didn't even bother to go in with a balaclava on, so of course the guard could have identified them.'

'OK,' I said. 'Next – do you know what connection Jackie had with that factory?'

'No, he wouldn't tell us, though I asked him, and I didn't press him. He'd grassed Hawes, which was the deal we'd made, and that was what mattered to us. But he must have been well in there somehow.'

'You knew he was gay?'

'Sure.'

'Did it ever occur to you that he might have had sexual relations

86

with someone up there and then threaten to blow the whistle on him if he didn't get certain information?'

'No, it didn't,' said Bowman. 'Look, I'm not the Branch. My job was to make arrests over that factory rip-off and the death of the guard. And I did, and the DPP was happy with it.'

'Pity you didn't push the boat out a little further, just the same,' I said.

'Look,' said Bowman patiently, 'you can't twist the arm of a man like that too hard. If you do, you're liable to lose him. A big grass like that, if you try to get out of him something he doesn't want to tell you, he'll just go and find some other officer, more accommodating.'

I sighed. 'Yes, well, it's too late now. But I think he was keeping a great deal back.'

'Why?'

'First,' I said, 'because if it was something really big, let's say it was security-linked, he'd have ended up having to go to the Branch. And if he'd done that, he'd have had to grass this theoretical boyfriend of his that he was putting the black on. And he might have had reasons for not wanting to do that. Also, take the guard. Come on, let's speculate – maybe the guard knew about Hadrill and Mr X. He may have been gay himself. He might have got ideas about putting the black on Mr X all on his own, of grassing Hadrill before Hadrill was ready. A horner-in, if you'll excuse the pun. That guard could have been a thundering nuisance to Hadrill.'

'You do pick up odd lines on the obvious,' said Bowman, 'and put another twist on them, I'll say that. Mind, gay – it's no crime to be gay nowadays,' he added regretfully.

'No crime – still, it could be awkward for a married man, say, doing top-grade security work in a government establishment. It's all theory, of course.'

'You're a funny man, you are,' said Bowman, 'there are times when you really freak me. You're difficult, cheeky, self-opinionated

– you don't try and get on in the force at all. Yet some of your theories, seeing this is a truce, well, I like them, I can't deny it.'

'You sound to me as if you knew something I don't know,' I said. 'Are you telling me every single thing you know or suspect about this robbery? Come on. Are you?'

'No,' he said, 'no, I'm not. There are certain things I'm not telling you because I haven't the authority to do it.'

I was truly astonished. 'Never, never in my life,' I said, 'have I ever heard you say a thing like that before.' I added: 'What's the matter with you? Something new on the ministry of defence?'

'No, Christ, why?' he shouted. 'Have you heard something?'

'No I haven't, only you look as if you had.'

'Look,' he said, grabbing me by the jacket, 'are you on to someone over this Hadrill killing? Anyone? Come on, speak up, fuck you!'

'Yes, I may be,' I said. I shook him loose: 'It's a lucky thing I only wear old clothes to work.'

He shrieked: 'Come on, I haven't got all day – who are you after for it?'

'It's more what my head tells me than anything definite yet.'

'The name, the name!' he groaned.

'Well,' I said, 'it might ring a bell with you at that. I'm not saying you deserve it, but the name's Billy McGruder.'

'Him? Christ! I thought he was in Central America or something.'

'For your information,' I said, 'Central America is now a bus ride from hell – cost you all of eighty pence, a housing estate over at Catford.'

'You think you can stick it on him?'

'Yes, I think I can,' I said, 'because frankly I'm convinced he did it.'

'Some information received?'

'Yes, of course,' I said. 'We'd none of us get far without some of that after all, would we?'

'Now don't start taking the piss,' he said.

'I'm really getting so interested in the rest of that factory,' I said, 'that I'm going to try and check it out.'

'Well, you won't get far.'

'What are they really making up there that's so bloody secret?' I said. 'Come on, Charlie, whatever it is, disguising it as a shoe factory was an incredibly stupid idea if you ask me.'

'Easy,' he said. 'Look, you could be talking about a government department.'

'What else could I be talking about?' It's a typical civil servant idea. They live in egg-boxes, these people – no one in his right mind'd ever swallow the notion it was a shoe factory. Shoe factory!' I shouted. 'You don't get people in white coats with heads like a goose's egg and a degree in physics making bloody shoes, not even in these hard times!'

'Look,' said Bowman, 'don't be the greyhound, son, give the hare a chance. Don't be deliberate, see? Just leave that factory alone.'

'But how can I, if Hadrill's connected?'

'Don't be so fucking holy!' he shouted. 'Do I have to draw you a map? Give them a bit of flannel, pass it back upstairs. Do what I did. Please 'em, please 'em, all you have to do is to please 'em! I'm trying to help you, son – just concentrate on your plastic bags.'

'You're not running this case, Charlie – I am.'

'Oh, for God's sake,' he said, 'you are a right nut and I'm humouring you for it, but you're stretching it, calling me Charlie. I hate it: I'm always telling you.'

'You're cunning,' I said, 'and it's what makes you stupid, Charlie – I like you but you do get on my nerves.'

'Well, I don't like you, sergeant,' he said, 'it's no good, I just don't – there's something about you, like arrogant or something, that gets right up my nose.'

'It's not arrogance,' I said, 'it's my plain thinking. I've got no rank to win, none to lose, I think clear.'

We stood up at the same moment; the truce was over.

20

I had been checking on Pat Hawes through the computer, but it wasn't easy, because a lot of what I wanted had a Branch star on it, and that meant you had to get far up to the top before you could get access to the file. But I was interested why the Branch had ever been on to Hawes at all, so I went as far up as the voice which, after I had told it why I wanted the material, reluctantly went further up still. This enabled me to find out that for a good while Hawes (with his brother Andy, dead now down to a villains' shoot-out in Stockwell) had been mixed up with the Soviet Trade Delegation over at Highgate. Trade Delegation was the polite Russian name for their espionage services in this country. Normally, that was none of my business, but I was interested to see, in this context, that we had been giving it a great deal of attention lately. What one of its branches did (the one I cared about) was subvert our higher-ranking politicians if they could, and that was where Pat and Andy had come in. If there was one thing those two specialized in aside from downright naked villainy it was running moody companies. The companies were nothing but expensive notepaper and a kosher letterhead, with registered offices in a shed in the brothers' back garden in Greenwich. Then they got hold of idiot punters, greedy MPs attracted by easy money, and put them on the board. All the punters had to do – anyway, that was what it looked like at first – was commit themselves by signing share certificates, then carry on and just draw directors' fees. But quite soon things would get more complicated for the punter. He would find himself having straight questions put to him by 'fellow directors'; the subject would invariably be classified information. It was really tricky for the punter. If he kicked across with the answers, fine, well then he had betrayed his country and could carry on drawing his fees again in peace for a while. If he refused, Pat and Andy would reveal that the company that was paying him was completely bent, and would threaten to pull the rug out. This happened often, because these moody companies were financed from Highgate; and if there was one thing the Haweses hated, it was having to pay anyone money for long. Neither were the Russians a charity organization. Then there would be a sudden by-election, the sitting member having resigned through 'ill-health'.

The Fraud Squad and the Branch had had a lot of trouble so bad that at one point Chief Inspector Verlander had put up a notice in his room that read: The Following MPs Will Not Be Served. Once, a junior minister had had the rug pulled out too soon – as Andy Hawes remarked at the minister's trial, 'just to see what would happen, like'. What happened was that the junior minister, who was on bail pending the verdict, blew his brains out on the steps under Albert Bridge, while the cabinet minister involved strolled off for a bathe while on holiday in France, 'drowned', and then turned up in Cape Town with a bird. All that was arranged by the brothers, because the Soviets had decided that they might still make use of this minister after all. It didn't work out, though, because the South Africans blew the whistle on the 'swimmer' and two officers from the Yard went out and brought him home on the next plane. The public thought it was a terrific giggle but they hadn't been told everything, otherwise the government would have looked even more stupid. A large quota of Soviet 'trade delegates' was returned to Moscow marked Not Wanted, and that appeared to be the end of it. In my view the ex-minister should have drawn a good ten; he unfortunately only got three, though, and did two at Ford open. Still, it was the end of his political career, and so I should bloody well hope.

When asked at his trial how he had managed to swim all the way from Antibes to Cape Town the accused replied bitterly: 'Well, I had my water-wings on, didn't I?' At least he had learned things – he knew better than to implicate the brothers, who had turned some evidence for the occasion, but by no means all of it.

Now, though, over in Stoke Newington, people with nothing better to do could still gawp at the padlocked gates with weeds under them where the two Haweses had originally started up in business. The writing on the gates read: HAWES BROS, DEALERS IN NON-FERROUS SCRAP. There used to be another inscription underneath in semi-literate white letters: This Firm Runs The Manor, No Coppers Here.

But the whole lot had been painted out now, similar to the folk that had run it.

I went to see Pat Hawes; he had just moved to Wandsworth, so I didn't have far to go. I saw him by appointment in an empty cell in the Punishment Block. The customary scene – section 43 and a screw outside.

'Hello, Pat.'

'What do you want?'

'Whatever I like that you've got to give,' I said, 'might be a little, might be a lot.'

'If it's questions you won't get any answers. I'm not very easy,' he said, 'no, I'd say I was a difficult man.'

'You must be a masochist to talk like that,' I said, 'because this is going to be sheer agony for you, I've come here to loosen you up a great deal.'

He looked at me full of age-old lies. He still looked big, but not so fit – not like back in the days when he still had an iron bar in his hand. He seemed to me now a man for whom the murderous rush across a pub at someone he thought was being deliberate was now over – and I hoped for good. He was a London whelk out of its shell that therefore stood no chance: a clever man, resourceful, oversexed like the rest of us and who, as well, trusted no one. Violence, his only cover, had consistently uncovered him, discovered him. But in my role I was watching him, seeing how jail life, jail food and jail inactivity were in the process of turning him to jelly. Yet when I thought of how he had taken life and maimed it, that separated us, and then I stopped bothering about his state.

'You know a man called Jack or Jackie Hadrill?'

'By sight, yes. Who doesn't. But not to know him, no.'

'Now look, you're trying to take me for a cunt,' I said, 'which as far as I'm concerned proves that you're one. Now don't fuck me about – Hadrill was practically on the firm. I say practically because after he marked your card for that shoe factory he then grassed you to Serious Crimes.'

'Oh well,' he said, gazing away at the wall, 'no hard feelings, that's how it goes.'

'You mean how it went,' I said. 'Hadrill's dead.'

'Yes, I saw that on telly,' he said. 'Nasty.'

'Right, there's nothing much worse can happen to you than winding up boiled and stapled into five plastic bags. You know anything about it?'

'Me?' he said. 'In here? You've got to be joking.'

'I just don't know what's happened to my jokes,' I said, 'and yours are pretty flat too. The fact that you're in here has nothing to do with it. Hadrill's dead, you've got a motive for wanting that, I'm the man who's been told to find out about it, and I'm going to.'

He didn't say anything straight away, just stood looking ahead as if he wanted to have a stiff shit. 'I know what they really make up at that factory in Yorkshire,' I said. (I didn't know.) 'Where it says they make shoes. It isn't shoes.'

'It was shoes the night I was there,' he quipped. 'But maybe they've started on something else now.'

'Don't be cheeky,' I said. 'Are you still saying you just took the wages?'

'Right.'

'Well, that's funny, because Hadrill knew there was a fucking sight more to it than that. That's what got him interested in you. I know, because he left a note. More than a note really. More like a letter.'

'I don't believe it,' said Hawes. 'Hadrill was just a grass. He got us bang to rights; now he must have grassed someone else, got up their nose and was topped, and who fucking cares?'

'You might find yourself doing a lot of caring,' I said, 'because I'm beginning to reckon that you thought you'd better top Hadrill before he came to us about what got lost at the factory besides the money.'

'I'm really sorry,' he sneered, 'I'm completely and totally mixed up, what you're talking about.'

I attacked on another front. 'What it is,' I said, 'you're sick with fright, because you've heard that we're not going to stop until we've found out who did Hadrill, who had him done, and why. You hoped his body was going to get dumped out with the garbage, didn't you? You didn't think the bags were ever going to be found, did you? Well, now you know what's happened – your man made a right royal fuck-up, had to leave his signature, had to leave the bags for the caretaker to find. Also the job had "done for money" written all over it, a right villain's work, and that's dropped you straight in the shit, as if you weren't in it already.'

Hawes started to look unhappy, and it didn't surprise me. 'I've been through all the people who've had visiting orders from you,' I said. 'There's your wife and your eldest boy, who's doing borstal now I hear, a real chip off the old block. And then there's your brother-in-law, Tony Williams, he pops in and out too.'

'Well, why not?' Hawes said. 'He's family, ain't he?'

'You're not being helpful,' I said, 'which wouldn't be so bad, except that I know you could be helpful if you wanted.'

He shook his head. 'I can't help you at all, copper.'

'Look, you're not being very bright either,' I said, 'so I'm going to put this simply. You've got a lot of bird to do yet, a lot – and you can take it from me that the parole board's not keen on you, so you might find yourself in the death having to do practically all of it, particularly if we give the board a push. After all, you've killed three men and badly damaged a lot more, so why not?' I looked round me. 'Still, I suppose it's not that bad in here, not for you. I hear you just about run the maximum security wing. You've got some screws bent. You've got money outside, plenty of it, and then you've got Williams; after all, he's the governor of the Nine Foot Drop, and I bet he's always good for a bit of the ready.'

'What's Tony got to do with it?'

'A lot,' I said. 'That pub of his was the last place Hadrill was seen alive. We'll come back to that. Meantime, though, speaking of governors, I believe the governor here's not a hard man. Not hard with you anyway – he doesn't want a riot on his hands. Then you're a snout baron. I've had a long talk with the principal officer and it seems you've been in front of the governor for working a few tabs in, a bit of shit. Sells well in here, doesn't it? Why, Christ, for a killer, you're leading the life of Riley in here.'

'Well, it could be worse,' he smirked. 'All the same, it's bloody bad.'

'You moody bastard,' I said, 'if you don't cooperate with me I'll make it fucking impossible. How would you like to do the bird you've got now, and then double it?'

'You can't work that, you bastard!' he screamed. 'There's a fucking law in this country!'

'That's right,' I said, 'and I'm it. And if you won't help me, and if I have to prove the hard way that you had a connection with Hadrill's death, then you'll find yourself back at the Bailey before you've even had a chance to do up your shoes, do you hear? If I can show, as I mean to end up doing, that anyone ever even mentioned the name Hadrill to you, well then, a word with the DPP's office is all it takes. And here you are – it's not as if I even had to go to the trouble of arresting you. None of it's difficult for me. Dicey for you, though. You mightn't be able to take all that extra bird. Suppose you drew thirty altogether, why, you'd be seventy-two by the time you came out, Pat, do you realize that? Think of it! You could go mad in here; folk do. And think of all that money you've got koshered away outside, and never a chance to spend five p of it till you're an old cunt on a stick. And again, who knows, they might have changed the currency or something by the time your release comes up; things happen fast outside these days.'

'You bastard!' he shouted. 'Fuck you!'

'That's OK,' I said, 'let it rip. What matters is, when you've finished, are you going to help me or not? How was that Hadrill meet set up? Who arranged for McGruder? Tony? You?'

'Get stuffed!' he bawled. 'I've never heard of McGruder!'

'I was told downstairs that you were having roast duckling breasts with green pepper sauce on them for dinner tonight,' I said primly. 'Now that's a very rich meal, and I wouldn't want it to go repeating on you.'

He went white. 'You can't interfere with a man's food!'

'I can interfere with anything I like,' I said, 'there's always a way. Anyhow, when it comes to leaning on a villain I'm tailor-made, so don't push me.'

'I'm not,' he said after a while. 'I'm just telling you I don't know what you're on about.' He took a roll-up from a tin and lit it with a trembling hand. He held it craftily, the way cons do, hiding the weed behind his hand and drawing on it in a furtive manner. I called through the peephole to the screw outside. When he came in I said indignantly: 'Look, this man's smoking.'

'Yes, I see he is,' said the screw. 'Still, it's not against regulations, that isn't.'

'It is if I think it is,' I said. 'If the new act goes through I'll be able to think what I like. And I think it's bad for this man's health,' I added in a concerned way. 'I don't think he ought to be allowed to ruin it, smoking like that – look what a bad colour he is. After all, the State's responsible for him.'

'Very true,' said the screw uneasily, 'yes.' I could tell he was one of the ones Hawes looked after, and looked after well, so that between Hawes and me he didn't really know what to do next.

'Also he's eating too much of this rich food,' I said, 'I've been checking in the kitchen. For a man leading a sedentary life like he is, that's very bad for his health too – oh, very bad. I think you'd better come along with me when I leave, officer, and we'll see the MO about it.'

Hawes was staring incredulously from one to other of us. 'What are you talking about?' he yelled. 'What do you mean?'

'What I mean,' I said, 'is that you might prove to be a valuable prosecution witness in another trial, and I wouldn't want you to go ruining your health smoking and eating too much rich food, you might have a heart attack.' I said to the screw: 'OK, leave me alone with him for a few minutes more.'

When the screw had gone I said to Hawes: 'Well?'

'Look, for Christ's sake, will you get off my back!'

'That depends,' I said. 'Who was the man standing next to McGruder that night in the Drop? Youngish, solid, scar across his left earhole, fancy dresser, tends to be careless with a set of car keys?'

'I don't know a thing!'

'Was it a man called Merrill Edwardes?'

He looked at me with anguish. 'Even if I knew anything, I couldn't sell a geezer!'

'Why not?' I said. 'You kill people and have them killed. What's so special about just selling someone?'

'I don't know anything,' he said, turning whitish.

'You're getting deeper and deeper in,' I said, 'and the less help you give me, the more trouble you'll get.'

He screwed his eyes up. 'Isn't doing bird bad enough?'

'Duckling breasts tonight or bread and water?'

'Look, I suppose it could of been him, I mean I don't know if it was him.'

'You know bloody well the two of you, you and your brother-in-law, planned to have Hadrill topped,' I said. 'You've got a motive as bright as a bunch of red roses. When I make it stick, by the way, that makes Williams an accessory before the fact – you're coming unravelled all over the place. Now tell me the rest of it. Christ, get your bloody mouth in tune, or I'll tune it for you – I'll put you away for ever.'

'Look, if there was a contract out for this geezer,' said Hawes, 'and I say if there was, I suppose it could have been Edwardes, this geezer you say left the keys. I say I suppose it could, that's all.'

'You prepared to make a statement?'

'No.'

'What went out of that York factory besides the money?'

'Nothing.'

'You're lying. You're guilty right, left and centre.'

'Prove it.'

'I'm going to, don't worry about that. It's how much help you're going to give me, that's what you need to worry about.'

'No help, copper. These people you're on about, they're just names.'

'Bread and water, then.'

'Yeah,' he said, 'but at least I'll stay alive to eat it.'

Going back across the river, the day was sweet and sharp, the sun like bursts of music. The weather that day had no flaws; only the people were flawed.

21

I went into the Nine Foot Drop and leaned against the bar. It was early, just after opening time. A big bloke in a striped blue and white shirt came over. He was fat and chirpy. He had thick white hair and a white Turkish-style moustache.

'Evening, squire, what'll it be?'

'It'll be a few questions,' I said, producing my warrant card. 'You Tony Williams?'

'That's right. What is this, a census poll?'

'It's the kind of poll that could get you in a hell of a lot of bother,' I said, 'so you'd best mind your manners.'

'Bother?' he jeered. 'Me? Look, I've been running this boozer for fifteen years and I've never had no bother.'

'That could all suddenly change,' I said, 'though if you were helpful it might just be passing clouds.'

'I don't know what you're on about.'

'I wish I had a pound for every time I've heard that,' I said. I put a pound on the bar. 'OK, serve us a pint of that Hofmeister you've got there.'

'My treat.'

'Not a chance,' I said. 'I always pay for my rounds.'

He brought the beer and a ring-a-ding for himself and his tone grew conciliatory. 'Look, I know the Drop's a tough pub,' he said, 'but what else do you expect in a place like Hammersmith? Anyway, I've never had any bother here that I couldn't handle.' I believed that, because as he spoke one of the hardest-looking youths I've ever seen came up through the cellar trap, carrying a case of beer as if it were a packet of biscuits. 'I've got a good staff,' said Williams approvingly. 'Like nimble.' He had, all right. Williams picked up his drink and said: 'Well, cheers.'

'I'm not sure about the cheers,' I said. I pushed my glass away. 'Something nasty started up in here three nights back.'

'That's funny,' he said. 'There haven't been no fights.'

'This wasn't a fight,' I said, 'it was the lead-up to a topping.'

'Christ, when was that, then?'

'The evening of April the thirteenth. And don't look so innocent.'

'You must be coming the acid,' said Williams. He was around fifty, but he still looked hard behind all the jollity. He certainly looked as if he knew what his fists were for, also his feet. 'What's all this about, then?'

'Well, it's about this bloke who wound up in a warehouse in Rotherhithe in five plastic shopping bags,' I said. 'Did you ever know Jack Hadrill?'

'Never heard of him.'

'Look, you're not trying hard at all on this one,' I said. 'You're going to have to do a lot better. Hadrill was sitting at one of your tables here practically all evening.'

'I don't know everyone who comes in here,' he said. 'Why should I?'

'Because it's strange,' I said, 'I've been asking around a lot – that's my job, isn't it – and it seems he did come in here.'

'Well, I think I might know who you're talking about vaguely,' he admitted after some thought. 'I read about him in the linens, of course. Dreadful business.'

'And it will be for you too,' I said, 'if you don't open up on full throttle and tell me everything you know about it.'

He thought some more, then shook his heavy white head and said with his lips pursed: 'No, that night, I honestly can't say I noticed him, squire.'

'Well, I've got a witness who did notice him,' I said. 'He states that Hadrill was in full view of you, and don't ever call me squire. Now, there was also a man called Merrill Edwardes standing here at the bar, just about where I'm standing now. I suppose you'll be telling me next you didn't notice him either.'

'Oh no. I know who you mean by Merrill Edwardes.'

'Well, we're making a start at last,' I said. 'Now then, there was a bit of moody with a set of keys Edwardes left on the bar when he left. Right under your nose, my bloke says.'

'I'm sorry, I really am. But I don't remember about no keys.'

'You must be one of the most unobservant governors I've ever met,' I said. 'So of course you didn't notice who picked the keys up, either.'

'That's right, I didn't.'

'Well, I know this place is thick with villains, solid with them. After all, you're not Pat Hawes's brother-in-law for nothing. But even you must take some notice when a man like Billy McGruder comes into a pub.'

'McGruder? Name means nothing to me.'

'Well, that's probably just as well for you,' I said. 'No man Billy takes an interest in ever stays healthy very long. You been visiting Pat lately?'

'Well, if I have been,' he said, 'it's only natural. It's family.'

'I'm getting more and more tired of you,' I said. 'You know a hell of a lot about all this. You do know Hadrill, or you did, you know Edwardes, and since all your best mates are hard villains it wouldn't exactly amaze me if you turned out to know McGruder as well, anyway by sight. Did you know Hadrill was a grass, by the way? A big-time grass?'

'No.'

'You're lying,' I said. 'You're telling me nothing but lies, Tony; you're white with lies, and I really hate that. I think you fixed up this meet for your brother-in-law all right, and if it turns out that you did, you realize that makes you an accessory to murder, don't you?'

'Look, I just don't know what you're talking about,' said Williams anxiously.

'Oh, don't you?' I said. 'Look, I've a bloody good mind to go straight back to the Factory and get a W out for you, and by the time I've finished with you the charge will be what I just said it was. You'll go down with a bang you could hear from Hammersmith to the Elephant. Now, I'll give you one more chance. If you're helpful with me, we might be able to kosher some of this up. I'm not promising anything, mind. I'll also tell you another thing. I'm the sort of man, once I get started on something I never let go, and I'm into this Hadrill business hard, hard. Now then, how well do you know Edwardes?'

'Edwardes? Hardly at all, not really.'

'What does "really" mean?'

'Well, he just comes in here. Like, he lives locally.'

'You got an address for him?'

'Christ, no, I don't know him that well.'

'Well, you know a lot of other funny people, starting with Pat Hawes; I'm surprised, surprised you don't know where Edwardes lives. You seen him since the night Hadrill was topped?'

'No.'

'You say he comes in here regular? How regular? Tonight, for instance? Today's Saturday. Might he come in here tonight? I want to see him badly.'

'Well, a Saturday is often his day. Why don't you just sit and wait for him? Excuse me, I've got a customer to serve.'

'You just wait a minute,' I said, 'and let your staff there do the heavy toil. I haven't finished with you yet, anywhere near.'

'What more?' screeched the landlord. 'For crying out loud?'

'Look,' I said, 'you're related to a heavy criminal serving a life sentence, and I don't know whether you ought to be really keeping a pub at all, I'm not at all sure.'

'Christ, look, if I had an address or a phone number for Edwardes, I'd give it to you.'

'I'm not convinced of that,' I said. 'I think you know most of this story from beginning to end. I also think you're frightened, and with people like Edwardes, Hawes and McGruder mixed up in this I'm not surprised. But at the end of the day you're going to be just as frightened of me as you are of them.'

'You're not going to do me over my licence, are you?'

'I don't know,' I said, shaking my head. 'You mightn't have form, Tony, but you have got some very bad contacts. Really naughty.'

'I can't help who comes into the pub!'

'It's not that, it's what you say to some of them, especially in that flat of yours upstairs. I wonder. I wonder if I just oughtn't to ring your brewers and talk to someone fairly high up there.'

'You people abuse your powers, you do!' Williams screamed.

'Only if other people abuse my common sense,' I said. 'You tell me more about Edwardes. He a heavy spender in here?'

'Well, he likes a drink, yes.'

'He's got form,' I said, 'did you know that? What does he do for a living, apart from crime and villainy?'

'I don't know! I don't ask those sort of questions!'

'That's your bad luck,' I said. 'You should. You ought to be more careful for your own sake, especially as you've got Hawes as a brother-in-law. Yet for a man who doesn't ask questions – Mr Trust-'em-all, doesn't see things, doesn't see people when they're right under his nose – you seem to know a good deal all the same. But getting you to talk about them's like trying to turn over a seized-up engine, and that gets up my nose. You sure you can't help me with Edwardes? I'm going to find him, and if I do it without any help from you – well, I tell you again, you've got your licence to think of. Afterwards will be when it's too late, Tony.'

'Well,' he said reluctantly, 'I know he likes a battle. Funny kind of geezer, went to some posh school. Not for long, though. Wears glasses, but don't think he ain't tough on that account. It's when he takes them off that you know you're in bother. Tells people he's a company director.'

'Don't they all,' I said. 'Till when was he on the firm?'

'Firm? What firm?'

'On the firm, the firm! The firm, for Christ's sake!' I shouted. 'Don't try and take the piss out of me – you know bloody well what firm I mean! I mean Pat and Andy Hawes – *that* firm!'

'God, you really are riding me,' said Williams.

'What I'm doing,' I said, 'is investigating a disgusting murder, and if you can be any use to my inquiry I don't give a fuck if I ride you to hell and back. Now, if Edwardes shows in here tonight, you point him out.'

'What about my licence, though?'

'I'll think about it.'

I stayed till closing time, but Edwardes didn't appear, so I went back to Earlsfield and made myself some powdered coffee.

Then I went to sleep.

At ten past one I was woken by a call from Serious Crimes, who I'd requested to keep a look-out for Edwardes. His body had been found on some waste ground behind Olympia; he had been shot through the head.

'Some of his teeth came right out through his earhole,' said the officer on the phone eagerly. 'How about that, sarge? Shows what a common-or-garden twelve-bore can do, eh?'

I let that one go.

'You been over to his place?'

'We just done it. It wasn't easy to get the address but we managed. The killer had removed everything he had on him, but we got Edwardes through his prints; he'd done bird. Then we run him through the computer to see what else he'd done. Only took a few seconds.'

'I don't like that bloody computer,' I said.

'Oh, I don't know,' he said. 'Christ, it does save time.'

'What are we saving the time for?' I said. 'Christmas? You find anything interesting?'

'No. It was just a flat. Squalid. Letters. Bills – plenty of them. But nothing to make you sit up.'

'Even so,' I said, 'I'm coming over to look at it.'

'What?' he said. 'Now? Can't it wait till morning?'

'No it can't,' I said. 'This one, nothing can wait till morning.'

'You got any idea who it was?'

'I've got one idea that's so powerful that it practically amounts to a conviction,' I said, 'in both senses of the word. It's the same man who did Hadrill. Be a good lad and send what you've got over to me at the Factory, will you?'

'The chief inspector won't like that.'

'Then he can come and see me about it, can't he?' I said mildly, reaching for my trousers. 'And how's his bank case coming along?'

'He don't seem to like talking about it, not at the moment.'

'That means he's on the verge of cracking the man,' I said. 'And thanks for ringing.'

I doubted if any of Edwardes's belongings would tell me anything and I was right, they didn't. But I didn't care. The fact that he was dead told me a great deal, and I had someone else on tap who could tell me even more.

22

'Who's that?'

'Me as usual. I'm coming in.'

McGruder opened the door and stood there. I studied my Billy for a moment; I looked at his thoughtful eyes, and at the little ears that stood up like white question marks against his curly hair.

Billy Zero.

I didn't say anything straight away. I walked past him to the window and stood looking out at the high-rise blocks opposite.

'You know something?' he said behind me. 'I like you.'

'That's lucky,' I said, 'because we're going to be having a crunchy conversation.'

'You're chancing your arm coming in here alone,' he said, 'you realize that.'

'I'm not a bit worried,' I said. 'You'd never do a copper like that with nothing prepared unless you really have gone off your trolley. You've got enough on your plate as it is.'

'Nothing's proved.'

'No, but it's coming along; both of them are. I'll get the proof.'

'Both of them? Both of what?'

'What were you doing last night, Billy, from ten o'clock on?'

'I was here. A quiet evening I spent on my own.'

'That could be heavy for you. You know a man called Merrill Edwardes?'

'Never met him.'

'Well, you won't have a chance to now,' I said, 'because he's been topped – half his head blown off with a twelve-bore. You a sporting man, Billy? Got a sawn-off shotgun lying around, recently fired?'

'No. Course I haven't.'

'You know, Billy,' I said, 'your major problem is that you were seen the night Jack Hadrill was in the Nine Foot Drop – the night he was killed.'

'Who says so?'

'Never mind that. You were in there, Hadrill was in there, and Edwardes was in there. Which mightn't have been so interesting if Hadrill hadn't been killed immediately after.'

'Makes no difference, it's a coincidence. I don't know either of these men you're talking about.'

'What makes the whole incident even more peculiar,' I said, 'was the business with the set of keys. Edwardes left them on the bar, kind of by mistake on purpose, and my witness saw you pick them up. What sort of keys could they have been now, Billy? Car keys?'

He started to shake his head again, but I shook mine first. 'It won't do, Billy,' I said, 'a mere headshake's too thin, darling.'

'You haven't a thing on me,' he said easily. 'No proof at all.'

'I'm not bad at proving things once I get going,' I said, 'and I'll prove these were keys to a stolen motor. Edwardes stole it, and you used it to take Jack Hadrill over to Rotherhithe, where you and Edwardes murdered him, cooked him and stapled him up in the bags.'

'You know, you're pushing me too hard,' he said, shaking his head and staring at me. 'You realize that, don't you? It isn't safe to do that with me. I'm a private man, noted for it, and I get in a rage if my privacy's interfered with, anyone could tell you.'

'As a copper I don't care about your privacy,' I said, 'your rages even less. To me you're just an operation – find 'em, nail 'em, wheel 'em in!'

'Must be dull, same operation all the time.'

'You should know,' I said, 'you're the disease.'

He didn't like that. There was a rustle in his entire expression, like a striking snake. 'Face me,' he said. 'Come on, turn round and do it.'

'Wouldn't you love it if I did?' I said, with my back to him. I was watching him in the shaving-mirror he had left on the window-sill.

'That's what you made the others do. *Turn away. Turn and face me.* Thoughtful expression, kind voice – I'll bet you leaned over that corporal almost tenderly.'

'Face me!' he said. His voice rose a pitch. 'Go on!'

'You're about as funny as Hitler,' I said, 'and that's only part of your trouble, you poor slob.'

He started to take quick breaths; at last I turned round. He had a cut-throat razor in his hand. 'See this?'

'I see it,' I said. 'What am I supposed to do?'

'I could take your head off with it!'

'You could, but you won't,' I said. 'You're far too clever.'

'Are you serious,' he said, 'I mean about my being clever?'

'No,' I said, 'not in the least.'

'I am clever, though.'

'If you hit a single note on a piano very hard,' I said, 'you just ruin the sound, also you get the tune wrong. I've got my wife in a lunatic asylum, and I hear the patients on the piano every time I go down there, in the day room, doing that. It's one of the saddest sounds I've ever heard. Now put that razor away – and I should look out if I were you, you've just cut your finger on it.'

He looked down at his finger, surprised. It was bleeding fast – faster, anyway, than he could lick the blood off.

'Go and put something on it, Billy,' I said, 'park the razor, then come back and we'll talk some more. There's lots to say.'

He walked slowly out of the room, looking at his finger. He looked ashamed of what he had done to it. A moment later I could hear him moving about in the bathroom.

When he returned he seemed quite calm; it was an illusion. I looked at him and thought, you're gone, Billy. They'd never take you back in the red berets now.

'What did Edwardes do wrong on that job?' I said.

'I'm not saying anything.'

'It's possible, of course,' I said, 'that he just got scared; I'll bet he never expected the flap that went up over Hadrill's death. Probably you didn't either, and I'll bet that balls-up, leaving the bags in the warehouse like that, didn't make Edwardes feel any better. And then when the bags were almost immediately found, I daresay that's what tipped the balance; I think Edwardes said something to you, or gave you the impression, that he was going to grass, and that meant he had to be wasted.'

'Well, don't look at me,' said McGruder, 'I'd never have made a mess like that of it.'

'Maybe,' I said, 'maybe, only you didn't have time to plan Edwardes, did you? If he was going to grass you he was going to do it quick; neither of you had any time the way things turned out. It was you or him on the hurry-up; you were up shit creek otherwise.'

'I'd never have panicked like that if it had been me, I tell you.'

'No, not normally you wouldn't,' I soothed him, 'but this wasn't a contract, it was safety-first. If it'd been a contract I agree – you'd have made a lovely clean weird job of it.'

He stood looking at me, pale, fit and crazy. It was early evening, but there were no lights on in the room; the only light was in his eyes, which caught the reflection of the park lights from the window.

'The best thing you could do, Billy,' I said, 'is to confess to these murders, Hadrill and Edwardes. You're going to have to.'

'You're still at square one when it comes to proof,' said McGruder. 'A dozen people could have been after Hadrill and Edwardes.'

'It was handy, though, Edwardes being topped like that just when he was, wasn't it, Billy?'

He just shook his head slowly, staring at me. 'That's no proof,' he said kindly. 'That's just circumstantial.'

I kept my temper all right: I think now because we'd both got into that cosy kind of chat where we both knew he was guilty. I thought I could probably crack him right now just by taking him down to the Factory and confronting him with Smitty. But the trouble was, I didn't want to, not yet. For I was in a dilemma. If I pulled McGruder in now, broke him down, say, and then charged him with other officers present, as there would have to be, then I might never find out what else it was that Hadrill had known. I might do a Hawes/Bowman. The Crown might well say, let's just do him for Hadrill – that puts McGruder away for ten. But I felt sure McGruder knew a lot, if not all, of what Hadrill hadn't told. Yet on the other hand, if I didn't pull McGruder in now, or soon, he might disappear, and that would be my head on a platter. I didn't care, though. It had been on a platter so often that it practically lived on one.

I decided to distribute his photograph to all national points of exit, and have him watched; but behind my thinking was the conviction that the case was getting too big to be dealt with by a department with resources as limited as A14's.

The time had come to tenderize McGruder again. 'I'll tell you what we're going to do now,' I said.

'You're never going to try and take me in to the Factory.' He shook his head again. 'Not on your own, you're crazy.'

'Nothing like that,' I said, 'not today, anyway.'

'Not any day.'

'What we both need is time to think.' I was aching to ask him some more questions about Hadrill, but I knew it was too soon. 'Why don't we just sit down and relax?' I said. 'You got anything to drink around the place?'

'There's some beer in the fridge.'

'Get us a couple of cans.'

He came back and poured it carefully into glasses and sat down. I noticed he barely touched his. 'OK,' he said, 'so what are you going to do? Get off my back?'

'No, we've got to go on talking about these killings; I'm going to treat you to a hypothesis.'

'What the Jesus is that?' he said warily.

'It's when you don't know the answer to a problem. You construct a set of assumptions for it and test them to see if they work. My first assumption: you did kill Hadrill, also Edwardes. Now why was Hadrill killed? Do you know?' Inwardly I sighed with frustration. I could see the knowledge there in his brain. But I couldn't get at it, because McGruder couldn't give it to me without admitting the murder. There must be a way round the problem, but I just couldn't see it.

'If it had been me that had done it,' said McGruder, 'I wouldn't want to bloody know.'

'Oh yes you would,' I said. 'That's my second assumption. You'd want to know all right if you thought Hadrill knew something that could do you some good. It'd be to do with money, Billy, and everyone knows you're into that.'

'You think you're a smart bastard.'

I said: 'I've got a nickname for you, you know. When I have a nickname for a killer it means I think he's something special.'

He flushed with pleasure. 'What's the nickname?'

'Billy Zero.'

'Now that's amazing!' he said. 'That's what Nacker Harris used to call me.'

'Who was he?'

'Man I used to go shooting with in the army. Shooting people,' he said easily, 'because that's what an army's for.'

'Where was that, then?'

'Down in Oman there; Harris was the only mate I had.'

'You treat him well?'

'I looked after him. Only man I ever looked after, I was like a mother to him, because he suddenly told me he was afraid; we were in action.'

'And what did he have to do?'

He sneered at a corner. 'Let's say he looked after details. Easy things. Cleaning my gear. Running errands.'

'You sleep together?'

'With Nacker? Yes.' He was still looking away. 'He's dead now. He wasn't right for a soldier nor a villain.'

'You miss him?'

'I don't think about him.'

Yet I was reminded of a poem I had learned at school called 'Sorrow Lane':

> I'll just turn down this lane here
> Into our sorrow;
> I'm afraid today is lost
> And we've mortgaged tomorrow.
>
> I've got us into Sorrow Lane
> Through darkness and thunder;
> I'll shine our lights again,
> But I know we're going under.
>
> Don't put on black for our grief
> Or wear a veil;
> But pray for us, we entreat,
> As the nights grow pale.
>
> Lift us and save us both, Christ,
> After the horror;
> We've fallen through today
> And won't make it tomorrow.
>
> How sweet life was,
> How deep its truth and love;
> Like the water we kissed by
> With August above.
>
> Then we gave all we had
> Till we had to borrow;
> Now we're alone and sad
> In the grove of our sorrow.

Farewell, sweet hours of night,
Farewell, sweet air;
The others are out in the light
But we aren't there.

Help never came
And now help never can;
Pray for my woman's soul,
Pray for the man.

'I'm not a copper right now, Billy,' I said, 'I'm just a man. Forget I've got a job to do for a minute; why not just talk to me?'

He stared at me without any expression at all, and I knew it was no use. He would always come out in pieces, in fury and despair, his way of describing a sense of loss. He would feel for a second, or a minute, if you reached out far enough to him; but he was too far gone, with violence behind him, violence in front and beside him. Like a broken piano, he could only make discords.

'I spend a lot of time on my own,' McGruder said, 'people like me always do. I'm no good at talking.'

'Maybe you read.'

'Yes,' he said, 'I'm a great reader. Most of what I read's a load of rubbish. I could write better than most of them. The things I've done, I could write a book that'd knock them all out.' It was surprising, the number of psychopaths that told you that. Their intelligence, usually high, remained unimpaired, whatever their problems. It was also completely divorced from those problems, and that was what made them so bloody dangerous. 'One time,' he said, 'I got nicked in South Africa. There was a little trouble in Johannesburg – never mind that. I got hold of a book on hand-reading, palmistry it's called; it was in the prison library. You know anything about hands?'

'I go by their shapes a lot,' I said, 'but that's just an instinct.'

'There's more to it than that.'

He put out his own hand flat, palm upwards. In his weird way, he was trying to reach me through hands, and I was prepared to let him. I was prepared to try anything to get at the truth. I was in my usual false position; I was a copper with a job to do gaining a killer's trust so that I could nick him. I couldn't see Bowman talking to McGruder or anybody else about hands; I could almost hear his peals of ridiculing laughter. Yet any way was a good way if it got you ahead, and I had to get a man with a brain just as good as mine to commit himself. This wasn't like dealing with Pat Hawes, or a devious landlord – straight force wouldn't get me anywhere with Billy McGruder; he knew about straight force all too well, and he laughed at it.

The first part of catching a man is easy – the part when you know who it is you want. It's when you get to know him, that's when I find it difficult. I don't like deceit, even when it's a killer I'm dealing with. I was pretending I was trying to help him, when all I wanted to do was to help him into jail.

'This part of my hand,' McGruder was saying, 'see, this line, it's called the head line. It's straight and true. I know it looks bent, it takes a downward curve at the end there. But that's imagination and desire.'

I knew he had neither. That was knowledge I could see he had buried; its absence was as plain as murder itself.

'There's the violence in me, of course,' he said with a touch of pride. 'You can see it here, look. And here. Look at the life line,' he said, indicating it to me and gazing at it. 'See? It's bad; I could die any day! At thirty-three! The line's short, the same on both hands. That makes it worse. I'm also very mystic.'

He droned on, completely – and what was worse, unconsciously – absorbed in himself, and suddenly I realized what hell it meant, not only to be a killer, but a bore. You think nothing of taking life; but your own existence fascinates you, and that's the imbalance that we mean by evil. Paolacci, or Edie, even that I could understand better. But this neat, dull man crouched in a sort of mass over his own hands, that freaked me.

114

At last he let his hands fall to his sides. I was about to yawn with relief when he raised them to his face to look at just once more. 'These have to do the work,' he said, nodding raptly. 'Yes.'

It was the angle of murder the public never sees unless a member of it is just about to be topped by one of these maniacs. I remembered – I seldom forgot – the murdered old lady I had found by the side of the motorway years ago. I said: 'The hands do it to just anybody, do they?'

'Just about.'

'Do they do it to old women?'

'What?' he shouted. He looked horrified. 'Me do a thing like that to an old lady? Never!'

'Suppose she was well off. Money in it.'

'Not at all!'

'You lying, self-deceiving cunt,' I said, 'if the money were right you'd top a handicapped child in a wheelchair, cop for the lolly and bank it. You're full of shit, piss and death, McGruder, so don't try and launder yourself with me, friend.'

He danced towards me, eyes glittering with fury.

'Get off, get away from me,' I said, 'you wanking berk. If a girl came up to you in the street with heartbreak in her face and said please help me, my man's shot himself, you'd walk straight on to improve your image, you pitiful egoist.'

He stared at me for a long time; nothing in his face moved. At last he shook his head slowly, his eyes never leaving mine. 'You are so close to the edge, copper,' he said, 'you just cannot know.'

But I didn't care. I remembered Jim Macintosh who used to work with me at A14. He's been dead since 1981, killed in circumstances like these, by a bastard like this.

'The trouble with you,' I said, 'is that you never tell me anything new – get us another beer.'

When he came back with them he poured them and said: 'While I was in the kitchen I was thinking of what you were saying about that bird, the one that shot her bloke.'

'What a slip,' I said. 'She didn't shoot anybody. The man shot himself.'

'Well, anyway,' he said. His eyes took on that sharp yet absent look that they often had, and he began one of his great quiet tirades. 'Women? I don't need women. I shit women. I use them. Me, I'm unique. I'm going to change the world; it says so in my hand.'

'You've changed it for some people,' I said. 'They're out of it.'

He took no notice. He had his hand out in front of his face again and he said: 'I'm a black Christ, a white Satan. I take what I need from folk, just passing through, see? I could be tender to them, I could threaten them, but I get it from them. I'm bound to get it. Anyone tries to make Billy McGruder look small – no one tries to make me look small.'

'I do,' I said.

He flicked his razor a millimetre in front of my nose; that's a psychopath for you. 'Belt up and watch your step,' he said calmly. 'I haven't finished. I read this book in the nick once, at Wandsworth, that a screw got in to me, there's one man like me born once every 666 years.'

I thought that was often enough, but all I said was: 'I read somewhere, I think it was the Bible, that that number was the mark of the beast.'

'You're taking the piss out of me,' he said softly. He came up to within half a pace of me and stared into my eyes. 'Don't you ever do that.'

'So you're telling me you're special, not like other men.'

'That's right.'

'And so you are,' I said, 'you're a convicted killer, and proud of it. How many people have you killed altogether, Billy?'

'I'm not saying; I'm a very private man. But – and this is off the record, right? – I reckon they all ought to be glad. They were all a pain in the arse to themselves and a lot of other people.'

'I like it when you moralize, Billy. Tell me, if you were looking into the dark end of my pistol now, would you be glad? Would you be thinking, I'm glad I'm going to be shot dead after all, I'm just a pain in the arse to myself and everyone else?'

He gazed at me motionless, his eyes like stones. 'A man on his own like you are,' he said at last, 'ought to have more sense than say a thing like that to me.' He half took the razor out of his pocket again.

'Cut out the crap,' I said, 'and for the last time, put that fucking razor away. Now then. You killed that army corporal up in the Midlands, Brownlow. The whole world knows that. So who else are you responsible for, Mr fucking Six Six Six? Jackie Hadrill?'

He didn't say a word, just stared at me with the unblinking eyes of a snake, his face dead between his tight, questioning little ears.

'Merrill Edwardes, now,' I said, 'when you blew half his head away with a sawn-off shotgun. Do you reckon he was sold on that as a way to go?'

'I've never met either of them,' he lilted, 'I keep telling you. Mind,' he added, 'from what I've heard of folk like that around the manor, I'd say they were no great loss to the world.'

'Look, I know we've all got to go some time,' I said, 'but what amazes me is the way you manage to miss out the terror of the moment. You almost manage to make it sound a great way, your way to go.'

For some mystifying reason, that cheered him up. He had no sense of the ridiculous whatever, and that made him ridiculous, like some sexual perverts. He made a proud little noise in his throat.

'You did those two men all right, Billy,' I said. 'I'm satisfied. All I need now is the proof. You bled off and cooked Hadrill – the job you had time for. You did it with Edwardes. But Edwardes was a rush job; you had to just catch Edwardes and chill him. I'll find out why, but my guess at present is that he tried to grass you. And another reason why I like you best for Hadrill, Billy, is the way your pad looks – neat and prissy. You're so tidy in your habits. Yes, you and Edwardes did Hadrill in cold blood on orders from Pat Hawes. And you did him for money, the way you always do.'

'Get out of here fast,' said McGruder suddenly, coming up to me again with his right hand in his pocket. 'I'm patient, but right now I just mightn't care what I did. Get out; do it now.'

'All right,' I said, walking past him to the door. 'Still, one of these days you're going to tell me why you were in such a sweat over Edwardes, and soon now you'll be telling me just how it happened to Hadrill down there by the river.' I opened the door. 'I'll be going, Billy. Just for the time being.'

23

The next day, Monday, I was ordered to sit a board. I knew what the board was for.

'I don't want to sit it,' I told the voice, 'I haven't time. Everybody knows I'm in the middle of this Hadrill business; it's mad.'

'That's not for you to say,' said the voice, 'and boards can't wait.' He paused and then said, 'Besides, don't you realize it's to do with your possible transfer to the Branch?'

'You know I've been turned down there once,' I said, 'but I'm not bitter. I'm fine here at Unexplained Deaths.'

'Maybe you are,' said the voice, 'but that isn't the point. If the board decides you're fit material, it'd be your duty to transfer. Christ, what am I arguing with you for? Any police officer would give his teeth for it.'

'I'll hang onto my teeth,' I said, 'the false ones cost me nearly a hundred quid; I had them done privately after I lost my own that time over at Arnos Grove when it went the other way.'

'I'm not interested in that now,' said the voice.

'OK,' I said, 'well, I'm not interested in the board.'

'Are you telling me that you're refusing to take it?'

'Yes,' I said, 'I'm not going to take the board. I'm quite entitled to refuse.'

'All right, then,' said the voice, 'you're obviously going to have to have this the hard way – it's an order that you sit the board.'

'I don't care whose order it is.'

'But it's the Commissioner's order!'

'No,' I said. 'Tell them it's the plastic bags; I can't drop that now. Tell them I don't want to know about any board.'

'I'm transmitting an order to you, sergeant.'

119

'I know,' I said, 'and I'm telling you I won't obey it.'

'Now look,' said the voice with a trace of uneasiness, 'you've got to take the board, do you understand?'

'It's no use threatening me,' I said. 'No one's going to force me to take it.'

'Force?' said the voice. 'Force? That's far too strong a word.'

'Listen,' I said, 'let's play this again, what are you all doing? I'm just getting warm on this business, then I suddenly find I'm obliged to take a board I've already failed once, maybe because of what happened in my personal life − I had a mad wife who murdered my daughter, remember, there's no secret about it. But why do I have to retake the bloody thing? I accepted their decision the last time; I don't care, I tell you.'

'I haven't all day to discuss this,' said the voice. 'You'll do as you're told and take the board, that's all.'

'And if I won't, I resign. Is that it?'

'Don't be ridiculous. It's been decided at a high level that you don't want to remain a sergeant at A14 for the rest of your days. Everyone, including myself, has recommended you. And that's that − you're going to be promoted and transferred.'

'And Hadrill?'

'I imagine they'll send that back to Serious Crimes.'

They hold these boards over at the Yard, and I was sent to a neon-lit waiting room. Other candidates were already sitting there on steel chairs. I sat down, but I was unable to think of anything but McGruder.

They called me finally; I was last. I dug my hands into my trouser pockets, went through a door with a green light over it which said Enter, and walked down a featureless room towards a table with people sitting at it. No one asked me to sit down, but there was a chair there, so I sat on it. There was a clerk present, busy being a clerk. He had what I supposed was my file in front of him, and his hands shuffled about with the contents while his eyes watched what his hands were doing in a needle sort of way. I thought Christ, what do they need people like that for these days? A home computer could have shot through it all and printed out whatever they needed at twenty times the speed. Then there were two uniformed officers, and one senior detective in plain clothes. I knew him by sight. He was Detective-Superintendent Reid, and I thought, you ought to be busy on something else, the murder rate we've got in this city.

There was also a psychiatrist. There's always a bloody psychiatrist.

One of the uniformed men leaned across the table and looked me up and down with distaste; I wondered if I'd left my fly open or what. He said: 'Well, sergeant, the problem you've got to solve is this. You've been summoned by a special committee at the Home Office; they want your reaction to a terrorist act that's just been committed against a sensitive embassy in central London. A vital point – East–West relations mustn't be upset. The PM's waiting for the committee's decision. Well? What do you recommend?'

'It's a silly question,' I said, 'when I'm in the middle of a real murder.'

'I beg your pardon?' said the other uniformed man. He was sitting in the middle, and was therefore plainly the chairman. 'Would you repeat that?'

I did repeat it, louder than before.

'You're not doing yourself any good, you know,' said the chairman, 'taking that attitude.'

'No, I know I'm not,' I said. I didn't say anything else. There was a silence which I was evidently expected to fill. But I didn't fill it, so the chairman, after fidgeting in his chair, finally said: 'You must say something, now.'

'I'm afraid mythical situations don't stimulate me,' I said.

'Even so.'

I yawned. 'Well, I'd do what anyone else would do – assemble a squad, men I knew well, draw the weapons we needed, and get in there any way we could.'

'East–West relations mustn't—'

'Fuck that,' I said. 'You've got to get in there fast. It's people's lives that matter, not East–West relations. Then, when you've done all that, some tweedy individual from the PM's office wanders along and tells you you've done it all wrong, so you don't get promoted, just bollocked, and that's it.' I looked at my watch and said: 'I'd like to get out of here now, if you don't mind; I've got a lot on.'

The chairman glared icily at me. Something more seemed to be expected of me so I said: 'And East–West relations? Don't make me laugh. I read the papers thoroughly enough to know that they only exist in people's minds, unless you call a nuclear arms race East–West relations.'

'You seem to see the future pretty black,' said the other uniformed man.

'Yes, that's right,' I said, 'and the longer I sit here answering a lot of idiotic questions, the blacker it'll get.'

'You're verging on insubordination,' said the chairman. He was a grey-faced, grey-souled man; I could tell he loathed me. Various hairs which he evidently couldn't get at with his electric razor grew in the furrows that obstinacy and capitulation to routine had long ago carved between his nose and chin.

'This is a police force,' I said, 'not an army. If nobody said what they thought for fear of offending their superiors, it wouldn't work. It doesn't work that well as it is,' I added.

I could see that Reid had a hard time not laughing; but then he was the only intelligent man there. He had quick, dark eyes that missed nothing, and wore a cheap suit with cigarette ash down the front because he chain-smoked.

'And I've been a copper long enough to know that if I tell a killer he's verging on insubordination, they'll likely be the last words I speak,' I said.

The psychiatrist poked his nose up like a ferret. 'Tell me, what sort of childhood did you have, sergeant?'

'Rotten,' I said. 'A lot of my family were killed in the last war, in action, and my father bored my mother to death.' I stared at him; he looked at least sixty. 'As for yourself, you seem about the age where you could have been treating war wounded. But I'll bet you weren't; I'll bet you were too busy examining pilots for signs of lack of moral fibre.'

There was another long silence. 'You don't seem anxious to pass this board, sergeant,' said the second uniformed man at last.

'That's right,' I said, 'I'm on a case – a little matter of a man found boiled and stapled up in a warehouse in five shopping bags, I expect you've read about it. I'm not interested in boards.'

After a pause the chairman said: 'You might well hear more about this.'

'Well, as long as I don't have to go through all this again,' I said, 'it'll be worth it.'

'It's a good thing you don't care about boards,' said the chairman, 'because I can tell you you've failed this one.'

'Fine,' I said. I stood up. Nobody said anything more, so I left.

I started walking; I felt better than I had done for weeks. I was glad I had failed the board – I had now proved to everybody, I hoped, once and for all, that I wasn't inspector material, or Branch material, but just Unexplained Deaths material. I took a bus up to Soho and bought myself an expensive pint of beer in the French pub. I watched three men in video nasties gnawing at their glasses of Aligoté and a black beauty queen refusing to give a grafter five pounds.

I finished my pint, had another and left, feeling not bad.

But in the night I dreamed that two figures appeared at the foot of my bed in Earlsfield. The one in front was a thickset, middle-aged man, heavy-featured and dressed in a cap and thick grey coat. He made as if to chop at me with his hand. Black matter seeped out of his mouth and nose and he had been dead for years. The figure behind was so evil that one glance was all I could stomach. It was very small, a collection of what looked like old peeled sticks wrapped in a sack; it radiated hell's own malice and groaned to get at me.

I put the light on and started to read an introduction to pathology.

24

'The minister of defence has contacted us,' said the voice. 'He's had a worrying note; someone's threatening to kill him. This is confidential, of course.'

'Worries like that usually are,' I said, 'but why tell me about it?'

'Because you're always nosing about in the dirt, and you might have heard something about the ministry of defence. Have you?'

'Well, this is confidential too,' I said, after thinking about it. 'I protect my sources, that's why; I wouldn't get any information if I didn't.' I told the voice what Cryer had told me about the rumours in Fleet Street over the ministry of defence, and the possibility that the recent massive expulsion of Soviets was connected with it. I didn't name Cryer, though the voice tried to get me to.

'What we've got to do,' I said, 'is find out what Hadrill knew about Hawes that was so big that it earned Hadrill a topping. I've been over to see Hawes at Wandsworth. I couldn't get the meat out of the whelk, but I'm convinced Pat got word out that Hadrill had to be done. I'm equally convinced that Pat's brother-in-law, a man called Tony Williams who runs a villains' pub in Hammersmith, made all the arrangements, gave the job to McGruder and a hood called Merrill Edwardes, and that the two of them carried it out. Well, Pat led the wages snatch at that factory up north and killed the guard – OK, that's what he's doing porridge for. Now I'm not sure yet, but I believe something else went missing besides the money. Something big – something Hadrill knew all about, that's why he was able to steam into Hawes so hard. So, two questions – you might know the answers. One, is that factory really a shoe factory?'

'Of course it is! Why shouldn't it be? What do you mean?'

'I was hoping you were going to tell me what I meant. All right, second question. You know Hadrill was gay?'

'You keep going back to that,' said the voice irritably. 'What difference does it make?'

'Maybe a lot,' I said. 'Look, if I were you, I'd grip Hawes and give him a bloody good grilling, the works, say two teams of three. Because after all, if I can trace a connection between Hawes and McGruder as I mean to try and do, that makes Hawes an accessory to murder yet again. But we need all the facts we can get, and in your place I'd get Hawes right by the goolies and squeeze him till he splits, while I get on with McGruder.'

'Well, McGruder's still a theory,' said the voice, 'but pursue it, quite right. Meantime, I think I'll send the Hawes angle back to the Yard; it's out of our line and I haven't the manpower for it right now.'

'OK,' I said, 'why not give it to Bowman? It's right up his street. God help Hawes by the time Bowman's finished with him; you won't even be able to find the pieces.'

'Yes, I'll tell Chief Inspector Bowman what you've just told me, and he can take it from there.'

My life, I thought, it looks as if the voice is actually going to have to do some work. 'That's fine,' I said, 'brief him like that; I've told you everything I know. Meanwhile I'll try and crack McGruder, but it'll probably take time. Did you know he was married, by the way?'

No, the voice hadn't known that.

'Well, he was, I haven't traced her yet, but I will. Klara McGruder.'

'Anything known?'

'She was treated for alcoholism a couple of years back. I've got lines out for her.'

'You going to see her?'

'When I've found her,' I said, 'I most certainly am. But I can't question her till I know where she is; that's the sort of thing that only happens in films. You know – cut to the next scene and there she is by magic.'

'Never mind films, sergeant. But this business about the note the minister's had is most worrying.'

'I'll bet it is,' I said, 'for him.'

'It must be a nut that sent it,' said the voice.

'I'd like to think so,' I said, 'but you never know. He may be a minister but that's not to say he hasn't been a naughty boy; it wouldn't be the first time.'

'I wonder if we ought to pull McGruder in now?'

'What's the charge?'

'No charge, just for questioning.'

'I'm not going to take him in for questioning,' I said, 'it would be crazy at this stage. McGruder really is a hard man, and you'll never crack him like Bowman might crack Hawes. Besides,' I added, 'I think if we let McGruder run about a bit, who knows, he might lead us to something.'

'He's dangerous to have running around, though.'

'I reckon he'll think hard before he kills anyone else at the moment,' I said. 'There's too much brimstone in the atmosphere.' I added: 'That is, anyone except me, if he thought he could get away with it. You've got to bear in mind, the whole of this is deeper than it looks; when a grass is topped for money by a professional it always is. Two grasses, as a matter of fact, because I'm pretty sure Edwardes was planning to grass as well, or had perhaps even tried to – that's why he was done on the hurry-up.'

'You're starting to get a picture?'

'Some sort of a picture, yes.'

'Well, let's make some more assumptions.'

'There are enough of them around as it is,' I said.

'We'll make them just the same. Names in a hat: Hadrill. Edwardes. McGruder. The Soviets up at Highgate. The defence minister. Pat Hawes.'

'Yes, OK,' I said, 'but you've missed one out – what's the name of that bloke who runs that factory up at York? I don't mean the front man who knows about shoes; I mean the brainy individual who heads whatever it is they really do up there.'

'What, Martin Phillips, you mean? Him?' It was one of the few times I had ever heard the voice lose its cool. 'Christ! Don't go anywhere near him. He's spotless; he's got top security clearance.'

'All right, all right,' I said, 'I was only asking what his name was.'

'What are you driving at?'

'Well, what I'm wondering,' I said, 'is if anyone up there was gay by any chance. We know Hadrill was. I wonder if Hadrill ever knew anyone on Phillips's staff, er, in a carnal sense. Anyone really responsible.'

'Impossible. Look, I've told you, don't start messing about up there, you've got no authority. The entire staff there has been cleared by the Branch.'

'Nothing's impossible,' I said, 'and our security record's terrible – ask any American.' I went on: 'Hadrill was a cunning sod; he had that nose for information that makes a supergrass – not that it did him any good in the end.'

'Sergeant,' said the voice, 'I am giving you a direct order; you are to have nothing to do with that factory or with anyone employed there, do you understand?'

'What I understand is that this case has got to be solved. If there's any connection between Hadrill and that factory that we don't know about, we've got to find out what it is. It's not only useless sweeping everything under the carpet, it might be bloody dangerous. I do admit one thing, though; it's right outside the scope of A14.'

'You will obey my order,' said the voice, 'and that's the end of it. You are authorized to continue your investigation into McGruder, and that's all.'

25

I knocked on McGruder's door and said: 'I'm back.'

'This is getting very monotonous.'

I said musingly: 'You do make the perfect hit man.'

'I've never done any hit jobs,' he lilted, smiling.

I suddenly lost my temper. 'Look,' I shouted, 'don't take me for a cunt! Hit jobs? The only reason we dropped the Wetherby case against you was lack of evidence. You had an alibi we couldn't crack, and the barman and the governor of The Case Is Altered were too scared to come forward, otherwise you'd be doing life right now. But this time it isn't the same. I told you about the witness I've got who's ready to swear he saw you over at Williams's pub while Hadrill and Edwardes were there.'

'The witness you had, you mean,' said McGruder. 'That was no witness, just a little grass on the make. Anyhow, he's had a bad accident, I heard in a pub.'

'Oh yes?'

'Yes,' said McGruder. 'Why don't you take a run over and have a look? I believe he's in Bart's. Sorry if he was a mate of yours, but he's in a coma. It seems he may live, only he'll never get his brains in straight again. Wasn't his name Smitty, something like that?'

'What happened to him?'

'Well, as I say,' McGruder smiled, 'it's only what I've heard, but it seems he unfortunately tripped and his face hit a wall with a terrible great bang. He can't hear or speak or see anything.'

I said: 'It was the Grossmans.'

'Well, of course, I wouldn't know anything about that,' said McGruder easily.

'It's not going to make any difference to you anyway, Billy,' I said, 'not in the long run. I'm going to get you one way or another, you'll see. But that's three men dead or as good as dead in as many days – you mob have really got your seven-league boots on, haven't you?'

'"Sail on, silver girl",' murmured McGruder, gazing at the ceiling, '"sail on through the night." I do like Simon and Garfunkel. Reminds me of the time I had to top a feller while I was in Africa; I'd been listening to S and G that day. Bloke who'd cheeked me.'

I nodded absently to show I was listening; naturally I was concentrating on the loss of my witness and kicking myself for it. The voice would spread me right over the wall for that, and serve me right. I said: 'It's a dangerous thing to do with you, isn't it, Billy, giving you a bit of cheek.'

'This feller was asking for it when he said I couldn't get it up in the sack,' said McGruder, 'I took that very seriously. Also he thought he was a hard man. He didn't know me – thought he could put me down. So we went out to fight somewhere quiet, a place where it was just bush and snakes, and I told him no, I can't fight you, I don't want my pretty face all marked up, you're too hard for me. So when he'd finished laughing at me and was turning away, I took out this two-five automatic I'd nicked off a dead golly and I just said to him *I'll kiss you where you've never been kissed before, darling* and gave it him straight up the arsehole. What a mess.' He added: 'Then I shot him in the head. I don't like it, people being cheeky with me, it's no good.'

'Yes, I get the message,' I said. 'Did you have any bother over it?'

'Bother?' He burst out laughing. 'Don't be stupid – there was a war on. I just told them back at Command that a golly patrol had got him – I shot him with a golly gun.'

'Well, it's about time I got you, Billy,' I said, 'missing witness or not. I don't like what happened to Smitty – no, I don't appreciate that at all, particularly as it's partly my fault, I was too eager. Anyway, I'll be in a position to feel your collar soon.'

He shook his head in the calm, obstinate way he had. 'If you ever want to take me, copper, you'll have to do it the hard way.'

'It won't be that hard at all,' I said, 'not once I'm ready for you, you'll see. My people wanted to pull you in on sus right now; but I said no, I'd prefer to wait until I could do you for murder.'

'You'll wait a long time.'

'No, Billy,' I said. I paused. 'In fact, I've changed my mind. I think it would be nice if you and I took a trip over to the Factory straight away to see if we can't crack you down there – make it all official. You could make a statement and sign it—'

He shook his head again. 'I told you no,' he said evenly, staring me in the eyes. He added: 'And I'll tell you you don't know how lucky you are, because I'd really like to kill you. Yes, that's what I'd like to do.' His lips trembled with desire. 'Badly.'

'Oh, come on,' I said, 'you'd drown in the shit if you did that, you'd have every copper in Britain after you and not a leg to stand on. No, that wouldn't be clever of you, Billy, and don't you just love to be clever? I'll tell you what would be clever, though,' I added. 'Why not be a big boy? Why not confess you topped Hadrill? Just to start off with. We might do a deal. We'll leave Edwardes for the time being. Come on, you'll feel a load better once you've done it. Easier in yourself.'

But he wasn't listening. 'I don't need anything to do you with,' he said dreamily. Then he held up his hands with their hammer thumbs and screamed: 'These! That's all I need, just these!'

I turned my back on him and walked over to the door, though it took some doing. He was making a strange noise like an animal caught in a trap. He took no notice when I opened the door to leave. 'I'll be back again as usual,' I said softly, 'but you won't know when, Billy.'

26

'Hawes is ready for you,' said the chief screw. 'He's over in the punishment block, I'll show you the way.'

'Good,' said Bowman with relish, 'let's get over there.'

We went quickly, because the one thing Bowman couldn't stand, ironically, was the inside of a nick. 'Putting 'em in here's enough for me, I hate having to come into this fucking awful place myself.'

It was pissing with rain as we crossed the exercise yard. He didn't like the rain either, and by the time we got inside the punishment block he was in a state of barely suppressed fury. Detective-Sergeant Rupt was with us, one of Bowman's mob. Rupt was heavy, with a reputation for liking trouble. What made him more dangerous, he had a very quick cold mind to go with his build.

'Nothing rough to start with,' said Bowman as we approached Hawes's cell, 'anyway, not unless I think it's necessary.' He added: 'Which I well might.'

'Do we do him one by one,' said Rupt, 'or three-handed?'

'I'll kick off,' said Bowman, 'and then we'll play it by ear.' I thought this quite comic because Bowman is tone-deaf.

Hawes stood up when we entered, then we all found some-where to sit – the three of us on the bed, Hawes on a wooden chair, and the WPC who had arrived with a tape recorder on another chair at a table. Everyone was silent while the WPC checked her machine and then recorded the time, place, date of the interview and the names of those present; that made the tape official in court. She was a hard-looking woman in her thirties with about as much pity in her face as an empty plate.

Hawes sat looking at us in his prison gear – blue and white striped shirt, grey wool trousers and denim jacket. His appearance had deteriorated since I had seen him. Perhaps he was getting fewer perks from the kitchen; perhaps he was more worried, too.

Bowman looked hard at Hawes; the expression in his eyes was cold. He was a chief inspector, he was ambitious and confident, and the whole lot showed. He was well dressed, well fed, well housed; Bowman could go anywhere, any time, do anything, do anyone. He nodded impatiently at the WPC and she switched her set on. Bowman said to Hawes in a let's-get-this-over voice: 'You realize you are not obliged to say anything, but anything you do say will be taken down and may be used in evidence. Do you understand?'

Hawes said: 'Yes.' He looked as if he knew what was coming.

Bowman said to the WPC: 'Switch off.' When she had he said to Hawes: 'Now listen, lover, and listen hard. This is the bit that doesn't figure on any tape. You can play this one of two ways; the one I strongly recommend to you is the one where you tell us off the record every fucking thing you know about this Hadrill business, including everything that happened up at that York factory which didn't come out at your trial. You play square with us, Pat, and who knows, you might do yourself some good. If not, and this'll equally be off the record, well, I'm wearing my old clothes, and Sergeant Rupt here, he's in the battering business as well. The other sergeant on the left here, he's easier tempered, but the thing with him is, he just don't like a killer; in fact he hates the bastards. Well, that's it. Now we'll just wait a minute while you make up your mind.'

Silence fell. It was very quiet that day in the punishment block; I still remember the ringing silence in that row of unoccupied cells. When Bowman had stopped speaking it got even quieter during those moments that can never be measured in time until Hawes, knowing he was beaten, broke the silence and began to talk – slowly at first, until he hit his stride.

27

I was interviewing Klara McGruder in her Stoke Newington flat. It was in a state of painful squalor. Through the kitchen doorway I saw piles of dead bottles; part of her unmade bed showed opposite and the floor beside it was littered with dog-ends. She talked unendingly in a deep, blurred voice, and the smell of garbage in the place wouldn't keep quiet either. On the lino-covered table between us a half-eaten plate of sardines wallowed in their oil; an empty whisky bottle towered above them.

Outside it was raining bitterly across a barren park where the grass had been trudged away by the aimless feet of the unemployed until the ground was just mud. I got up and went to look out through the rain. Below me a man spread his rags to show his chest as if it were a really fine day. His red lips gaped open inside his curly beard; the mouth closed only when it encountered the neck of the bottle that he kept picking up from the bench beside him. Rain ran over him, sliding down his ribs, subtle as a blackmailer.

Behind me Klara McGruder shifted on her battered couch.

'OK,' I said, still at the window. 'Let's go over it again. Your parents were Yugoslav. You were born in Paris. But you're not a French national.'

'I became British when I married that bastard.'

'You wouldn't have got it now,' I said, 'the British Nationality Act, 1981, would have put paid to that.'

'Who cares anyway?' she said. 'Drunks don't need passports. The only way they want to go is backwards, and there isn't a passport for there.' She started to daydream. 'When I was a child we used to go out into the countryside round Paris at weekends. Les Andelys, I liked that best. Do you know Les Andelys?'

'I'm afraid not,' I said. 'The few times I've been abroad, it's only been to unpleasant countries.'

'It was great in the summer.' Her English wasn't good. 'You could smell the grass – God, it was something, after Belleville. I used to chew a stem and dream of what I'd be when I grew up. And this is it!' she screamed. 'Look at it! This shithole! This, and social security!' She looked through me as if I wasn't there. 'Mum and Dad would be off somewhere nearby, screwing; they always did it in the country. But I used to lie on my back in another world, listening to the river, smelling the grass, dreaming.' She started to cry.

I looked at the wreckage he had made of her and it was one more point in my book against Billy. 'I'll be as quick as I can,' I said, 'but I've got to put these questions to you. First, how did you meet your husband?'

'In Paris. We met one night in a bar by the Austerlitz station. All right, I was on the game. We got friendly. *Friendly?*' She spat on the floor. 'With *him*? With that bastard devil?'

'You think of him as a devil?'

'I did after the start. When he began beating me up.' She was silent. 'It's no good,' she said suddenly, 'I've got to have a drink. Just thinking about it. You having one?'

'No thanks.' She disappeared into the kitchen and came back with a tumbler of neat scotch. She drank some, gagging over it. 'Billy McGruder? Christ, I must have been out of my mind. He tortured me, too,' she added. 'Cigarette ends on my hands and face. Red-hot needles, big ones, four inches long.'

'Yes, he's into needles,' I said, thinking of Wetherby. 'What was he doing in Paris when you met him?'

'He told me he was a paratroop sergeant with the British army and that he was on leave.'

'The kind of leave he was on,' I said, 'was being released after doing seven years for murder.'

'I know that now,' she said, 'but too late. It's always too late for me.'

'Don't say that.'

'Are you joking?' she shouted. 'Look at me! I'm thirty-three, I can't keep off the bottle, I'm finished, through, kaput.'

'No children?'

'I lost two through him. I miscarried with the first after a beating he gave me. He made me abort the other.'

'What a smashing bloke. Does he know you live here?'

'What?' she whispered. 'Christ, no, he'd kill me if he knew where I was.' Fear stole over her face like an old carpet-slipper. 'He always told me.' She pushed back her hair and shook it out in an attempt to be a woman again; the hair might once have been gold. She drank the rest of her whisky at a gulp, looked at me with half-cut steadiness and said: 'I know he did Jack Hadrill.'

'What makes you so sure?'

'It's got the devil's mark all over it. Christ, even I can read a newspaper, watch the telly. The humane killer? The plastic bags? That's Billy all right. Ah, he was always neat, the bastard.'

'You should have contacted us. Why didn't you?'

'I was too afraid. You don't know what he's like with a woman. But always neat, even when he came into you for a screw.'

'Perfunctory?'

'I don't know what that means. I don't know long English words. But if you mean he'd rather wank then the answer's yes.' She burst into frightening laughter. 'And to think he married me because I talked him into it!' Her face creased into what looked like merriment until you saw the expression that went with it. 'I thought I was in love with him! With *him*!'

'Why didn't you leave him? Right back at the time when he started hurting you?'

'You don't leave a man like Billy,' she said sombrely. She shuddered. 'He leaves you. You've no will of your own if you're living with him; that's the first thing he takes off you. After any money you've got. He's mean. And he left me. Often, and for a long time.'

'When he went off to an army?'

'That's right. He said it was business. And then just as suddenly he'd be back. In the night. Like that. Any time. He'd suddenly be there in the room, with that cold smile he had.'

'What did you do with yourself while he was away?'

A look crossed her face – the kind that always told me when there was a lie coming. 'Nothing. I just tried to get him out of my mind.'

'With alcohol?'

'That's right.'

'Nothing more?'

'No.'

'Well, I don't believe you,' I said. 'You're lying to me, and I know why; it's because you're afraid. But you've no need to lie to me, Mrs McGruder, it's the other way round. You've got to tell me the truth, because that way, by holding nothing back, you might tell me something that'll help me nail McGruder and put him away.' I waited for her to say something, but she didn't. 'All right then,' I said quietly, 'OK, there was a man now, wasn't there, while Billy was away?'

'Well, he was a lousy lover. Give a woman any pleasure? Him? Never.'

'Did Billy know about it?'

'I hope to Christ not,' she said. 'But sooner or later he finds out about everything. He might know, and just be waiting till he finds me, or till it suits him. Then I'll suffer. Battery cables. Terminals on my breasts and on my you know what. Needles. Fags. Fists too, of course. Everything he learned on interrogation courses in the army. Christ, I'm sick with terror just knowing he's around – can't you arrest him? You must be able to do the bastard for something.'

'No, I can't,' I said, 'not yet.'

'When will you be able to?'

'Perhaps soon,' I said, 'perhaps not. But the more you can tell me the sooner it'll be. Where did you live with him?'

137

'At a place we had over in Queenstown Road.'

'All right, Klara,' I said. 'Now, who was the other man?' I had the electric feeling I was onto something, but I spoke patiently, easily. She was already drunk. There was no point trying to rush her.

'Billy brought him back to Queenstown Road one night some years back. They told me to fuck off; they had business, Billy said, so I went out to the pub. When I came back at closing time the man had gone. But at different times after that he'd be back; sometimes we used to sit and talk, the three of us. And drink. I could tell he fancied me; a woman always knows. Then one night, after Billy had gone – abroad on business, he said – this bloke came round. We sat and drank for a while, and then it started.'

'I just want his name, Klara,' I said. 'That's all. Just the name.'

'I daren't.'

'Look, Klara,' I said, 'if it comes to the worst I can arrange for you to be watched. It's not easy, because we're always short of men. But I could do it.'

'You promise? You give me your word?'

'If you find you're in danger on account of information you've given me then yes, I give you my word.'

She sighed, closing her eyes and putting her hands on her knees. On the back of her hands I noticed red angry scars. 'Yes, it'll be a relief,' she said, 'if it'll help put that devil away where he can't do any more harm. It'll have been worth it, even if something happened to me.' She looked at me and said: 'Well, it was Pat Hawes.'

'Thank you, Klara,' I said. Excitement surged through me. Everything fitted. The business they were discussing years ago was murder – Wetherby's murder. I thought, if we could have got hold of Klara then, we'd have had the evidence that would have nailed McGruder for that. Meantime I had lost Klara again. She had refilled with scotch, and was talking about her father.

'Did Hawes tell you anything while you were going with him?' I said. 'Anything you think I ought to know?'

She shook her head. 'Pat Hawes was no talker,' she said, 'he was a grunter. All he wanted was a rough fuck. That's all they ever want, the men I get. Women with them, they don't get no credit for brains.' She started crying again.

'Hadrill was never mentioned? A man called Edwardes?'

Her reddened eyes gazed at me as though she were surprised I was still there. 'No,' she said. 'I never asked questions, they was always good for a smack with Billy.'

I thought, you don't surprise me. Billy's a psychopath; he laughs on the surface; often, I've seen him do it. But the expression on his face has nothing to do with what he's thinking or feeling at all.

'When we lived in France,' said Klara, 'I always used to have good feelings about the English. We used to watch them playing football on TV. Big, solid men. Kind-looking. Anyway, after Belgrade.'

I didn't say anything; I was thinking about what I had just found out.

Klara was wandering, but after a while she started up again. 'All music's like the wind,' she said. 'My mother was from Titograd; she worked on a collective there. She's been dead a while now. Yes, she used to say, music's like the wind. You hear it and then it's gone; it takes the people who played it, the people who listened, and its pleasure and damage with it. You could hear the same music, perhaps, at another time, in a different place; but it would be played by other people even though they looked like the same people, yet you would never hear it the same way again.' Scotch came back into her mouth raw, but she held it with her hand to her mouth, and a tear like a varnished fingernail slipped down her face. 'My father was from Despotovac, a village on the Zagreb–Belgrade road. In the winter it was buried under snow. The children had one dress, the same as for summer, and one pair of boots, and they crept out to go for the bread under a black sky full of snow, under pine trees loaded with ice.'

It should have been drunken melodrama but it wasn't, and I sat listening silently in the dark room; by talking of children, Klara McGruder had brought Dahlia into my mind.

I stood up. 'Well, I'll be going,' I said.

She gazed up at me blearily. 'Have a drink. Just one. It's so lonely by yourself.'

'I can't,' I said, 'I've got too much to do. Another time.' I scribbled down the number of the Factory and my home number on a page out of my notebook and put it on the table.

'Ring me at either of these numbers. Any time, if you feel afraid.'

But she had lain back. Her eyes had closed, her despair making her look like death, her face purple and swollen in the wicked shadows.

I went quietly downstairs. The weather had turned sick. It had stopped raining, but the air was like thunder over the puddles in the street. The heavy lorries were jammed solid and it was too warm for April, sickly warm; it was weather that made me sweat. I went over to the tube station to buy a paper, and the headlines were that Pat Hawes had gone on the hot cross. I didn't bother ringing the Factory; I just bought a ticket and went on down to the platform reading the story.

28

When I got in to the Factory, there was a man waiting for me from Serious Crimes, a sergeant from Bowman's crew.

'Christ, we've been looking everywhere for you!'

'Well, you didn't look in the right place.'

'You're meant to carry a bleeper so you can be contacted.'

'I'd look a bloody fool questioning a man,' I said, 'and then just when you're getting to the interesting bit that thing goes off in your pocket.'

'All the same,' he said. I could tell he always carried one like a good boy. 'Anyway, what the panic is, Pat Hawes is out of Wandsworth.'

'Yes, I know,' I said, 'I just read it in the paper.'

'Well, you've got to go up and see Superintendent George.'

When I got up there George said: 'Jesus, what a flap. Hawes — we've got every copper in the country looking for him. You saw him the other day — any idea where he might be?'

'I might have,' I said, 'on a hunch basis.'

'What did he go on the hot cross for? Jail fever?'

'You could put it like that,' I said. 'The man was sick with fright; he'd been well leaned on. He had to go where we couldn't get at him again; some of my questions were near the bone. Also, he talked to us.'

'You're on this plastic bags business.'

'Yes, it's all connected.'

'Well, we've got to get this bastard.'

'How did he get out?' I said. 'Usual? You bag the screw who sold him the key?'

'That's only a matter of time,' said George, 'there's four over at

141

that nick we've an eye on.'

'It doesn't matter,' I said, 'you can book him for flogging the key but that won't tell us anything more.'

'It's a right fuck-up,' said George. 'You're on the plastic bags thing, we're onto catching Hawes, we're all tripping over each other, it's like Charlie Chaplin.'

'Screws aren't millionaires,' I said, 'they'll take a chance where the money's right and their wages are wrong, and won't the heavy Sundays have fun with it? Hawes went straight out of the main gate, did he?'

'It's hardly worth putting them inside,' said George, 'not the well-heeled ones. Motor waiting right out there.'

'Well, it's pathetic,' I said. 'What they call a security wing in a prison these days, it'll hardly keep a sardine in its tin.'

'If you're going to tackle it,' said George, 'you'd better get your skates on, it's going right up the ladder this one is, you'll see – the brass is running about like a chicken with its head cut off.'

29

I knocked, and after a time McGruder opened the door.

'It's me, Billy.'

'What do you want this time? I'm really busy, copper. Why not another day?'

'You're never too busy to see me,' I said.

'What do you want?'

'To have a look round.' I was already doing it. 'You got Pat Hawes here?' I called to him from the bedroom.

'I never even heard of him till I read about that jail break he made in the papers.'

'You certainly read the papers, don't you?' I said, rejoining him. 'It's all right,' I added, 'I didn't expect to find Hawes here; even you're not that stupid.'

'I'm not stupid at all.'

'That's what really stupid people always say.' I'd only mentioned Hawes to give my Billy a jolt. Now I gave him another. 'Your wife around?'

'Wife? What wife?'

'Our records tell us you had a wife. Klara, maiden name of Godorovic. What have you done with her? Divorced her? Killed her? Cooked and eaten her?'

'That cow,' he said. 'I haven't seen her for years, I don't know where she is.'

'That's lucky for her.'

'Look,' he said, 'you're giving me a right pain in the arse.'

'OK,' I said, 'and now here comes a worse one. I'm taking you down to the Factory with me, McGruder. I'm doing it now. I'm taking you down for questioning in a nice peaceful room I've got there. Chief Inspector Bowman'd like a word with you and he doesn't like to be kept waiting. So get ready, I'm sick of going round the houses with you.'

He started shouting. 'You can't take me in! What could you do me for?'

'If you keep rabbiting on,' I said, 'obstructing a police officer would do to begin with.'

He managed to calm down again. 'Look, I just told you I'd got a lot on right now,' he said. 'I'll not be in the country much longer, and I've a lot to arrange. That's why I'm on edge, see? I'm sorry, really sorry if I come on a bit sharp.'

'Don't bother with the soft pedal,' I said, 'you're coming, sport. If it turns out you've never had a connection with Pat Hawes, nothing's changed. But if you have, then a lot has. If it turns out that you did business with Hawes over a period of years, then it could start to rain on you hard, Billy. And if I can establish a definite connection between you and Hadrill last Wednesday evening then it's going to come pissing down on you. I'm only thinking aloud right now, so I reckon we'll go on over to the Factory now and get everything in better shape.'

'I tell you, you must be a maniac coming in here on your own and saying things like that,' he said, 'you really must.'

'But I'm not on my own,' I said.

'I tell you I don't know bloody Hawes!' he screamed. 'Nor Hadrill!'

I had a strong feeling he was going to attack me; so I went to the door and banged on it. Immediately a big wooden-top came in. He was young and blond with hair cut short; he was pale and lean with training. He went up to McGruder, whom he topped by three inches, and said: 'OK. You want this the easy way, son, or the uphill route?'

McGruder stood in the middle of his neat room in a crouch for defence, and the officer said to him: 'I want you to touch me, son.' He spoke softly. 'Go on. Just once. Give me a pat. Go on, then. Just to see what I'm made of.'

The tension in the place was deafening.

'I hear you think you're a hard man,' the officer said. 'Christ, I'll have you licking my boots to stop the fucking pain.' He looked over at me and said: 'What's the matter with him? He broken a spring or what?'

McGruder just stood there, motionless.

'He usually carries a razor,' I said.

'Oh really?' said the officer. 'God help you if I find one on you, son.'

I said to McGruder: 'Come on, Billy. Get your coat, you can't win.'

From his stillness, McGruder did it to me. Moving in a blur of speed, he toppled me with a kick in the left kneecap that struck in a red flash of agony. As I was getting up, not feeling that leg any more, I saw McGruder had his razor out and I yelled at the officer, who took it on the arm, kicked McGruder in the genitals, got his wrist in a judo hold and caught the weapon as McGruder dropped it, doubling up and holding his wrist to his balls.

'All right,' I said to the officer, 'put the cuffs on him.' I added: 'That arm of yours really is bleeding.'

'I know it,' he said, 'that's me out of Saturday's match. Why I ever joined Special Patrol Group I'm buggered if I know.' He looked at his cut sleeve: 'Wrecked my tunic, the bastard has, and it was brand-new.'

30

Back in Room 205 I said: 'OK, Billy, now talk.'

He shook his head obstinately; I was getting used to it. 'No.' His wrist was bandaged, but it wasn't broken. He still sat hunched over, because of the kick he had had in the balls.

'I'd rather we sorted this out just between the two of us,' I said. 'But of course if we can't, we can't, and I'll have to turn you over to Serious Crimes, and no one seems to care for their methods much. So why don't you simply tell me all about Pat Hawes – how long you've known him, what you used to talk about, everything the pair of you ever got up to together?'

The WPC with the face like a plate sat at the other table with her tape recorder; a uniformed officer stood with his back against the door.

'I tell you I don't know this Pat Hawes.'

'It's a lovely tune, Billy,' I said, 'but you'll ruin it if you play it too often, also it's in a key I don't like. Look, I'm being reasonable, Billy, which isn't easy for me because I don't like being consistently lied to, and I know you've known Hawes on and off for years. Don't ask me how I know that because you won't get an answer; you can just take it that I do.'

He was silent. I thought about Klara McGruder. I had asked the voice for a watch to be put on her; I was sick of people being at risk from men like Pat and Billy. So that when McGruder suddenly said: 'I'm not telling you anything, you're just a sergeant,' I exploded.

'Now you listen!' I shouted. 'You're a cold-hearted bastard that's done bird for murder, and who knows but you're going to do some more – a sergeant's all you're fit for!'

He just looked at us. He reminded me of a picture I had seen once of a wolf surrounded by armed men in a forest clearing; his face was white, his eyes red where they should be white, and he seemed to have gone beyond argument but was turning on us because there was nothing else left for him to do. It was also suffocating in 205; everyone was sweating, and I got the constable to open the window.

'You've got to get someone down here that can talk sense,' he said at last.

'No, no,' I said, 'don't think I'm going to get my commander out of bed just on your account, Billy. Not at one in the morning.'

'Well, at least tell her over there to stop that machine, then,' he said, 'if it's you I've got to tell I don't want any of it recorded. Just five minutes or ten with you alone and no witnesses.'

'Yes, OK,' I said. I nodded to the others. They packed up and left; it was my bollock. 'Now,' I said when they had gone, 'we're alone again, isn't that nice? Now talk. I haven't got all night.'

'What are you holding me on?'

'Committing, or conspiring to commit, a murder.'

He shook his head again; it was a frequent trick with him now. 'You won't be holding me long.'

'You've got a bloody nerve, you have,' I said. 'You're right in line for the worst grilling anyone's ever had at the Factory. I've good reason to believe you topped three men, Wetherby, Edwardes and Hadrill, but any one of them will do. You assaulted two police officers this afternoon in the course of their duty, and what with one thing and another, you're going to look like a blown-out flashbulb by the time we've finished with you.'

'On your bike,' he sneered. 'I don't say I don't know a few things, but no ordinary sergeant can handle me.'

'I've handled you this far,' I said, 'I don't see any reason to give you up now; you're like the rest of my bad habits.'

'No,' said McGruder, 'you're too far down the scale – if I tried to play you as a card you'd make a noise like a mouth organ in a barrel of water. I need to talk to the bosses, people who can make binding promises.'

'Well, I truly am sorry I'm only a humble sergeant, Mr Bleeding McGruder,' I said, 'but all the same you're going to have to give me some idea what it is you want to talk about before I wake the bosses up at this time of night.'

He did give me some idea of what he was prepared to say if the conditions were right, and when he had finished I had him taken away.

'Don't give him cell 3,' I said to the constable on duty down there. 'Try and make the miserable bastard a bit more comfortable than that.'

When everyone had gone I sat drawing monkeys for a while on my ageing notepad. Then I finally did what I knew I had to do, and rang the voice. The time being what it was, though, I had to ring him at home.

'I don't know what the Christ I've got into here,' I said, 'but what I do know is, this is no more a matter for Unexplained Deaths than it is for Almighty God; it'll have to go over to the Branch.' I told him what McGruder had just told me.

'I don't believe it,' said the voice. The voice sounded as if it might have had a heavy evening. 'That's staggering, it's quite impossible.'

'Well, I know McGruder's cornered,' I said, 'and it's logical to think that he'll do anything he can to get himself out of the jam. But we can check a lot of it, or at least the Branch can.'

The voice swallowed. I was sorry for it. I had half a mind to call it sir – but how can you say sir to a voice in pyjamas?

'It would be a bit embarrassing all round if this information turned out to be straight up,' I said, 'impossible or not.'

The voice must have thought the same because it said sharply: 'OK. You stay right where you are; don't move out of your office until I call you back.'

'Not even to go to the karzy?'

'Toilet.'

'All right, then, toilet.'

'I've heard there's a method where you can hold it in, sergeant. Mind over matter. No. Not even to go to the toilet.'

31

The Branch man I had to go and see looked like one of those young majors we sent off to the Falklands who got interviewed on the box. He had two fingers on his left hand missing; he was well turned out, casually relaxed. He looked public school before he had even got his mouth open. Right now, however, he was starting to look less debonair than his turn-out.

'This is the most extraordinary business I've ever heard of,' he said. His name was Gordon, and we were sitting in his room at the Yard. The Yard again. It was remarkable if I saw the Yard once in five years. This time, counting the board, it was the second time in two days.

'Surely McGruder's just putting one over on you to get himself out of his jam,' said Gordon.

'That's what my deputy commander felt,' I said, 'but I see he took the trouble to contact you just the same.'

'Yes, well, because, Christ, if this is true,' said Gordon, 'some people could get badly hurt on this one – anything from their kneecaps to their careers. And if it broke in the press, even as a rumour, it could stay on page one of every paper in the land for ever and ever. All right, you know McGruder better than we do. How seriously do you really take it?'

'Seriously enough to make my call upstairs,' I said. 'And McGruder isn't naive – he knows we can check out most of what he's said. If we want to,' I added.

'That's the thing,' said Gordon. He coughed. 'Look, this is between you and me – it's embarrassing. It means checking things out that have already been checked out.'

'Even so,' I said, 'if they've been checked out wrong for any reason, the knife could go straight through the cheese.'

'Good image,' said Gordon. 'Jolly good. God knows how many maggots there mightn't be inside.'

'Well, don't let's get too depressed,' I said, 'anyway not yet.'

'What does McGruder actually know?' said Gordon.

'He says he knows what Hadrill knew,' I said, 'and what's more, I believe him, to put it crudely.'

'We're all of us used to things being crude.'

'Well, he maintains he choked everything out of Hadrill before he killed him. Grasses are no heroes. I dare say Hadrill thought that by telling McGruder everything he might save his skin. Christ – anybody might think that. But he didn't know McGruder. Once primed with money, McGruder's only a computer who works for himself. Getting to know what Hadrill knew was, well, reinsurance for McGruder in case something went wrong. And something did go wrong. And McGruder is reinsured. McGruder's a psychopath, but psychopaths are no fools; they wouldn't be so bloody danger- ous if they were.'

'So he bled Hadrill's knowledge out of him, then killed him as he'd been paid to.'

'That's it. and Edwardes too. Because remember that Edwardes heard everything McGruder heard, and McGruder wasn't prepared to share it with anyone. That's villains for you.'

'At least we've got McGruder's confession – he killed Hadrill.'

'He'd no choice. He was staring ahead into years of bird. He needed his reinsurance, but to operate it he had to talk – something had to give. Mind, I knew he'd done it the moment I got next to a little grass called Smitty.'

'It's what Hadrill did know that's so bloody worrying,' said Gordon. 'This has gone right the way up to the top, and you know where the top is. A wrong move here, and heads are going to roll in a way that's never been seen here before.'

'Heads are going to roll even if it's a right move,' I said. 'Fewer though, I suppose.'

There was a depressed silence so I said: 'Well, what are you going to do about McGruder's proposition? Do we let him go on running about and then give him a ticket out of the country when this is all over? Or do we bury him?'

'It's a diabolical decision,' said Gordon.

'Yes,' I said, 'but it's got to be taken.' I was tired; I yawned. 'Anyhow, luckily it's nothing to do with me.'

'What do you mean?' said Gordon. 'What do you mean, it's nothing to do with you?'

'Look,' I said, 'I want to be taken off this. I've done what I was told to do; I've got a confession out of McGruder and he's nailed up at the Factory. But espionage is nothing to do with A14 – we only deal with obscure deaths, the murder of people who are never going to make headlines. But now, what started off as a contract to waste a grass in South London turns out to be page one, and it's got nothing to do with people like me, nothing to do with Unexplained Deaths at all. McGruder's bottled up now. Anyone can deal with him.'

'Well, they're not going to,' said Gordon. 'You are.'

'I haven't the rank.'

'Fuck that,' said Gordon, 'you're co-opted on the Branch for this.' He picked up a phone. When the number answered he said he had to speak to the Commissioner. He got through and spoke for a long time. When he rang off he said: 'Well, that's settled, then.'

I got out of the building thinking, what a stupid thing to happen – I fail a board for the Branch deliberately and then within forty-eight hours I've got this on my plate, I'm working for them.

Later in the day I had to go back to the Yard again.

'The minister of defence has had another note threatening his life,' said Gordon, 'and we're taking it really seriously.'

'How seriously? You've got a watch on him?'

'You bet, round the clock.'

'What sort of a note?'

'Typewritten, on one of those old machines villains junk when they've done with them, not realizing they're a collector's piece.'

'McGruder knows something we don't,' I said, 'that's the thing to remember. He either knows who's got the contract to kill the minister, if there really is one, or he may have got it himself. Anyway, what I do know is, that thanks to what he choked out of Hadrill, he knows things that we need to know badly, very badly. Meanwhile, we've got to get Hawes back; he's the mainspring in the whole works. You take it from there.'

'I tell you, we've got every copper in the country looking for him.'

'He must know that too,' I said, 'and that's why, wherever he is, he won't be going anywhere, unless he tries to get out by private aircraft.'

'Our best bet is to soak McGruder for every bit of information he's got,' said Gordon. 'But how to do it?'

'We won't do it by keeping him slammed up in the Factory,' I said. 'The murderous little man fancies himself rotten; he reckons he's better than all of us put together any day; he's holding some very strong cards, he thinks.'

'How strong do you think they are? You know him, we don't.'

'It's a big case,' I said. 'But unless anyone loses their nerve here, a quite feeble card well bluffed could just pull the trick.'

'Christ,' said Gordon, 'I'm beginning to read your mind; you're not seriously suggesting we let McGruder out, are you? Yes, you are.'

'Well, I was leading up to it, yes. We'd take precautions like a tart of course. He'd be constantly watched; I'd be spending a lot of time with him myself. I've got his passport; it's an Irish one. I've turned his place over, but I didn't find anything else exciting.'

'Nothing written at all? No names? No addresses?'

'McGruder's a man who keeps everything in his head,' I said.

'You're really suggesting we offer this maniac a deal, are you?'

said Gordon. 'Offer to let him out of the country in exchange for this information?'

'Well, I don't see any harm in just offering him something,' I said. 'It doesn't mean to say we necessarily have to give it to him. It's a question really of deciding on the easiest way of getting to the bottom of this; but whichever way we play it it's going to be bloody difficult. Just the same, keeping him at the Factory and grilling him is going to make the job downright impossible. He's a much tougher man than Hawes; McGruder really is hard.'

'Also, we may not have much time.'

'Yes, that's another thing,' I said. 'Certainly not enough time to leave Bowman and Co. pounding away at him and getting nowhere. You could grill McGruder for five years if you wanted to, but you still wouldn't crack him. You've got to know exactly where to hit McGruder to make him react, and I know him better than anyone else here does. I've also had a long talk with his ex-wife, which he doesn't know I've had. He's threatened to kill her,' I added, 'to go by her own statement. She ought to have protection if we let McGruder out.'

'For Christ's sake,' said Gordon, 'we haven't time to worry about her problems. Does he know where she is?'

'No,' I said, 'at least, I don't know. I can only say that it's not likely. But McGruder's a man who can find anybody if he decides he wants to.' I added: 'Besides, I gave her my word I'd have her protected if she felt she was in danger.'

'You shouldn't have done that,' said Gordon. 'You had no authority.'

'I don't care about that,' I said. 'I just won't forgive myself if anything happens to her. After all, if it hadn't been for her, we'd never have had proof that Hawes and McGruder had dealings over a space of three years – it's certain now, from what she told me, that McGruder was responsible for the Wetherby murder.'

'Well, McGruder'll be watched the whole time if we go ahead with this,' said Gordon. 'I don't see the woman's in any danger.'

'There is such a thing as the mark getting lost,' I said. 'Losing the man.'

'Don't get metaphysical with me,' said Gordon. 'Once we start getting into the laws of probability we'll be sitting on our arses for ever.'

'Well, police work is four-fifths probability,' I said, 'at least, to start with. Anyway, what's your decision on whether to let McGruder go?'

'I don't know,' he said restlessly, 'it's your idea. You're really in favour of it, are you?'

'Yes,' I said, 'I am, because it's the only alternative to keeping him in the Factory – and grilling him there, the most you might achieve is putting him away for Hadrill or Edwardes. But even that's not certain; the DPP would have a fit if I went to him with nothing but what we've got now. Meantime, down to the minister, you'd be back where you were before. No, further back; because for all we know, long before we'd finished with McGruder, the minister might be dead, whatever's lying underneath this case might explode; anything could happen. No, I think we've got to let McGruder run about the board for a while.'

Gordon thought it over. Finally he said: 'All right, then, let's try it. But if anything goes wrong, it's my head on a platter.'

'Oh, you'll get used to that,' I said. 'My head's practically always on one; it's just waiting for the parsley sauce.'

32

I rang downstairs: 'Get McGruder up here to 205.'

When he appeared I said: 'We've come to a decision about you; we're going to let you out.' I watched his left hand slide up to his mouth to hide the smile of triumph. I added: 'But don't get ideas, there are conditions.'

'Never mind that for now,' he said, 'I've got my own conditions. I want a proper deal. I want out of Britain, and I want out with a lot of jack.'

'I don't know about money,' I said, shaking my head.

'Oh, I've got to have money,' he said, smacking his lips. 'Plenty.'

'Look, McGruder,' I said, 'I don't think you've quite got your brains in straight today; you can think yourself fucking lucky that you're not still in the cells wondering how soon we're going to charge you with murder.'

'Cut the crap,' he said, 'I'm not stupid, I know there's money in it.'

In the end I said: 'Well, that's not up to me. Anyway, everything will depend on what you've got to tell us.'

'I can tell you plenty.'

'You'd better be able to, it'll be your prison memoirs if not.'

'If I did grass,' he said, 'I'd need to be leaving Britain for a time, as I say. Naturally, I'd be coming back.'

'You cheeky bastard,' I said, 'our proposition is that once you get out of this country you never come back. And never means never. If any copper so much as catches sight of you here after this, I'll give you no guesses what'll happen to you.'

'You can't stop me landing in Britain for ever!' he shouted. 'Britain's my home!'

'And a horrible mess you've made of it,' I said. 'Besides, no one'll attempt to stop you landing. But where you'll land, I'll give you the address right now – it'll be HM Prison, Wakefield, Yorks. So don't come on like a barrack-room lawyer with me, see?'

He saw. 'OK,' he said, 'let's get back to money, then. What am I going to live on, once I'm abroad?'

'Well, not on your wits,' I said, 'because they're giving way, if you want to know what I think. And not on your pension, because you won't be drawing one here. Nor on your armies, because I'm going to card you up with every police force across the known world.'

'Well,' he sulked, 'there'll have to be some arrangement made, if I'm to cooperate.'

'And there will be,' I said. 'Incredible, but true. I hear it's to be a lump sum out of the special fund, and it'll be large. I don't know exactly how much, of course, because I'm only a sergeant.'

'Well, that's something, I suppose,' he said, 'though of course I'd have to know the exact figure first before I told you anything.'

I looked at him. I thought, this has to be the most extraordinary experience I've ever had as a copper, where the villain dictates the terms; this man's as guilty as hell and we're paying him to get lost in return for a word in our ear.

'I tell you I don't like this bit about not ever being able to come back here any more,' he was saying querulously. 'I mean, this is my native land, that's the bit sticks in my throat. I'm really not happy about that part. After all, I've every right. No, that part I'm not happy about. No. You'd have to drop any charges against me.'

'No charge is ever dropped,' I said, making a great effort at self-control, 'not once it's open and on the DPP's file. Only through lack of evidence – but that isn't the case with you.'

'Well, I think it stinks!' he said. 'To be told I'm not wanted and can just fuck off? That's nice! Very nice! Nice on you, friend!'

'Think yourself bloody lucky,' I said. 'But of course, if you're not interested in our terms as they stand, the officer here will take you straight down again.'

'Oh well,' he said irritably, 'as long as the money's right, I suppose it'll have to do.'

'It'll do better than a life sentence,' I said.

33

'I hear you let this bloke McGruder go,' said Bowman, 'that was fucking brilliant as a stroke that was, wasn't it?' He was leaning against the wall outside my office, his fat hands in his pockets.

'Yes, wasn't it?' I said. 'And what happened to your bank case, by the way? I heard a strange rumour they'd taken you off it.'

'Don't try and be clever, son,' said Bowman, 'it might make you ill and put you in hospital.'

'Well, I know you'd come and see me every day, Charlie, and bring me flowers and cream chocolates. Or would you just turn up for the funeral?'

He swallowed hard. 'Look, it's rank that matters in this game, sergeant,' he said. 'Rank. Not age, see? With rank you can get anywhere.'

'I know you can,' I said. 'Right up everyone's nose.'

'I could report you for that!' he shouted.

'You could, but you won't,' I said, 'because you'd look a right idiot repeating the conversation in front of the superintendent, and you know it.'

'What you know is going to get you in dead trouble one of these days,' snarled Bowman. He paused, curiosity getting the better of him. 'All right, all right, let's drop it for now. Is it true what I've heard, that you're working with the Branch over this Hadrill case?'

'That's correct.'

'You're all pussyfooting about with it,' he jeered. 'It was bad enough when Hawes scarpered from Wandsworth – but letting McGruder off the hook and all, that's just pathetic, that is, pathetic. Christ, if I'd been on it full time I'd have half murdered the bastard to get him singing and had him banged up for keeps by now. I'd have opened him up till he was on full chat.'

'Yes, you would,' I said, 'and what a total fuck-up it would have been.'

'I liked the way you failed that board the other day,' Bowman sniggered. 'That's gone right round the force, that story has. I never did think much of your brains, but what did you go and do a stupid thing like that for? Don't you care about promotion at all?'

'No, I don't,' I said. 'Time was, I wanted to join the Branch, but that was before A14 started. A14's to do with the murder of ordinary, unfortunate, obscure people, and you don't need any rank for that.'

'Christ' said Bowman, 'I just don't know about you. I wonder sometimes – under your knickers you're like Florence Nightingale or something.' He got a match out of his pocket and started picking his teeth with it.

'You seem to have plenty of time on your hands,' I said. 'I wish I had.'

'I'm waiting for Chief Inspector Verlander.'

'Going to have a few frames with Alfie?'

'I tell you, you want to watch your step,' said Bowman, 'because one of these days I'm going to very gently ask you to step outside with me, somewhere nice and quiet.'

'You'd just spoil your nice jacket,' I said.

'I see you've got a front tooth missing,' said Bowman, peering forward at me, 'so why not the whole lot?'

'I know they're not marvellous,' I said, 'still, I think I'll go to a better dentist than you.'

'God,' he said, 'you, you really push your luck. I think you really ought to come over and join me on Serious Crimes. You don't need to pass a board for that, and wouldn't we have some good laughs?'

'Maybe we would,' I said, 'but you wouldn't get any of your cases solved, we'd be too busy laughing; we'd never get anything done, and bang'd go your next promotion. No, you wouldn't really like it with me on your back, Charlie. Not really.'

34

I was having McGruder watched; I was also having him report to me at the Factory every evening at nine, otherwise straight back inside. He had just reported to me now and was turning to go. But I stopped him.

'Now what do you want?'

'A drink,' I said. 'With you. And don't worry about your bank balance, the State's paying.'

'I don't drink.'

'That's all right, you can watch me.'

'Am I going to have you on my back like this all the time?'

'Right on,' I said, 'and if you don't like it, you know what we can do.' We were outside the Factory by this time and walking west along Oxford Street. I waved at a cab. I could see the driver hesitating over McGruder, but he swerved in at the death. 'Take us down to the Painted Lady in Cromwell Road,' I said, getting in.

'What's this pub we're going to, then?' said McGruder petulantly. 'I've never heard of it.'

'You wouldn't've,' I said, 'because it isn't a villains' pub for once, just an ordinary one; writers and musicians and folk like that go in there. I know you're the jack in the pack, Billy, but I'm getting sick to death drinking with killers all the time, it's bad enough I've got one sitting next to me right now.'

'I could take offence at that.'

'Well, I wouldn't,' I said. 'Get your knees open. Let it all hang out.'

After a while he said, looking out of the cab window: 'Traffic jams, look at them, I'd like to put a bullet through a few of these motors.'

'Not yours, though,' I said. 'Anyone put a bullet through yours, you'd be too mean ever to buy another.'

He wasn't listening. That was the worst of people like that; they were a monologue – killers are like the army, dull and dangerous simultaneously. 'Bullets,' he was saying. 'Funny. I never thought of it before – what if I got one through me? Not to have my body. Not to be alive. I always reckon it's me's going to pump them in, not the other way round.'

'I know,' I said, 'and that's why we don't want you around, Billy.'

'Guatemala'll have me all right. That's where I'm bound next.'

'Good luck to Guatemala.'

'This money you're giving me, I could run my own outfit down there.'

'You haven't got the money yet.'

'But I'll get it,' he shouted, 'won't I? I will, won't I?'

I was too choked to say anything.

'By the way, I don't even know how much it is yet,' he said urgently, 'nobody's told me.'

'They're working it out.'

He was quiet for a minute. Then he said: 'You don't know what it means to be murdered when you're a child. Kind of murdered in your head.'

'Do we have to talk about you the whole time?' I said. 'I'll just tell you this much, Billy – the devil can never be murdered. You can nick him all you like; he'll always be back as someone else. I'm sorry for you, Billy. It must be terrible to be you, carrying someone like you around the whole time.'

'I don't know,' he said seriously, 'I switch on, I switch off, you know. Depends on my mood.'

'Hell never switches off,' I said, 'it works twenty-four hours a day.'

'I've got beliefs.'

'I know,' I said, 'killing for money, and it ends up you doing the breast-stroke in blood.'

162

'They've all got to die. Everyone has.'

'Maybe,' I said, 'but people like to choose when and how.'

'They don't feel anything.'

'They do before,' I said, 'while they're looking a sailmaker's needle in the eye, or waiting for a nail through the back of the head.' We got to the pub. It was cold outside, but nice and warm inside the place. It was a pub I came to sometimes, just for a lager. You could still see traces of what the décor had been like; it was a high room, and they had kept the old ceiling with its plaster mouldings, and there was a fan to cool the place down in hot weather. But that was all. The brewers had been in to gut the rest and had repapered the walls that I remembered, and put up the same repros of hunting dogs and old-time army officers that they had in a thousand of their other pubs. It was half past nine and crowded. A group of young men in bow-ties and suavely crafted clothes were saying ho ho, ha ha to three disparaging women in shapeless knitwear that had cost a fair bit; if they hadn't done a spell at Greenham Common yet or been on a CND march or sent a telegram of congratulations to Andropov on his accession to power, well, they looked as if they had. Some Irish regulars and Arab embassy chauffeurs were dotted along the bar, and there was a quartet of East End villains at a corner table near the bar; they liked to take a run up from Peckham in the jamjar of an evening to a nice quiet part of the town once in a while, somewhere where it wasn't a villains' pub.

'What are you drinking, Billy?'

'All right, I'll have half a lager and lime just for once.'

I got it for him, and a pint for myself, and we found ourselves a table. A big Australian barmaid winked at Billy as we carried our drinks over; he didn't wink back. It was strange, the way he spread coldness around him. We walked across the pub; Billy didn't say a word. He didn't look like anything special at all at first sight. Yet the bow-tie and woolly mob, two Irishmen with their arses parked against a fruit machine and even a villain on his way to the gents, all made room for him to get by. Also, once we sat down, the tables around ours vaguely started to empty. Only the handful of mean old buffers who were always in there, carrying someone else's *Times* importantly under one arm, took no notice of him; they were too busy looking out for anyone they could bum a half off or a ring-a-ding, might they be so lucky. Next I watched the governor in his corner behind the bar. He was only a tame edition of the governors I usually met, in a navy blazer with a regimental badge in gold thread over the top pocket. He was looking at us uneasily and the talk in the place, loud when we came in, seemed to have dimmed.

'OK,' I said, when we were settled, 'start telling me about Hadrill. You've nothing to worry about now; the deal's fixed.'

'I've got the money to worry about.'

'The way you go on about your piggy-bank,' I said.

'You would if you were me. Come on now, how much is it?'

'All right,' I said, 'it's fifty thousand. And don't try and bargain over it – that's it. If you don't like it you can go straight back inside. As keep-clear money, I don't think it's bad myself.'

He lit a cigarette, something he seldom did. When it was going he laid it in the ashtray and rolled it round and round. 'This is a terrible thing I'm doing,' he said. 'There are limits.' I didn't myself think it was anything like as terrible as the things he had already done, but I didn't say so.

'Money,' I said. 'Money and your freedom. Think about that.'

'I am doing,' he said. He coughed, he was so nervous, so off-balance. 'Well, all right,' he said, 'yes, OK, it was done for Pat Hawes. It had been arranged I'd wait for a phone call from Tony Williams – you know who I mean by him? – and when it came it was to say come over, it's been set up for Jackie to come in to the Drop on the night of the 13th. This was done in code, like there was an agreed code, you know? So when I got the call I went down to the Drop by tube, marked my punter, picked up the car keys Merrill had left on the bar, and pulled Jack into the motor that went with the keys, yes, I know Edwardes is dead, I'll come to that later, one thing at a time. What I mean is, I went off after Jack when he left the Drop; I got in the motor and followed him along the street; I wound the window down when I caught up with him and said hello, Jack, nice evening. I don't know you, he said. Oh, come on, I said, not so fast, why not come for a ride, Jack? Not on your nelly, he said. Look, I said, I hate disorder outdoors, on the street, we don't want a public scene now, do we, so be a good boy, just hop in the motor. I was holding him by his eyes like I was a ferret, you know, and then I took him by the arm hard. Thin little arm like it was driftwood. He said I knew all along this was moody and I said you're wrong, you're in on a big deal, Jack. I pushed him into the front beside me and away we went; nice motor, Renault 20, Merrill stole it and Jack said, where're we going? And I said, now don't you worry about that, Jack, I know where we're going right enough. Is it far? he squeaked. Far enough, I said, the far side of the river. I always think of it as death, the river, but of course I didn't tell him that. I don't like it, he said just the same, and started to blubber. Look, I said, there's nothing to this, you're going to be rich, what are you going on about − I always think eternity is riches, do you think that's why I am the man I am, sarge? − just listen to this beautiful tape. I found a Kim Carnes cassette under the dashboard, *Misbehaviour* it was called, I'll always remember that, and put it on, and all the while we was driving I felt, you know, like kind of above it all, very calm. I'm always calm when I've been paid for work, and it's to be done. Well, I had an easy trip with Jack. I didn't mind what I touched in the motor. I was gloved, wasn't I? I always go gloved, makes sense that, doesn't it? Jack, though, every time he went to touch the motor inside, I just reached over and smacked him like he was a naughty boy. You keep your hands in your coat pockets, Jack, I said, like you're big time − you know, you play the boss like you're used to, you're used to doing that. I said, I've got a terrible sharp toy here if you don't front it out and play the boss, Jack. I only had to show him the razor once. It was just blag, really, for him, for me – he knew in his guts what it was all down to, but he wanted to believe me that there was a deal at the end, see? Anyway, there wasn't a lot of traffic, and he only threatened to yell once, at a set of lights, but I just showed him the edge and told him I didn't care and he forgot it. So we slipped into Rotherhithe just as dark was coming, quiet as mice, and when we got there I said, OK now, Jack, out you get, I don't want to have to haul you out, it's undignified, that is. Well, in the death he half come out of the jam and I half give him a hand and I looked, and the street door was ajar as agreed. I didn't see Merrill's car. Jack said, I don't like it, I don't like it, I don't know who you are, and I smacked him to let the air out of him a little. But I promise you, I didn't like doing that, and I told him so; I only did it because he was bawling. I took him across the pavement and he looked up at this great old empty warehouse. Anyone live here? he said. No, just us, I said, you're moving into new quarters. Merrill, who had heard us, came down, took him over for a minute while I went and got my case of gear out of the motor. I never like them to see the gear; that's my pleasure of working. Well, I went up to the second floor (the first was old offices and not suitable) and there was everything we should need laid out; Merrill had put it there earlier in the day. We knew there'd be no trouble with the caretaker, we'd been careful about that. We'd studied him, weeks beforehand. He's a regular old pisspot and don't care to go round the place at night, not even with a skinful, and I don't blame the old cunt. So we all three went upstairs, and I got my gear out and put it in a corner and then Jack looked at the two of us and said, what is this? So Merrill let him have it straight. This is a topping job, he said. You've done two things, you've grassed Pat down to that factory job in the north where the guard was killed; also you threatened to tell the law what else was taken besides the money. You was too nosy and too noisy, and you got Pat twenty years. Jack wailed, I didn't, I didn't! I didn't care, I'd only come to do him; I let him wail. So we stood there, the three of us for a minute, and I could see Jack plainly in the light from the street; that light would be all we needed. I saw Jack so clear, I watched him fade inside his funny clothes when he saw the look on my face; he had a little peaked cap on and knee-length boots – he looked like a rabbit, a pest, something you've caught by the ears when you're going to give it the chop. I'd been over the whole procedure with Merrill beforehand; Merrill knew just what to do. Bring him over to this wall beside the window, Merrill, I said, but not too near. I don't want to come, Jack bleated, I don't want to. We know which copper you went to, Merrill said, and we know how much you were paid, because we paid to find out; it was a bent copper, and that's all there is to it, Jack; the firm don't like a grass. I repeated to Merrill, right over here, here, that's right, not too near the window, just by it, that's right, that's right, get him up against the wall. Then I noticed that the big pans I'd ordered were bubbling away over the camping gas, and I was right pleased to see that. We had time; still, there's never any point in wasting it. So the water was coming up to the boil nicely. I asked Merrill had he got the plastic sheet and he said, it's over there. The bags were there, the tub to bleed him into; everything was there and I was satisfied. I said to Merrill, OK, we can go ahead then. Put his face to the wall, bang his face on the wall if he gives any trouble, I'm nearly ready. Jack didn't give any trouble, he was like jelly with terror. Fear's a strange thing to see in a man; smells almost like piss, makes you cry out to do it to him. All the same, Merrill put his face into the wall hard and there was some blood and I said to Merrill careful now, that'll have to come off. I said to Merrill, now, when I come up, take him by his ears so he don't move his head. Merrill said something like he didn't think he could look and I said, don't be ridiculous, with one of these there isn't any mess. Merrill said that once something was dead he didn't mind any more, it was just that moment. I didn't think much of Merrill for that. That was when I began to have doubts about him. I needed him now, though. Well, I turned to Jack with my gear all ready and said to him, look, this isn't going to hurt, see. You won't know a thing. Jack had been quiet up till then but when I said that he started to make a noise like a sheep or a chicken or something into the wall, sort of farmyard noises, and I knew I was going to have to be quick. Also, between ourselves, I had a hard on, and I can judge when I go off just nicely. One thing I noticed while I was going up to Jack; through the window I saw a ship crammed with people and every one of its lights blazing, moving slowly down the Thames just outside, going down with the ebb tide. There were bands playing, you never saw anything like it. You got him? I said to Merrill. Yes, he said, looking away, see, I've got him by the hair and one ear. Take that cap off him, I said, he won't need it where he's going. Merrill brushed it off Jack's head, still without looking at him. Jack was quite bald on top. I thought again, I don't think much of you, Edwardes, underneath you're just piss and wind; I don't trust you, you've bottled out. I loaded my gear while I was thinking that; I'd oiled it so well you could hardly hear the click. I said to Jack, OK, now stand still, take it like a man, Jack. I pulled the trigger and he was gone, smack; he just slid down the wall. I caught him and held him to the sheet in case, but there was hardly a drop of anything, just a bit of the grey; then Merrill got ready with his knives and we started. Well, you know what happened after that.'

'What you haven't told me,' I said, 'was what Hadrill knew. You've left a piece out, and I want it.'

'All right,' said McGruder, 'the factory that Pat ripped off, that's no shoe factory. I learned interrogation techniques in the army, all right? I know just how to work the carrot and stick – the weapon or the kind word, the offer of the smoke that breaks them. Right up to the last second Hadrill thought that what he knew might save him. But I reckoned I'd be better off with his knowledge than a dead man – it might do me some good; knowledge usually does. And it has. The place is a government electronics set-up, and Hawes was paid to rip it off. That is, their share was all the wages – no one to split with. The government was asking for it as usual, I reckon.

Whatever it is they do in there it's so secret that I imagine they thought well, if we pretend there isn't any secret, people will think there isn't one. How daft can you get? What? Locals watching gay white-coated eggheads trying to pass themselves off as operatives on a factory floor? I laughed my head off when Jackie got to that bit. Well, Jackie's gay if you didn't know, and he got right into one of these intellectual miracles at the end where his brains aren't. The two of them liked a piss-up besides; don't tell me gays don't like a drink, I know better. Jackie's sweetheart tried to keep it quiet, of course; but talk gets about in a little place, orgies with little male mysteries Jackie brought up from the Smoke and the rest of it. The only thing I don't know is the feller's name; Jackie tried to deal with me over that but I got fed up with him, I was getting a hard on and I was getting pushed for time. Myself, I like to come just as the target goes; what screws it for me is if I come too soon. So I said to Edwardes, bang his mush on the wall, will you, shut him up – so I never did get the boyfriend's name. He was a high-up, though.'

'What was taken besides the wages?'

'Microfilm. Only they didn't take it, they just refilmed it so that nothing was missing when the law came round, see? Anyway, in the death, when Jackie had got all this out of this poofter of his who'd set it up, he went to see Hawes and asked for his cut – and he wanted a big cut, seeing how the guard got himself topped. So when Hawes told Jackie to get stuffed Jackie went to the law; he had contacts there like you wouldn't believe. OK, you know the rest – Jackie copped and Hawes drew the bird. The only mistake Hadrill made when he agreed to that meet on the thirteenth was that he thought he was safe, even though he knew the governor of the Nine Foot Drop was Hawes's brother-in-law.'

McGruder stopped, swallowed a little lager and said: 'It's amazing the way folk who ought to know better will stick their necks out for money.'

'You, for instance.'

'I never stick mine out.'

'You stuck it out for fifteen hundred quid to top a grass.' I added: 'Why did you risk boiling him away?'

'Don't be stupid,' said McGruder. 'We didn't want any traces, that's why. It was my idea, I planned it all out.'

'What about Edwardes?'

McGruder looked into his glass and said gently: 'He knew too much. You know he was there while Jackie talked. He might have tried to win the race. Also, he was frightened after Hadrill. There was all that publicity, and he bottled out. Mind, I knew he would before that.'

'You'd better tell me about it.'

'Oh, I don't know,' he said, 'I don't know if you get all that information for fifty long ones.'

'Don't try and bargain with me,' I said with sudden fury, 'or your feet won't fucking touch.'

'Don't you welsh on me!' screamed McGruder. People near us looked round.

'Don't fuck me about,' I said. 'No information, no deal.'

'All right,' said McGruder when he had calmed down, 'well, it was a short cut he took across to his flat in SW5. I knew he always took it because he told me he always did. So I waited for him there, on that piece of waste ground behind Olympia where you found him. There was enough cover. It was risky, but in that area people take cover if a cat farts. I didn't like it, as I say; blowing a man's head off in central London, even at night – it's clumsy, it's careless. Still, I reckoned I was in a fair way to get away with it.'

'And you might have done,' I said, 'if there hadn't been a link between Hadrill and Edwardes.'

'I had to do it,' said McGruder. 'I told you I started not trusting Merrill while we was doing Jack; that was the main reason I shot him. He could have gone to the law, the linens – I couldn't take the chance.'

That was the moment the landlord looked at the clock and rang the bell again before coming out from behind the bar. It was a quarter past eleven, and everyone was leaving. When the landlord saw that McGruder and I didn't move he made a serious mistake: he dug his hands in his side pockets and strolled over to us. 'OK, you two,' he said, 'move. It's well after time. Haven't you got no homes to go to?'

McGruder said: 'We was just talking about murder in a general way, and I haven't finished my drink, darling.'

'I don't fucking care,' said the landlord. 'I've had my eye on both of you all evening and you look like a couple of wrongo's to me.'

'And you're dead right,' said McGruder, 'but that's no reason to make a spectacle of yourself. What's that yellow thing on your pocket there? Someone throw an egg at you?'

The landlord boiled in the face: 'I'll let that pass, now drink up, on your bike, fuck off, the two of you, and don't come back.'

'When an East Ender like you dresses up,' McGruder said to him mildly, 'he usually goes to the right tailor. But you're an exception, you look a real mess.'

'Christ,' said the landlord, buckling his fists, 'you're really pushing your luck, you are.'

McGruder just placed the tip of his forefinger on the rim of his glass and moved it gently round and round till the glass rang. 'You know what that means?' said McGruder. 'It means I'm ringing for service, lackey. And what an angry glass it gets if it don't get any. Understand, cunt?' He picked the glass up and poised it against the edge of the table, ready to smash it. 'You ever been bottled?' he said. 'Well, my life, I think you need to be, you've certainly got no bottle, you're just piss and wind.'

At last the landlord began to understand.

'You've gone soft down here,' said McGruder, 'that's your trouble.' The air around him was cold and silent. A fridge hummed, then started making a noise as if it was trying to bugger something. But it seemed far away. Somewhere behind the bar, on the floor, there would be a bell the governor could have trodden on to get help. But that, too, was far away.

'Well, look,' said the landlord, 'now please, gents.'

'That's better,' said McGruder. He picked up his glass and threw the contents in the landlord's face. 'You never know who you're dealing with when you're serving the public; you can be in a dangerous game there, sweetheart, without even knowing it.'

'Right, that's it,' said the landlord, wringing out his sodden shirt, 'I'm calling the law.'

'No need for that,' I said, 'I am it.'

'Well then, fucking do something!' screamed the landlord.

'OK,' I said. 'Come on, let's go, Billy, that's enough.'

McGruder grumbled, staring down: 'Scots and Irish blood don't mix. They make a terrible mixture.'

'That's right,' I said. Out on the street I could see the man detailed to watch McGruder for the rest of the night pacing around.

'I don't like to upset the law,' said the governor. 'What about a private drink, the three of us, friendly like?'

'Go and piss in your sponge-bag, nig-nog,' said McGruder. He went over to the door, kicked it open and went out. The man waiting for him followed after.

'What was all that about?' said the landlord.

'I'm afraid I can't explain,' I said, 'but you'll get a new blazer.'

'It isn't just the blazer, what about my shirt? There's a ton's worth of gear there.'

'Send the bill over to Poland Street, I've said I'm sorry.'

'I've a good mind to make a complaint.'

'I wouldn't,' I said, 'it won't get you anywhere.'

35

I had nightmares again, frightful dreams I dreamed of Dahlia. She was wrapped in her shroud. It was stained with earth; she flew over me with her arms out and touched my head, shaking hers and saying sadly: Oh, Daddy, come to me, Daddy, come quickly. She was bleeding all over again. Where are you, Daddy? she cried. I've come to find you for you to kiss me and hold me tight. It's so cold and lonely there in the graveyard, it's so dark in my grave.

There were a lot of us in a green uniform. It was long ago; but in the dream it was now. We started to advance down a mountain slope in the face of dirty white bursts of fire from medium cannon parked on the opposite spur. I wasn't in our army. Men went down everywhere but I kept firing. It was about four o'clock; I had the sun in my eyes. It was a hot summer's afternoon and a bloody one. I went through a putrid gust of smoke and changed, yet passed through it still as a flame, then came back to myself at last and lay in a strange state of awakening.

I had a stranglehold with both hands on the edge of the mattress; I had dreamed that I looked death straight in the face.

36

In the morning I went back to the Factory and asked for any news about Hawes.

There wasn't any. 'You'd have been contacted quick enough if there had been,' they said, 'don't worry.'

But I was worried. I went up to 205 and dialled Klara McGruder's number. I had had a horrible idea. There was no answer when I dialled, and that made the idea worse. I rang the Yard and said: 'Have we anyone watching Klara McGruder?'

They checked and said no – shortage of men. 'You idiots!' I shouted. My fear for her made me furious. I got the tube and went over to the Yard. I said to Gordon: 'I know where Hawes is,' and when I explained he said: 'God, wretched woman.'

I said: 'We've got to do something at once.'

'But what?' he said. 'Suppose we assault the place, Hawes'll be armed in there. He could do anything, he could kill her. Mind,' he added, 'it's my bollock. You said we should put a man on her and we didn't. Christ, what a balls-up, it's always the same – not enough men. Well, all we can do is put men on it now; after all, someone'll have to come out and buy food.'

'No, don't bank on it,' I said, 'they're not cretins, they'll have enough in there to last them a while. Besides, Hawes'll never let the McGruder woman out. She's his guarantee and anyhow she knows too much.'

One of his phones rang. 'This'll be bad,' he said, picking it up, 'this phone always is.' He listened, hung up and said: 'Yes, well, that's it, it couldn't be worse, the man who's been following McGruder's gone and lost him at a double-entrance pub in Piccadilly.'

'Well, get an alert out,' I said, 'Met, City, chief constables, the lot, he's got to be found.'

When that had been done Gordon said: 'Well, now there's Bartlett, the defence minister.'

'Yes,' I said, 'and he's the haemorrhoid in the fucking imperial arse, because if it hadn't been for the death threat to Bartlett, and the necessity of finding out what was behind it, I'd have had McGruder banged up already. Hawes would never have made his jail break, and the woman wouldn't be in danger now.'

'It's quite pointless indulging in self-pity,' said Gordon, 'we've made a balls-up and we've got to pick up the bits. Now look – I'm going to tell you something about Bartlett that no one outside the Branch is supposed to know. We've got our eye on him. There's nothing positive, but we have had for some time.'

'Oh, come on,' I said, 'stop hedging.' That was the Branch – getting them to say anything, even to a copper, was like questioning a criminal; to get at the truth was like tearing the page off a stiff calendar. 'Positive or not,' I said, 'you must have a reason.'

'More a suspicion.'

'Well, let me tell you this,' I said. 'I might just as well sock it to you, although it's your job to know. Like it or not, Hawes has definitely been working for the Soviet Union, I got that from McGruder. A lot of microfilm was snapped at that factory during the raid. I don't know just what those people are really doing up there, but I do know they aren't making shoes. Hadrill knew it too. And why snap film if it's not classified? And where would classified microfilm be going except to the USSR?'

'OK, OK,' said Gordon wearily. 'Why shouldn't you know it all, you're in so deep now? What those people are doing up there is designing and building the software for the President 2 missile. It was supposed to be an all-American job, but then they found that this man of ours, Phillips, was better at it than anyone they'd got in the States, for once.'

'Well,' I said, 'the Russians have got the film now anyway; how much damage has it done?'

'Enough to put us back five years; the Americans are thrilled, I don't think; we had to tell them.'

'Let's stick to the criminal angle,' I said. 'Just where does the minister come into this?'

'Money,' said Gordon, 'he gambles. Mostly at a very select club for big punters, the Rio de Janeiro in Bruton Street. In a private room. Not many folk, but a lot of money. Right now he owes them somewhere around two hundred thousand. Politicians seldom make good gamblers,' he added with a wan smile, 'that's over-confidence for you. Anyway, that put us onto him, when we found out he was owing – we put a croupier in, also a bird to see if she could chat him into telling her where the money was coming from. It didn't work,' he added. 'She got him to bed but all he did was talk about himself.'

'That's the trouble with politicians,' I said.

'Still,' said Gordon, 'He does like the girlies. He gets them to do all kinds of funny things to him, and that costs him as well.' He slid a drawer of his desk open and showed me some pix. I had seen it all before while I was on the Vice Squad, only more often with a lorry driver goggling underneath in his socks and wristwatch, not a minister.

'Fancy,' I said, 'a minister of the Crown having things like that done to him. Look at this one where he's being dragged around by his cock.' I added: 'How far does all this go back?'

'It goes back.'

'Did your folk ever check to see if he was on the board of any of the Haweses' moody companies at any time?' I said. 'Long before he was a minister; back in the days when he was just a humble MP?'

'Christ, no,' he said. 'We never did. You might have something there.'

'I can't understand how he ever got security clearance to take that job,' I said. 'Security isn't up my street, but still.'

'Well, our people get the points switched on them,' said Gordon
gloomily, 'that's what politics in this country are all about. It makes
us a jam puff for the Russians. You're an ambitious MP, you're well
in with the PM, you've got your cronies at cabinet level, the job
comes up – bang, you're in it. And if we or MI5 say hey, wait a
minute, we're told to go and get stuffed. In the nicest possible way,
of course.'

'And so now somebody wants to kill him,' I said. 'Why?'

'That's going to be a melancholy story,' said Gordon, 'when it
comes out, and he's going to have to tell it – the Russians have
seen to that. I've read the notes he's had, and they're bloody
terrifying – he had to come to us with them. First, the Russians
used him. Now they're ditching him. He didn't expect that. They
never do; they're like children. He can't believe he's going to lose
his job – maybe even his liberty. Just a little treachery to support
the old tastes; but a little treachery goes a long way if you're
minister for defence.'

'Where he came in really handy was over that robbery,' I said.

'It'll have to be proved,' said Gordon, 'even though the horse has
bolted. This is only how we're thinking so far, but let's put it this
way – a minister can find out anything he wants to. He was often
briefed on that factory – on the face of it he had to be, for cabinet
discussions, statements to the House. We know exactly how often
he's been up there. There wasn't a whisper of publicity, of course.
Dark glass on the car.'

'Get all the dates,' I said, 'we might as well find out how far up
and down this goes. This Phillips now, who runs the place, he
bothers me.'

'Well,' said Gordon, 'he was checked.'

'That doesn't seem to mean much, and I don't see what use the
minister would have been if Phillips wasn't in the deal, and vice
versa. I'd like to check Phillips. My way.'

'OK,' said Gordon, 'we may as well try and get it right this time.
I'll tell you about Phillips. Phillips is a software wizard – the sort

of microchip guru who makes a British government foam with excitement, like a snooker amateur with black over the top pocket. A chance of upstaging the Americans? They'd go to any lengths to punt him into the job and no questions asked. And punt him in they did. And ask us about him they didn't. As for threatening the minister, I tell you, it has to be the Russians that are trying it on. Look at it like this. They read our papers, watch our TV like everyone else. They see the coverage this Hadrill job's had, also the Hawes jail break; they know fucking well what it's all about. Also, they've just had forty-four of their folk kicked out of here – and now, if this goes to the end of the line, Christ, there'll hardly be a Soviet left in the UK by the time the dust's settled. So I reckon they followed this case step by step in the press; they watched us getting closer and closer to the minister, to Phillips, and they said to themselves, we reckon Bartlett's going to panic, let his knickers down and reveal all. We can't do a Philby on him these days and have him turn up in Moscow as a major-general in the KGB, so he'll have to go, that's all there is to it, he's gone unsteady. They won't use their own men, though; they know we're too sophisticated for that. Christ, these days, you get a native-born Russian ferreting anywhere around where there's no reason for him to be, he sticks out like a sore cock at a wedding, poor sod with his funny-hat accent – he comes unstuck at the first fence. It's the Soviets' own fault. They won't let their own people out of the workers' paradise to train, and they won't trust anything British a bit more up-market because it *is* up-market, no matter how it drags its feathers around in front of them. That, by the way, is where the Russians are really feeble when it comes to the West – they fear our society like the devil fears water right across the board. We know that – and this time it's against us – and that makes us take liberties with them. We just can't take them seriously enough, and that's where we come unstuck.'

'Are coming unstuck,' I said.

'All right,' said Gordon, 'all right. Don't criticize for a moment, this is my sphere, I'm just briefing you on this, you know nothing about intelligence work.'

'I'm learning fast,' I said, 'it looks just like police work to me.'

'Maybe you should join us here.'

'No, it's too abstract,' I said. 'I like to see the body and work everything right back. From back to front.'

'OK,' said Gordon. 'Now you're the Russians. You've got to top a British minister who's bent, before he grasses you. What do you do?'

'They use our villains,' I said. 'They haven't much choice. But they're taking as much of a risk using the hard mob as they would be with any of their other solutions.'

'The Russians just don't understand the way we work,' said Gordon, 'that's why, I tell you. Take Hawes. No one but a lunatic would ever have used him to rip off material like that. The Russians never took into account that Hawes might be grassed. But he was, and we put him away. OK, now Hawes is in the nick. But if the minister's caught and starts singing, Hawes thinks, Christ, that's another load of bird for me – fuck the Russians, they're too fucking slow, I'll do the berk myself. Hawes knows we'll have him on such a bundle of charges when we catch him that he might as well make his will and leave everything to Wakefield; he'll never get out.'

'We do know the Grossmans were working for the Russians, though.'

'Well, we think we do,' said Gordon gloomily, 'they said they were. But supposing they were working for Hawes too? They're old mates. Or supposing Hawes made his break just to top the minister himself, also to stop you questioning him? Or the man scheduled to top the minister may be an entirely different villain. We just don't know, and what a fuck-up it is, if you'll excuse the phrase.'

'Don't worry,' I said, 'I'm always using it.'

'The worst of the business is,' said Gordon, 'we've got to wrap it up in silence. No publicity, those are the orders; we've got to sweep every bit of this shit straight under the carpet.'

'Normally we've got a national genius for it,' I said, 'but this time it's going to be difficult. Fleet Street's got a sniff of burning wires already, and some of that mob feed stuff to mates at lunchtime to such a degree that it's virtually public before it's even been printed.'

'I'll see to the press,' said Gordon savagely. 'This is going to be done the way we want it done, and any half-arsed journalist that doesn't see it my way can take a bus ride down to the Manpower Centre, he'll be on the dole.'

'You could slap a D-notice on.'

'I've got no authority,' he said. 'Anyway, we don't like them – this isn't Poland.'

'The angle the press'd like best,' I said, 'is this angle on London villains working for the USSR – Hawes, the Grossmans. They'd find that incredibly juicy, the Sundays would go potty over it, especially the highbrows, what is our society coming to etcetera.'

'Well, I tell you they won't get a chance,' said Gordon, 'not unless the whole of this thing explodes on us like a defective rocket. This new man they've got at their embassy here since Andropov came to power. Gureyevich. He's a cunning sod. It must be his idea; he's the KGB resident these days. Yes, I bet it looked pretty good to him to start with. But he doesn't know villains as well as we do; what Gureyevich forgot was that once a villain's into a really good punter he'll never let go, why should he? They haven't admitted it yet, but I can just see the Grossmans having a go at putting the black on the Russians. They sent those notes for them; they smashed up your little grass for them, Smith; they may even have been approached over this contract to do the minister for all we know. You met the Grossmans?'

'I saw them clocking us the night I met Smitty,' I said. 'Heavies from Plaistow, but they go all over town. They're thorough. What have you had out of them?'

'Only that they sent the death notes so far, but Serious Crimes hasn't finished with them yet; they're at it now.'

'They'll be feeling very hard used,' I said, 'by the time Bowman's finished with them.'

'Yes, I sat in for a while,' said Gordon. 'There was nothing delicate about it.' He added: 'Well, how are we going to tackle Hawes and McGruder, then?'

'I'll have to trust to this double hunch I've got,' I said, 'if we're going to play it my way. One, that I'm right about Hawes being shacked up with Klara McGruder. Two, that McGruder's looking for them.'

'It must be electric in that flat,' said Gordon, 'if the three of them are together. I can see why Hawes would be in there OK, but why McGruder?'

'Revenge,' I said. 'If Klara really thought Billy knew nothing about her fling with Hawes, she really did have her head in the clouds. That doesn't surprise me, mind; nothing about alcoholics surprises me. Still, I feel terrible about the woman now. I promised her that I'd have her protected.'

'This sounds a pretty hideous thing to say,' said Gordon, 'but if we had protected her McGruder couldn't have gone there, and we'd still be looking for him.'

'Yes, it is a hideous thing to say,' I said, 'and I've exposed her by mistake on purpose, the way you expose a goat to a lion, I've seen that on TV. Yet, seeing that you've got the Grossmans, there's a chance that either Hawes or McGruder have the contract to top this minister.'

'Well, if they have,' said Gordon, 'they won't have a chance to carry it out. I tell you, the Russians aren't going to do it. Christ, if a Russian did it and was caught, they'd have a diplomatic forest fire on their hands that they'd never put out, and we're supposed to be trying to get back to the age of détente.'

'You'd better make sure neither Hawes nor McGruder get out of that flat if they're in it, though,' I said, 'over the roofs, say – you'll be in trouble if they do. I reckon the best thing would be to take the minister into protective custody, a safe house somewhere.'

'But that's just what I can't do!' Gordon shouted. 'What? Have him just vanish? It would go straight onto page one of every paper in the Western world, which is exactly what we're trying to prevent. No, we've got to take a chance.'

'OK – so have I the authority to play it my way?'

'As long as it's quiet. Will it be really, really quiet?'

'If it turns out right,' I said, 'you'll only hear the tune in the distance.'

He sighed. 'Yes, all right,' he said, 'we'll do it your way. You know the bastards. Men to watch and cover, we'll see to that. There have been two cabinet meetings over it, and it's all agreed; the PM's taking a personal interest.'

37

I went out into the street and stood on the pavement watching the traffic. Soon a squad car passed; I stopped it.

'All right, sport,' said the blond young copper beside the driver, leaning out, 'what's it down to?'

'It's down to me,' I said. 'I'm in a hurry.'

The copper started to laugh in an incredulous way, but the CID sergeant in the back put a stop to it. 'Hello, Sid,' I remarked, 'well, it's been a while.'

'I should think so,' he said, 'seeing you're dead and buried over at A14.'

'Sid, get me over to the Factory,' I said. 'I'm on this Hawes–McGruder thing.'

'Christ, that? That sounds hairy.'

'Will you do it?' I said. 'I'm in ever such a hurry, and I'll buy you a pint one of these days.'

'A whole pint? What, have we had a raise or something? Get in.' He said to the driver: 'Make it to the Factory, Dave. Put the wailer on.'

On our way we overtook a Planet car returning empty and going too fast. 'I'd like to have booked him,' said the blond young copper, 'them bleeding minicabs.'

'I wouldn't mind your job,' I said.

'You'd take a drop in wages, sarge.'

'It might be worth it,' I said, 'for the relative peace and quiet.' We stopped at the Factory and I got out. 'Thanks, Sid.'

'Always a pleasure to do business with Unexplained Deaths,' he said. 'Is it all right if we piss off and get some sleep now? We've been on since midnight.'

'Yes, dismiss,' I said, 'and sharpen your darts game up.' I walked into the Factory past the usual bag of thieves, whores and pisspots who were being assembled for the Black Maria to take them to Great Marlborough Street. I went downstairs and said to the girl on duty at the computer: 'I want you to check a name, it's McGruder.'

'We've been busy with that name,' the girl said. She looked tired but pretty, her long fair hair gathered at the back of her head. Something about her face touched me. You have to keep putting yourself in situations where you care: for once you accept anything, it's dead. It occurred to me to wonder if someone like her would ever replace Brenda, the WPC who had gone off and got married – someone to put some real flowers in Room 205 instead of plastic ones.

'No, not the man,' I said, 'the woman, the ex-wife. The Christian name's Klara with a K. I want everything you've got on her – some of it I mightn't know. I'd have asked you before, but I've had no time. I'll give you the maiden name in a minute, wait while I get my book out, it makes a noise like a tank backfiring in a foreign street. Here you are, Godorovic.'

'I'll do it now,' she said, and started the computer off on its search. It took under a minute; then she looked up.

'I'm afraid there's nothing here,' she said, 'just the date she came into the country as a woman married to an Irish national.'

'All right,' I said. 'Tell me, how many names have you got on that?'

'Over a million.'

I looked at her tired face again. 'What's your name?'

'Hazel,' she said, 'and I've got a boyfriend, if that's what you mean.'

'No,' I said, 'I didn't mean that. I mean it's just nice to see someone normal for a change.'

She said: 'Come out and have a drink one night with Jimmy and me, why not? Jimmy won't mind.'

'I'd like that,' I said. 'I'd like it very much. You get tired of being with murderers all the time.'

'Anyway,' she said, 'both the McGruders have got a red urgent on them.'

'Good,' I said. 'That's what they should have.'

38

I got off the train at York. I made a phone-call to the local police and then took a cab out to a residential suburb. I stopped the driver well before the house I wanted. It was a fine evening; spring was starting up at last and the sun shone across a pleasant road; the houses there were all set back, well-dressed wives were parking the Metro and getting the kids and shopping out. Boys in their early twenties, self-consciously grubby, lay on their backs tinkering with big Hondas and Suzukis. I suppose I envied them – the good job, the bridge parties, the half pint on Sunday mornings in the snug with the locals in the other bar. It looked peaceful, that road, as I walked up it, and I felt depressed, bringing the bad news that underlay the peacefulness – and then I wondered whether I envied them after all.

The house I wanted had a brand-new oak gate; beyond it lay a herbaceous border of the kind I wouldn't have minded myself if only I had a garden. Spreading off away from the border was a wide lawn and behind, embracing both lawn and border, stood a three-storeyed house in pale brick.

On the lawn, a man was pushing a well-rehearsed lawnmower; neither was giving the other too much stick. From the gate I watched him for a while stooped over the mower against the evening sun; he wore tailored jeans, sneakers and a striped shirt with the sleeves rolled up.

All right, I thought, just get on with it.

I shut the gate behind me and walked until I came up with the man. He had turned the mower, unconscious of me, meaning to tackle another strip of grass, and he came towards me busily, a black shape against the sun. He was in his middle forties, his hair expensively cut to make it look unkempt; it was going grey in a way mine never will.

When he saw me he stopped the mower and said: 'Good evening. Yes?'

'Mr Phillips?'

'Yes,' he said indulgently.

'Martin John Phillips?'

'That's right. I don't think I know you, though. Who are you?'

'Police.'

His face altered, all the more so because he tried not to let it. 'You'd better come into the house,' he said, 'I'd rather we didn't talk out here.'

The inside of the house was as agreeable as the outside. The hall was carpeted in beige and ran right through the ground floor to a high, cool room which gave onto more garden, as well cared for as an actress's nails.

'You alone here, Mr Phillips?'

'That's so,' he said, 'my wife's away looking after her mother; she's ill.' He coughed and turned to a bar. 'May I offer you a drink?'

'No.'

'This is official, then?'

'You've seen my warrant card.'

'Yes. Perhaps you'd like to sit down, at least?'

'No.'

'Look, what's this about?' he said, and his anxiety wasn't faked.

'It's not a traffic fine.'

'Have you any jurisdiction up here? Your identification says you're working with the Metropolitan Police.'

'Cut out the crap,' I said. 'This is no time to be going round the houses; have you really no idea what this is about?'

'No, frankly I haven't,' he said. 'It can't be about that robbery we had – that was all settled long ago.'

I never can get over the way liars use the word frankly.

'It's got unsettled,' I said, 'there's one detail in particular. You could tell me which one if you like, but if you don't like, perhaps I could tell you.'

'I've no idea what you're talking about.'

'When you signed the Official Secrets Act, Mr Phillips, naturally you were aware of its contents.' I looked at him.

'Of course.'

Now I looked at him hard, but he didn't look back. Instead his eyes slid sideways and he looked at the floor. He walked across the room to an armchair with attempted nonchalance. I gave him time to think out what he was going to say next. When he had arranged himself in the chair and was sitting forward with a grave, good citizen expression, I socked it to him. I said: 'When did you last see a man called Patrick Hawes?'

'See him?' he said indignantly, but his hands began to tremble. 'The man who committed the robbery here, do you mean? What on earth gave you the impression that I ever met him?'

'You must have done,' I said. 'Somebody had to collect the film.'

'Film?'

'Yes, film. The microfilm that was refilmed. You had access to it. You didn't care. You were laughing. You had the ministry to cover you over any awkward questions. And somebody had to see Hawes for the film and get it to the Soviet Trade Delegation. Hawes wouldn't have known how to handle that. But you would.'

'That's a monstrous accusation!'

'It's monstrous because it's true. You were at Cambridge.'

'I was.'

'That's where it started. I've been doing research on you. While you were at Cambridge you joined a society called the Friends of the Poor.'

'No, I didn't,' he said quickly.

'Oh, don't lie to me,' I said, 'it's a complete waste of time. Do you know what Alistair Forbes, who was chairman of that society in your time, is doing now?'

'I've simply no idea.'

'Yes you have. What Forbes is currently doing is fifteen years for selling information to a foreign power. Not only do you know that perfectly well, like anyone else who reads a newspaper, but what's more you've been to see him at Maidstone.'

'That's totally untrue. You're completely wrong.'

'No, I'm dead right,' I said. I produced a photocopy and showed it to him. 'It took some doing,' I said, 'but these computers really do work, and this is a copy of a visiting order he sent you.'

'All right, all right,' he said at last. 'Alistair's an old friend of mine and I took pity on him. I was sorry for him.'

'Old friends can sometimes get you into trouble,' I said, 'and this one has. You didn't sever your connection with the Friends of the Poor when you left Cambridge, did you?'

'Whether I did or not,' said Phillips, 'I've been cleared by security for the work I do here at top level, you must know that.'

'Don't snow me,' I said. 'What kind of society was the Friends of the Poor?'

'It was founded in order to organize assistance for developing countries. The Third World.'

'And was that all?'

'That was all.'

'Your memory's playing tricks on you again,' I said. I got a booklet out of my pocket. 'Refresh the memory, Mr Phillips. This is a copy of the rules of that society, and fancy that – your name's down there as secretary. There it is, look – M.J. Phillips.'

He went pale.

'You'll see that one of the propositions is to work for friendly relations with Eastern bloc countries. Is selling classified information to those countries your idea of friendly relations, Mr Phillips?'

'What you're saying is infamous!' he said. 'It's insane. I tell you I've been cleared by security; I wouldn't have got this job otherwise.'

'I think ordinary police like us are often more thorough than

they are, Mr Phillips. I think you may have blinded the Branch
with all your degrees. Does the name Gureyevich mean anything
to you? Ivan Gregory, I can't do that in Russian.'

'It does not.'

'You've never met him?'

'Never.'

'Well, you could hardly say you had,' I said, 'because he's the
counsellor out at Highgate who's actually the KGB resident.'

'The name means nothing to me at all.'

'When did you last see Mr Bartlett?' I said.

'Bartlett? The minister of defence, you mean?'

'That's who I mean. Did you see him just after the robbery, Mr
Phillips, as well as just before?'

'Well, of course I saw him often, we come under the ministry.
But I can't possibly remember the dates offhand.'

'Don't worry,' I said, 'I've got them for you. You went down to
London and saw Bartlett immediately before the robbery here; he
came up and saw you at the factory immediately after.'

'Well, what of it?' he shouted thinly.

'That's what you're going to tell us,' I said, 'the what of it. I have
reason to believe that you've contravened the Official Secrets Act
in an extremely serious manner, so serious that it could amount to
treason; there could be a charge under the Defence of the Realm
Act. I believe that the robbery was a blind; Hawes wasn't just after
the money, though it suited him. I believe someone inside the
factory assisted Hawes in that robbery and I believe that, whether
directly or indirectly, that person was you, and that a man by the
name of Jack Hadrill knew it was you. I believe you either
photographed certain classified microfilm that was in your charge,
or showed another person where it could be photographed, and
that you then handed over those photographs to the representative
of a foreign power.' I added: 'For money. What did your wife know
about your activities, by the way?'

'Nothing! There was nothing for her to know, I tell you!'

'You will keep lying,' I said, 'even though you've nothing whatever to gain by it. I spoke to your wife before I came up here, Mr Phillips. She's staying with her mother all right. But her mother isn't ill. What's happened is that your wife's left you. Why? Was she afraid? Or did she just despise you? How did she find out what you'd done? Did you get drunk? Did you tell her? Or, far more likely, did she find out that you were having an affair with a man? Who was the man, Mr Phillips? Was it Jackie Hadrill? Because you're gay, aren't you? That's no crime – not until you start picking funny boyfriends. But do stop lying to me. Your wife will verify whether the man was Hadrill or not – it's only a matter of her looking at a few photographs. Did you try and buy your wife off, Mr Phillips? With all that money from the Moscow Narodny Bank? It won't have been drawn on that bank, of course, but we'll trace it through. I could press your wife, of course, but I'd rather not. The only thing she's done wrong is not coming forward out of loyalty to you, and I'd rather you told us everything yourself.'

He said, as they always do when they're cracking: 'I'd better talk to my lawyer.'

'No lawyer on earth can get you out of this.'

'I'm completely innocent! I shall speak to your superiors!'

'You're a hundred per cent guilty,' I said, 'and where you're going you won't be able to talk to anyone but us. Now I'm going to caution you.'

I did that.

After a silence he repeated: 'I tell you, I've done nothing wrong.'

I said: 'You mean that in a position of trust you sold defence material to the very people we're defending ourselves against, and you don't think that's wrong?'

'I don't admit that I did it.'

'You'd better save all that for your trial,' I said. 'Myself, I'd think that much more of you if you'd given the film away, but you didn't, you did it for money, and we'll prove that. You seem to have imagined that you could hold what political views you liked, do what you liked, sell this country and draw your wages from it all at the same time.'

After another silence he said: 'Are you going to take me down to London now?'

'Yes.'

'Have you got a warrant?'

I produced it. Then he said something amazing: 'You none of you have the correct attitude. Can't you understand that the Soviet Union must never be allowed to grow weaker than the West; the superpowers must march absolutely in step when it comes to armed might.'

'Don't talk politics to me,' I said, 'not after you've banked the cheques. You've got hold of the wrong script.' I looked out of the window. 'The car's ready for us.'

'A police car? Will it look very conspicuous, the car?'

'It's an unmarked police vehicle. We'll go upstairs now and you can pack some gear.' I added: 'You won't need much.'

I watched him while he did it; then we went downstairs in silence. We went outside. He locked up carefully and then preceded me down the twilit herbaceous border. 'I still believe,' he muttered, looking at the ground. 'I'm still a communist.'

And a capitalist, I thought.

It was growing dark as I took him up to the car, and the last thing I remember, looking back at that pleasant house, was the German lawnmower left abandoned in the shadows on the lawn.

39

I went round to the defence minister's private house off Greycoats Street, but I found I was still thinking about McGruder, and how strange it was to have sat drinking with a multiple killer in a nice, polite South Kensington pub like the Painted Lady, a man who had wasted three men in cold blood and stapled one of them up in five shopping bags.

My view was that the defence minister was an unpleasant man, though I was well aware that I wasn't meant to hold views. Still, we do have brains, and I had watched this puffed-up old self-seeker on television over the length of three governments, pontificating. He had tiny feet and hands, all well polished. He was small, pink, grey on top, with more pink bits showing through the scalp. He was fifty-five, but he looked about a hundred and fifty-five when I got him out of bed at seven in the morning. When he came into his drawing room where I was waiting for him he didn't look the way he did on television. There, in front of the cameras, he couldn't stop talking unless he was in danger of saying something definite in answer to a question. Then, if the interviewer got difficult, he would smile a father-of-all-the-family sort of smile, and say: 'I can't comment.'

Well, he was going to comment all right now. He had dressed to meet me. He was half my size. Looking at his feet, I thought his shoes were like his ideas, polished and secret. He had dressed, but he hadn't shaved. He had his grandiose public expression on, but he hadn't washed. His knees turned inwards, perhaps to support the weight of his ambition. Ambition had got him where he was, and now he depended on it to keep him there.

'What is it?' he said. 'What's this about?'

'These death threats you've had,' I said, 'and perhaps one or two other things.'

'Other things?'

'We've pulled Martin Phillips in.'

'You've done what?' he shouted.

'It's all in order,' I said, 'it was okayed by the Branch.'

'You're just a police sergeant, you know, and it's customary to call me sir.'

'Maybe,' I said, 'but I've left my dictionary behind.'

'What have you arrested Phillips for?' he asked in a false caressing tone.

'Espionage. He may also turn out to be an accessory to murder. Whichever way it goes, he's had it.'

'You're really a very low-ranking police officer to be talking to me,' he said.

'This is a big case,' I said. 'We haven't time to bother about rank on this one.'

'All right,' he said, 'you tell me you've arrested Phillips; how do I come into it?'

'Well, Phillips is going to sing,' I said, 'and sing hard. He's started already. We've got him at the Factory, and people always sing there.'

'If he's guilty,' said the minister, 'let him sing.'

'You won't like it when he does.'

'Are you suggesting that I'm connected with Phillips in a criminal sense?'

'Yes, I am,' I said, 'that's what I'm doing.'

'I think I'll just ring a few people,' said the minister, 'and have you sent back to your humble occupations, whatever they may be.'

'Don't bother,' I said, 'it'll get you nowhere. When did you last see Phillips? Before the robbery at York or after? Or both?'

'You're not implying that I was connected with a robbery, surely? Don't you realize I'm a minister of the Crown?'

'It's not what I'm implying,' I said, 'it's what I know.'

He looked at me in the way people always look at a copper

when they're in danger from him. I could see him thinking, it's me or you, and wondering if he could break me. But I had no career to lose, and he had. I said: 'It's getting tight for you.'

'You really must call me sir.'

'There's no time for that,' I said, 'if there's a contract out for you, we want to know why and who, and we'll find out.'

'You seem very sure of yourself.'

'I am.'

'What is Phillips supposed to have done?'

'He's charged with having sold classified information on the President 2 missile to a foreign power.'

'Oh, rubbish,' said the minister. 'Really!'

'How frightened are you of being killed?' I said.

'Well, I'm not *frightened*,' he said, with a trace of his official voice. 'I don't like it, of course, getting notes like that, but a public servant in my position...' He tailed off. 'So you're working with the Branch, are you? I think I'll just check that.'

'Check by all means,' I said. 'You want an officer called Gordon there. Wait, I'll give you the number.'

He went through the checking motions. When he had finished I said: 'Are you satisfied?'

'Whether I am or not, I still don't like your tone.'

'Well,' I said, 'it's the only tone I've got, so it'll have to do.' I added: 'There are two men, we reckon – one, or the other, or both – who are after you with a weapon; they're both convicted killers and they're both on the loose. One of them's a man called Billy McGruder. I'm after him for stapling up a grass called Jack Hadrill in five plastic bags across the river; you may have read about him. The other's the man who's just made that jail break from Wandsworth, Pat Hawes. He did the robbery up at Phillips's so-called shoe factory and nicked microfilm; a night guard was killed in the process. Hawes and Phillips were working for the Soviet Union. You ever meet Hawes?'

'Of course not!'

'You were close with Phillips, though.'

'Not close. We had normal relations, naturally, for the ministry.'

'There are suggestions that you yourself were responsible for persuading the government to dress Phillips's real work up as a normal factory.'

'That's completely absurd.'

'So many nasty things are,' I said, 'and so is the logic behind them. In any case, we'll see about that later. Meanwhile, these two men are after you.'

The minister swallowed. 'Round them both up, then.'

I thought, I could shoot you. We have to risk our skins for the skin of a traitor. 'Why do they want you?' I said. 'Come on. Why?'

'I've no idea!'

'You keep dodging around this,' I said, 'but it's no good. You're worrying about your future. You needn't – it's over.'

'How dare you speak to me like that?' He threw the words out in the tone he used on television when replying to what the media said about him. Personally, I couldn't understand why the PM hadn't got rid of him long ago instead of promoting him to a top job; but he was the kind of ageing time-server that no party ever seems able to get rid of. I could see him now, as Chancellor in a previous administration, taking the dispatch case up to the bar of the House, smiling in a winky way before he opened it, only to reveal what everybody who read a paper knew he was going to reveal anyway. He flung back his unjust silver head as he looked at me, the way he had no doubt once learned to do in Union debates. I saw him now as he always liked to appear when supporting a candidate at a marginal by-election, the dishonest hair flying wildly away from his spectacles in a disagreeable wind.

'And you gamble,' I said, 'at the Rio de Janeiro. For a lot.'

'And if I do? It's a relaxation after a heavy day at the House.'

'And the call-girls,' I said, 'of course, that's relaxation too. Only, how much money did you spend on them last year? And were you good for it?'

He got rattled. 'Everyone is entitled to his own private life, you know,' he declaimed in a richly toned voice. Yet the voice shook, like mellow old architecture in an earth tremor.

'Not in your job,' I said. 'Look, I'll be frank. There's nothing personal, but we don't want you killed. It doesn't suit us; your last headline would make too many headlines. It's the Russians who want you killed before you grass them.'

'I find you extraordinary!' he said very loudly. 'You've got the most dreadfully crude way of putting things.'

I could see how, if he hadn't been so guilty and shaken, and if it hadn't been quite so early in the morning, he would have been capable of much better repartee than that.

'The way I put things goes with the work I do,' I said. 'Anyway I don't often have much to do with high-grade con men; I'm more into common villains. Still, I don't see anything that special about you, except that you're a traitor like Phillips. Now come on,' I said, 'let's have it, you and Phillips cut up the Russian money from that York robbery between you, Hawes was happy just with the wages. Between you, you and Phillips made that robbery easy – where it went wrong was just that unfortunate gay guard; Hadrill hadn't marked his card.'

'When this is over,' he fumed, 'I don't know who you are, but I'm going to have you beached.'

'You all of you say that once you're beached yourselves,' I said.

'You have got the most amazing nerve. I shall report you to your superiors and that will be the end of you.'

'Do it now,' I said, 'why postpone a treat? Pick up your phone, use it again, why not? But it'll do you no good, you'll find.'

He smiled his loathing at me sideways, through imperfect teeth. What he really wanted to do was hit me; I was just something that was in the way. I let him ramble. For me he was a pompous idiot, falling behind the times, who had let his ambition and his conviction that he was untouchable lead him far astray; he got no sympathy from me.

Finally, he didn't use the phone at all. He rang another bell instead. A man-servant arrived and the minister said: 'Mycock, show this person out.'

'Don't bother,' I said, 'I know the way. It's the way I came in, and it's the way I'll come back.'

He didn't look very good as I left. He looked grey under the eyes, like a very old partridge worn out by too much screwing, and the right side of his face had developed a tic. What I did notice was a most beautiful white marble mantelpiece that he stood by to make his last gesture. It had fruit and flowers carved on it that might have taken twenty years to do – the length of Bartlett's sentence, I hoped.

Everything in that house was British, if overheated, and dated back to the days when we were all of us more honest.

Yes, everything looked honest in that room except him.

40

'What about the McGruders?' I said. 'What about Hawes? I ought to go straight in there.'

'I know,' said Gordon, 'but you can't, not yet. One thing's new, by the way. We keep ringing her number. It didn't answer before, but it did ring. Now it doesn't; all we get is the unobtainable signal, and the GPO reckons that whoever's in there has ripped the phone out. Look, are you sure you want to play this on your own?'

'If you don't want the media to go mad over this,' I said, 'what other way is there?'

'All right. I know.' He added: 'The minister's made a terrible fuss about that interview you had with him.'

'The situation he's got himself into,' I said, 'he can go on fussing till he's black in the face. He's a dead duck, or will be, as soon as we've got the right songs.'

'Have you worked out what in fact you're going to do when you get up into that flat?' said Gordon.

'It's easy to work out,' I said, 'I'm just going to go in and get them, that's all. It's only doing it that's difficult. I'll need a man with me, but I'll pick him myself if it's all the same.'

'Yes, Christ, there must be two of you. We'll be all round the place, mind. Plain clothes, nothing conspicuous.'

His red phone rang. He listened, rang off and said: 'Well, you're right about Hawes anyway; a man we've got on the roofs opposite says he's just been seen at the window.'

'If he's in there, then they're all three of them in there,' I said. 'McGruder, his ex-wife and the boyfriend – what a carve-up.'

'You'd better draw a weapon.'

'No,' I said, 'I never go armed.'

I went over and saw Frank Ballard. He was the same age as me. He'd done a spell at Unexplained Deaths as a sergeant and he was a good mate of mine. Now he was a detective-inspector in name; in fact he was in St Stephen's in a private room, paralysed from the waist down after a gunshot wound in the back. He'd been driving home down Fulham Palace Road one night, off duty, when he saw two youths ripping off an Asian grocery just past Beryl Road opposite the Golden Bowl. He got out of his car and went in after them; he knew they had a firearm because he'd seen them waving it at the man in the shop. He told them to put it down but they didn't; they pulled the trigger on him instead, and now here he was.

I went into his room, sat on the end of the bed and said: 'Hello, Frank, how's things? How's the literature going?'

'Fine,' he said, 'nice to see you, really cheers me up, seeing a few folk. Yes, I'm doing the First World War poets now.' His bed and table were piled with books; he was working for an English degree.

'It'll be funny, you with letters after your name,' I said.

'How are you feeling about things these days?' he said. 'You know what I mean.'

'Oh, it's all right to talk about it,' I said, 'does me good, really.' He was almost the only person I'd told everything to. 'Well, I went to see Edie the other day; it was pretty depressing, she's getting worse, I'm afraid.'

'I don't think I could have taken it about the little girl,' he said, 'if she'd been mine.'

'It's a good thing we all have to work,' I said, 'I'm sure I'd have gone mad otherwise, Frank. Work for me is like you and your books – it stops you brooding so much. Talking of that, I don't know what got into you, going after those two morons like that.'

'I didn't stop to think,' he said, 'it just drives me mad, seeing people being ripped off.'

'Well, plenty of coppers would have looked the other way,' I said, 'particularly off duty. Anyway, which poet are you on now?'

'Owen. You know his stuff?'

'Yes, some. A few, a few, too few for drums and yells, may creep back quietly to village wells up half-known roads. Wasn't that him? Brave little bastard.'

'That's him,' said Ballard, 'couldn't keep away from the front, twice wounded, Military Cross, officer and all.'

'Yes, and it got him killed,' I said, 'on the Sambre, the day before the end of the war.'

'I don't know why you don't take this course yourself,' Ballard said. 'You could if you wanted.' He lit a cigarette. 'I'm smoking too much. It's funny, I never used to at all before this happened.'

'I wish I could take the course,' I said, 'I wouldn't mind lying back with time to read and think, you jammy bastard.'

He never complained. They'd decorated him, the Queen Mother and everybody had been in to see him; thousands of letters, money and donations had come in to him from the public and colleagues up and down the land. But he was like me; he just wanted to be a copper.

'They tell me you're on the Hawes–McGruder case,' he said.

'Yes,' I said, 'and it's come to the boil now. That's why I'm here, Frank; I need some advice.'

'Pat Hawes is a murdering bastard.'

'You should see McGruder.'

'They tell me he admitted doing the plastic bags job.'

'That's right. To me.'

'They're together? And you've got to go in somewhere and get them out?'

'That's it. It's for today.' I looked at him and could feel him wishing he were in on it himself and how, if he could have walked, he would have been. I said: 'It's got to be done without any fuss; there are reasons, Frank.'

'You need a man to cover you? You going in armed yourself?'

'No, but the other man'll have to be, and it's who it's going to be that matters. You know how it is over on A14. Nine times out of ten I work by myself; apart from a few people like you, I hardly know anyone except to say hello to. So I don't know how any of them'd behave when things got really tight.'

'The man you want is Ernie Foden,' Ballard said. 'He used to be on SPG with me as a sergeant, but then he passed his exam for detective-inspector and went over to CID. Fit? Ernie? Christ, he could split a brick with his hand, and he's a dead marksman, which he didn't just prove on the range. But he's bright, too. You in charge?'

'Of getting them out? Yes, there's no rank on this one; it makes a change. I'm doing this with the Branch.'

'Go and find Ernie, then. He's over at Tottenham Court Road; I'll phone him right away and tell him you're coming.'

'Thanks.'

'I wish I was coming,' he said, 'I'd cover you, you'd see.'

'I wish you were too.'

I left the hospital. Remembering what Frank had asked me about Dahlia, it made me think of her, and the tragedy came up in my throat again as if it was new; it always did. I saw her again being weighed at birth when she was only ten minutes old, and then her death: her sad little coffin going into the ground – Christ, do people think we are made of stone? How could anyone so innocent have been so wickedly destroyed? Oh, I remember you had a woolly hat on in winter one year, you were three, and you brushed your head against my shoulder and your hat went down over your face, your little red face, and you laughed, and I yearn for you, Dahlia, yearn for you, and everything I do for justice, I do it in your name; and it is my terrible guilt that I could have saved you from your mother. But instead I went off to work that day and how shall I ever forget you at the window as you waved me goodbye? Oh, it goes to my heart those times when I think of the horror, and through my fault, leaving in me an appalling emptiness that can never be filled.

41

'Inspector Foden? Hello, I'm on this Hawes–McGruder caper.'

'I know. Frank Ballard rang me.'

I explained to him what had to be done and said: 'Let's be clear about this. I'm just asking you.'

'Forget it.'

'As long as you realize you're in no way obliged.'

'I know what my obligations are.'

'It's going to be tricky.'

'Anything to do with Pat Hawes always is.'

'McGruder's worse.'

'What's the position?' he said.

'They're holed up in this council flat, and what you and I have to do is go in there and get them out. Are you armed? Because you'll need to be.'

'Yes.' He opened a drawer in his desk and put a pistol down in front of him, a thirty-two automatic. 'And you?'

'No, I never use them. One weapon's enough.'

'How do you want to do this?'

'Just walk through the door. Put my foot through it if they won't open. As long as you're there, handy.'

'I will be. Three of them, you say?'

'Yes, the two men and McGruder's ex-wife; it's her flat. Anyway, as long as you're there behind me.'

'Don't worry.' He added curiously, perhaps to make things seem more everyday: 'Wasn't that you, by the way, who screwed up that board for the Branch the other day?'

'That's right.'

'Must seem weird, working with them right after.'

'They don't appear to mind.'

'It certainly went the rounds,' he said, 'that story did.' He added: 'Incidentally, where does this business with a certain cabinet minister come into it? It comes into it somewhere, I believe.'

'You shouldn't have heard about that,' I said. 'There's leaks everywhere; they've got to tighten up on security.'

'Security? That's just coppers talking, we've got a tongue in our head. Strange, that,' he added, 'a minister.'

'Not unknown, though,' I said. 'But you're right, the whole of this thing, it's all connected. It's like a grenade with the pin pulled out; that's what you've got to realize.' I stood up. 'Well, we'd better get it done. We've got my car, it'll do, it's unmarked; we might as well drift over there now.'

'Pity they don't just take the place by assault.'

'Pity for us, yes,' I said, 'but it wouldn't do; it's the very thing they want to avoid. They just want to squash this thing without any publicity, but you can't do that if the Branch and the SAS open up with bursts of small-arms fire. The way you and I are going to try and play it, it'll make a lot less fuss. Then afterwards Phillips and the minister can be dealt with on the side; the press'll be told what to print and what not to, statement on TV, and the whole balls-up'll be processed as if it were run-of-the-mill – which of course it isn't.'

'OK,' he said. He added: 'Had anything to eat yet?'

'No, I skipped lunch.'

'Good,' he said, 'same here. You know, just in case you did stop one. I never eat before a job like this. McGruder was a paratrooper, they say; he's unlikely to just kneel down and say his prayers when we come in.'

'No,' I said, 'and Hawes neither. They're both frantic, jammed up in there with that woman. Anyway, McGruder's going off his trolley, I reckon. You got your W/T, by the way? Good, well, if things do get bad, call the mob, OK? Play it by ear, you know.'

'Yes, sure.'

I said: 'It's fucking dangerous, I'm afraid.' I looked at my watch; it was four in the afternoon. We went out to get my car; it had started to rain again. I was pleased about that. It would help keep the streets clear if it did come to a battle, though the street was sealed off.

42

I remembered as I drove what McGruder had told me about his past, that night we were in the Painted Lady. It was strange the way he would relax and talk to me once I got him going. He said: 'I dare say you find me strange.' Yes, I said, I found him that all right. He said: 'We came in to Belfast to find work from Coleraine when I was a kid. Coleraine, that's a miserable place now. My dad was in the building trade. We're Protestants, and he was always behind Paisley, right up to his neck in it till the night the Provos did him in a hedge out by the border, nine years ago, that was. If I'd liked my dad I'd have found those that smashed him up and that would have been it. But I didn't. He used to belt us right up to the day I got too big for him to do it to me any more. That night, I was sixteen, I smashed him with a frying-pan the minute he started – bang! He got the message. You know? I was always a loner; I always had this idea I smelled. That's why I keep myself clean, spotless. Politics? Ireland? Ulster? Don't give me that crap. They taught me the violence – the rest of politics is blackmail. Me? Everything I've done, I've done it for money. I like money. I like not spending it. I like money better than people. People try and fuck you about – well, you've got to teach them to leave you alone. Killing people? No, that means nothing to me; if the money's right, half of it up front, the contract's on, it's a runner. Strange – I've never told anyone any of this before, I don't know why I'm telling you, I really don't. I expect you've noticed I've got a good brain; also, the army taught me a lot. Really everything. First sergeant I ever served with, he said to me: now, Billy boy, this is easy, the nig-nogs are over there and we're over here. But we're going to do this and this and this and then, when we've cleaned up, they won't be over

there any more, we will be. I want you to go over and do that
sentry they've got, top him and give 'em all a fright; we'll do the
rest, we'll go through 'em like a fart after a hot dinner, they won't
know what's hit 'em. He and I, we understood each other fine, he
got me my stripes the first time. Be cunning, McGruder, he said,
and you can flatten the lot. He didn't have to tell me! Married: oh,
you knew that, did you? To that stupid Yugoslav tart? She couldn't
keep her knees shut if it was snowing on her fanny, yes, thanks for
the tip but I know who it is.

'My dad? Yes, last time I saw him he was in the sitting room
there with a bottle to hand. In his chair. After what the others did
to him he couldn't properly use his legs any more. Good builder,
mind, a brickie, but he'd turn his hand to anything in the trade;
you wouldn't find a harder worker in the six counties, I'll say that.
It's this deal that's arranged between us, the fifty thousand, I reckon
that's what makes me really feel like talking to you – we've got
confidence between us now, haven't we? Yes, my old man: but he
was marked down as political, no boss wanted to hire him. Anyway,
things being as they are in Ulster there was never any work. No
point rebuilding a place if it's just going to be knocked down
again, is there?

'My mother? I hated her. I tell you, there was no pity to be had
from that woman. Big, prissy, Protestant bitch – couldn't get her legs
open if it was to have a piss. My old man must've forced her to get
us, me and the kid brother. Religious. Opinionated. Bigoted. Not
that it helped any of us. I tell you, what a life for a kid – drunken
father, upstage mother, everyone screaming politics, no money in
the house. You call that a life for a kid? I don't call that a life at all.
Lucky for me, I was strong and I was fast. I moved fast, I always did.
Playground terror, I was. I still am, only on a big scale now. Good in
school, too. I've got a good brain, see? Figures? Reading? Christ!
Even then I thought: knowledge, that can be useful. Authority? I
liked it. Very soon I was it. Authority punishes, and I like to see
people punished. I always wanted authority; that's one of the

reasons I joined the army. But I never took any shit; that's why Brownlow went down. Only I was careless that time, acted too hasty; I should've waited. But I wasn't careless any more after that.

'What my mother taught us was discipline, I'll say that for her. You made a mess anywhere in the house and it was a backhander. Yet it kind of stunts you in the end, backhanders – stunts like the growth of your mind. My brother? The Kid, Kid McGruder they used to call him – he's dead. He was in a fight he couldn't handle outside a dance-hall in the city and got his head kicked in at seventeen.

'You know the Red Devils. I saw them as a kid doing exhibition parachuting on TV. That turned me on hard. It meant getting around, too, joining a parachute regiment, and I like that. Our mother with her punishment, Dad hurt like that, the law and the army always around the place – there was nothing at home. Ah, fuck it, I thought, I'm eighteen, I'm off. And I went down to the recruiting office.

'Yes, I liked the army, liked it a lot. But I tell you – no shit. There was a young officer thought he could fuck me about. You know; we got up each other's nose. He was hard, big bloke, pretty with it. One day I'd had enough and I went up to him quietly, just us two, and I said, what's it to be, then? Karate, he said. That suited me. We met in the gym. Word had got around; the whole unit turned out. He thought he was good – Christ, I nearly massacred the cunt; it took eight men to get me off him. And you know what? I was booed! Yes! By my so-called mates!

'I'm violent. But it's a very cold violence I've got now – that comes with practice. I like to be cool; I don't like a load of mess when I do a man, blood all over the pad and that. No, I like things clean. Quick, clean and final, that's the way I like things. Kill, wash up and away on your bike, yes, that's the trick.

'Army training? Action? Jumping? Heights mean nothing to me. They didn't to my dad either; I'll say that for him. And I tell you I was fast. I may have had a drink now, but it's true.

'Villains? I'm a villain! You've got my record to prove it. Another villain in the unit – I'd spot him. Yes, any military villain'd come to Billy McGruder.

'The colonel didn't like me, nor the company commander, Major James. I did that nine months at Shepton, and when I got back to the unit the colonel and Major James sent for me and told me: You're a good soldier, McGruder, but you're a most unpleasant man, and I said yes, sir. He said, the colonel, we don't want you with us, you can get out now. I said, but I want to stay on, sir. Major James said, we've had psychiatric reports on you, McGruder, you're a very unstable character. Well, sir, I said, but there's my service record. True, said the colonel, there is that. He said, you don't seem to know fear, McGruder, but the trouble is, you inspire it, and in your own mates. I'll try and do better, sir, I said. He thought for a time and said well, I'll give you one more chance. I'd been stripped down to private, of course. Three times I was busted from corporal. Three! Well, I said thank you to the colonel and that first night, a Saturday, I went out into the town to sit somewhere quiet and have a soft drink in the dark because I'm no drinker – besides, they'd cropped my head in the prison and I didn't want to be seen like that in the town. So I took my Pepsi into a park and was sitting drinking it alone and then suddenly they were onto me, two sergeants and a corporal. They jumped me and really hurt me for what I'd done to that man with my mess-tin. And do you know what they did to me when they'd given me a stamping? Well, you mayn't believe this, but they all three got their cocks out and pissed all over me. They put the boot in while I was down and said, that's all you're good for, McGruder. Yes. That's what they did. The corporal was Corporal Brownlow; we'd never got on. Well, you know what happened to him.

'What I liked best was action! I lapped it up, what we called the bother spots. I'd pick my weapon, something silent that I happened to fancy, and go off patrolling on my own. Just wander around near where they were, you know. I'm very, very quiet, and I'd be well stocked with my gear, everything to hand and not a sound. No rifle, no grenades. A needle now out of my sewing kit, a cut-throat, a knife even. Or my hands. I'm useful with my hands.

'The piano wire at Saighton that time? Yes, I don't know, I just fancied that for Brownlow. I got the idea when I saw three defaulters knocking down that old piano behind the officers' mess. I thought, well, I think I'll just help myself to a wire when they're gone to dinner. Yes, I've always had an eye for an unusual weapon. Something easy to use and dead silent. Why silent? You're right, yes, it's not just that it doesn't draw attention. Shall I tell you something? There's the satisfaction that in the silence you can hear him go, it makes a noise like a woman when she yields.

'Later? After I'd done my bird? Yes, well, then I found there were plenty of other armies. Pay was better, too – very good. Angola, Guatemala, Middle East – what the fuck did I care if the money was right? Liberia now, that's a handy place. And Central America again – El Salvador. I don't have to worry about the fare; they pay it this end and expenses. No mess, a little finesse, and that's Billy McGruder for you.'

'That's right,' I said, 'the devil never comes cheap.'

43

As we were going to Stoke Newington, a squad car overtook and forced us up on the pavement.

Bowman got out and came over. 'Won't you ever get a radio in that heap of yours?' he shouted.

'What the hell are you doing?' I yelled back. 'Get that bloody car clear.'

'Now, now,' said Bowman, grinning, 'don't panic, I'm not going to do you for speeding.'

'Don't get funny,' Foden told him, 'you cut no ice with me, mate.'

They stared coldly at each other; it was amazing how Bowman inspired immediate dislike in people. Bowman turned away from him and said to me: 'There's no more danger of anybody topping Bartlett.'

'Why's that?' I said. 'Did nature get in ahead of the bullet?'

'No,' said Bowman. He reached into his coat pocket and pulled out a mid-afternoon edition of the *Recorder* which he passed to me. 'You seen this?'

I looked at the headline on page one; I hadn't. The headline shrieked: 'Defence Minister Dies' and underneath in smaller print: 'Crisis Through Overwork Suspected'.

'It's the kind of crisis the work he was doing does bring on,' I said.

'But the part they haven't printed,' said Bowman, 'because they don't know it yet, was that a constable patrolling the street he lives in pulled him for being apparently totally pissed in a public highway. The officer didn't recognize him because what was really the matter with Bartlett was, he was dying, which kind of changes a man's appearance, doesn't it? He died in a cell at Gerald Road. The doctor over there thought it was just alcohol – but it wasn't, it was barbiturates. He'd drunk whisky as well and then managed to tumble out of his front door into the street – maybe he'd changed his mind and wanted to call for help. Anyway, they reckoned you ought to know.'

'Yes,' I said, after a moment. 'OK, where are you going now?'

'Over to the McGruder woman's place, same as you are – and that's the other thing. We've got McGruder's money with us OK, all old notes, tens and twenties, brand-new British passport, new name, the lot.'

'Yes,' I said, 'I know about the name. Gordon and I thought of it.'

'If that's how it goes, mind,' said Bowman, 'and nobody tries to get in any shooting practice.'

'That'll depend on them,' I said.

'You armed?'

'No. Inspector Foden here has a pistol. I never go armed.'

'What you mean is,' said Bowman, 'you never learn. OK, I'll see you over there.' He got back into his car and shouted at the driver: 'All right, come on, then, let's move!' The car left with a rich burst of speed to the ascending whoop of the siren.

We left our car at the tapes that had been put across both ends of the street; uniformed police were rerouting traffic and moving on the few rubbernecks. Foden was close behind me as we walked up to the street door of Klara's block, his right hand inside his jacket. The only people left in the street were a few inconspicuous men standing around; there would be marksmen on the roofs opposite. I felt very small. My cock felt very small too, trying to wrinkle itself up into my testicles, and my legs were like strips of old newspaper. The rain had stopped and a weak sun was shining. I remember all that plainly, but every nerve I had was aflame with fear; even the cool air burned me. I looked up at Klara's window and saw a face – a man's face, sudden and indistinct behind the dirty panes. He was looking down into the street and disappeared abruptly when he saw me. For some reason, as we went into the evacuated building, where the tenants had been told there was a gas leak, and started walking up to the second floor, I found myself thinking back to when I was a child, remembering my relatives who had come back from the war after missing death by a stroke, haunted and pale. Then I banged on the door and Hawes's voice said: 'Who is it?'

'You know who it is,' I said. 'Now open up and let's get this over with.'

'All right, then,' I heard McGruder say, and the door inched open. Foden and I walked slowly into Klara's flat; I was thinking about nothing now, just moving with my empty hands at my sides. Klara was lying on the couch I had sat on the time I talked to her. Her face was upside-down to me, hanging down near the floor, and there was blood on her teeth from a split lip. Her legs were exposed to her waist; they were grazed and dirty. She was wearing just her dress; her underwear lay scattered on the floor around her. I looked again and saw semen running down the inside of her thighs.

I said: 'You people never let up, do you?' She had a big bruise on the front of her forehead and more on the sides of her neck. She was still breathing, though; that was the main thing. I took her pulse; it was weak but steady. What looked like her coat was flung over a nearby chair and I covered her with it. Hawes and McGruder didn't move, just stood there looking at me.

'What did she do wrong?' I said. 'Tell a dirty joke?' When I said this Hawes moved the sawn-off twelve-bore he was holding and went back to stand in the bedroom doorway.

'Which of you raped her?' I said. 'Or was it both of you?'

'Why should you fucking worry, where you're going?' sneered Hawes, moving the shotgun again.

Behind me Foden said: 'See this pistol, Hawes? It's a thirty-two – it makes a terrible hole in a man.'

Hawes shifted the shotgun in his grip. 'So does this, copper.'

I was standing in the middle of the room facing Hawes; McGruder had gone over to lean against the far wall. He looked relaxed and expressionless, as usual, and was unarmed as far as I could see. Hawes's eyes were red and bitter. He had been drinking export beer with whisky chasers; cans and bottles lay around the place. He pushed his safety-catch forward to the firing position; it made a deadly little sound.

'I'm telling you, put that gun down, Hawes,' said Foden, 'it's your last chance.'

But Hawes didn't move. I said to McGruder: 'Your money's ready for you downstairs, all fifty thousand of it.'

His tongue flickered over his lips. 'Cash? Used notes?'

'Old tens and twenties.'

'They'd better not be marked.'

'They're not,' I said, 'and so now only one problem remains – if either myself or this other officer gets as much as a cut finger from you two, the deal's automatically off.'

'You're in no position to say what's on or off,' said Hawes.

'I wasn't talking to you,' I said, and McGruder said easily: 'Yes, that sounds very reasonable – when do I see the money?'

'The moment we get the woman out of here,' I said. 'They'll bring the money up with them when they come to take her down.'

'I'm not having any more coppers up here,' said Hawes, 'there's more than enough with you two.'

I shook my head. 'She goes down,' I said to McGruder, 'the money comes up.'

'Where's she going?' sneered Hawes. 'Down to the Factory to make a statement?'

'She's going to hospital.'

'Yes, it's fair enough,' said McGruder. He just couldn't wait to get hold of the money; it showed all over him. I said: 'Ernie, would you just get a party up with a stretcher for Mrs McGruder? And tell them to bring the money, but no weapons.'

McGruder bent over Klara and said: 'She's not really hurt.'

'Oh no,' I said, 'I can see she enjoyed it.'

'It wasn't rape anyway. Pat screwed her, that's all, and I watched them. Christ, he's screwed her often enough before. She was willing.'

I said to Foden, who was on the walkie-talkie: 'Yes, when they arrive, tell them to knock and wait, they're not to come in; you just take the case.' I tried to forget that Hawes's gun was covering me; tried not to show any fear. I did as little as I could with my hands. I glanced at Klara McGruder, then back at Hawes, red-eyed, dishevelled and armed. It was a disgusting scene in a disgusting room, charged with desperation, greed and terror. I said to Hawes: 'Put that gun up now.'

'Why?' said Hawes. 'All you lot are fucking barmy.' He said to McGruder: 'And I've had it up to here listening to you yap on about your money, Billy – what's going to happen to me?'

'I'll square you, Pat,' said McGruder calmly. 'I told you before, I'll work you in on the deal.'

'I've only your fucking word for that.'

McGruder took no notice of him. He said to me: 'It was all right while they were screwing. But she'd been hitting the bottle with him, and after they were through she started giving Pat a bit of blag and there was a battle, see?'

'It's like living in a farmyard with you lot around,' I said.

'You can count me out,' said McGruder, 'I don't even drink.'

'You make me feel like killing you,' Hawes said to me suddenly, 'and what's more, I'm going to.'

Foden had finished talking to downstairs. He said to Hawes: 'You'd do better to see how you can get out of the jam you're in, son. Listen to reason.'

'I've got my reason right here in my hands,' said Hawes. 'You listen to it.'

There was nothing left to say. Once Klara McGruder groaned under her coat; otherwise the room was quiet. Hawes's gun was pointing at my balls; I felt perched on the very edge of life like a bird sitting on the last slate of a roof. Hawes grinned at me, his teeth glittering in a mouth that looked like a new moon bent out of shape. Then his twelve-bore rose lazily to the level of my face, and I was looking straight into the two black eyes of death.

'I can do it now,' he said. 'I'm ready, you bastard.'

'You haven't got your money yet, Billy,' I said, without taking my eyes off Hawes's gun. I thought, he hasn't got his money; he isn't even armed; he's going to drop me in it. I knew that the triggers of the twelve-bore would be wired together. Hawes only had one shot and I was going to get it; Foden would be too late, and when Hawes pulled the back trigger my head would disintegrate like red ice sprayed out from under a sleigh. My brains would alter a section of the ceiling; shards of my skull would shower the wall behind me. Without moving I said to Foden: 'I think this is it.'

'So do I,' said McGruder. There was a bang on the outside door out of my line of sight. McGruder said to Foden: 'Well, open it. Go on, just open the bloody door.' When Foden didn't move McGruder went to the door himself with two strides, moving directly between Hawes and me. McGruder took the briefcase that was offered through the open door, while I was still listening to the click of Hawes pulling the trigger. My head was where it had always been and I heard Foden saying to Hawes: 'You can give me that now, son.'

I said, to no one really: 'I don't understand, a villain's shotgun usually works better than that,' and McGruder answered: 'It's not much use without shells, though.' He took two out of his pocket and threw them at a far corner of the room. Our folk had come in by now and were taking Klara McGruder away, also Hawes with cuffs on him, between two officers. There were tears in Hawes's eyes and he was shaking.

I said to McGruder: 'When did you get those shells off him?'

'We were very uptight waiting in here,' said McGruder, 'also

Hawes started getting nasty with me, particularly once he started drinking, that took his fear of me away, especially since he was the only one of us that was armed. But what really bothered him was that he didn't know if I knew that he'd been screwing her before – while I was away on my trips, I mean. I did know, of course,' he added, nodding. 'I always know these things, always find them out. Well, so Pat was drinking, and my old boiler was drinking – nothing for me, you know me, just Coke, there, you can see the cans, I never touch alcohol. So, when the two of them were well pissed, sitting together on the divan there, he said to me, I fancy your old woman, Billy, so I said, go ahead, we're all mates, aren't we, have a go, feel free, no charge, Klara means nothing to me. You can watch if you like, he says, we don't mind, do we, Klara, and I said, all right, I'll do that, then, it'll be something to do till the law gets here, won't it? Well, it cost him dear, that charver did. I meant it to. He had to take his clothes off and put his gun down to have it. He had his work cut out to get it up and all, he was that pissed. So when they were finished they both had a nice little bit of kip. I unloaded the gun and that was it, he never thought to check it again.'

'Supposing he had?' I said.

'Well, it wasn't loaded any more, was it?' he said. 'Besides, I've always got this.' The razor was out in his palm again.

'You might as well have taken the gun right off him while he was asleep,' said Foden. He paid no attention to the razor.

'Why bother?' McGruder said. 'Pointing a gun at a geezer the whole time, it's tiring. Besides, he might have tried to have a go – he was pissed enough – and then I might have shot him. Been a shame to do that – might have screwed our deal up. Anyway,' he added, 'I thought it was a right giggle to play it the way I did. You never sussed there was nothing in the gun, Pat never sussed it – nobody did. No one ever bunks up with Billy McGruder's women,' he said, his eyes empty. 'Not even when he's finished with them.'

'You could have let us off the hook a lot earlier,' I said. 'I don't like that, I don't like it at all.'

'Well, I don't like the law either,' he said. 'Besides, you're both all in one piece, aren't you, what are you moaning about?'

'Watch your mouth,' said Foden, 'or I'll take both hands and shut it for you.'

'Well, I was enjoying myself,' said McGruder, 'let's just put it that way.' He sat down with the briefcase on his knees. 'And now I'm going to enjoy myself some more,' he said, and snapped up the latches. 'Ah, isn't that lovely?' he whispered when he saw the notes. He started to count it. When he had finished he said: 'That's correct, it's all there.' He picked up a twenty-pound note, kissed it, put the note back in the case and shut it. 'Money?' he said gently. 'Best thing there is. Better than a woman, does just what you tell it and it never talks back – you can take it anywhere.'

Foden gave him the envelope with his nice new British passport in it. McGruder opened the envelope and took the passport out. 'It's like Christmas,' he said, 'isn't it?' He opened the passport. 'Angell,' he read aloud. 'Frederick William Angell, company director. Now isn't that nice! Angell, Mr Freddie Angell, life and soul of the old bistro. Yes, now that's a really nice name, that is; I can just fancy going round calling myself that.'

After a moment, though, his face darkened and he said: 'I suppose no one was being deliberate over that name, were they?'

'Well, as a matter of fact,' I said, 'yes, I was. I thought it was about time somebody else cracked a joke around here.'

Derek Raymond's
Factory Series

"No one claiming interest in literature truly written from the edge of human experience, no one wondering at the limits of the crime novel and of literature itself, can overlook these extraordinary books."
—JAMES SALLIS

He Died with His Eyes Open
978-1-935554-57-8

An unflinching yet deeply compassionate portrait of Margaret Thatcher's London—plagued by poverty and perversion—and an unnamed police Sergeant from the Unexplained Deaths department who may be the only one who cares about the "people who don't matter and who never did."

"Raymond is a master..."
—NEW YORK TIMES

The Devil's Home on Leave
978-1-935554-58-5

The unnamed Sergeant stands up to both mobsters and his superiors while engaged in a harrowing game of cat-and-mouse with a psychopath who seems to have ties to the highest levels of the British government.

"Superb ... an English Chandler."
—DAILY MAIL (LONDON)

How the Dead Live
978-1-935554-59-2

With growing desperation and enraged compassion, the nameless Sergeant fights to uncover a murderer—not by following analytical procedure, but by understanding why crimes are committed.

"Powerful and mesmerizing ... With spare, often lyrical prose, Raymond digs beneath society's civilized veneer to expose the inner rot."
—PUBLISHERS WEEKLY

I Was Dora Suarez
978-1-935554-60-8

Gentle Dora Suarez was already dying of AIDS. So why kill her? As the Sergeant digs deeper into a diary she left behind, the fourth book in the series becomes a study of human exploitation and institutional corruption, and the valiant effort to persist against it.

"Everything about I Was Dora Suarez shrieks of the joy and pain of going too far."
—MARILYN STASIO, THE NEW YORK TIMES BOOK REVIEW

Dead Man Upright
978-1-61219-062-4

In the fifth, final, and most psychologically probing book in the series—unavailable for 20 years—the nameless Sergeant attempts not to solve a crime, but to keep one from happening.

"Hellishly bleak and moving."
—NEW STATESMAN

Ⓜ MELVILLE INTERNATIONAL CRIME

Kismet
Jakob Arjouni
978-1-935554-23-3

Happy Birthday, Turk!
Jakob Arjouni
978-1-935554-20-2

More Beer
Jakob Arjouni
978-1-935554-43-1

One Man, One Murder
Jakob Arjouni
978-1-935554-54-7

The Craigslist Murders
Brenda Cullerton
978-1-61219-019-8

Death and the Penguin
Andrey Kurkov
978-1-935554-55-4

Penguin Lost
Andrey Kurkov
978-1-935554-56-1

**The Case of the
General's Thumb**
Andrey Kurkov
978-1-61219-060-0

Nairobi Heat
Mukoma Wa Ngugi
978-1-935554-64-6

Cut Throat Dog
Joshua Sobol
978-1-935554-21-9

Brenner and God
Wolf Haas
978-1-61219-113-3

He Died with His Eyes Open
Derek Raymond
978-1-935554-57-8

The Devil's Home on Leave
Derek Raymond
978-1-935554-58-5

How the Dead Live
Derek Raymond
978-1-935554-59-2

I Was Dora Suarez
Derek Raymond
978-1-935554-60-8

Dead Man Upright
Derek Raymond
978-1-61219-062-4

The Angst-Ridden Executive
Manuel Vázquez Montalbán
978-1-61219-038-9

**Murder in the Central
Committee**
Manuel Vázquez Montalbán
978-1-61219-036-5

The Buenos Aires Quintet
Manuel Vázquez Montalbán
978-1-61219-034-1

Off Side
Manuel Vázquez Montalbán
978-1-61219-115-7

Southern Seas
Manuel Vázquez Montalbán
978-1-61219-117-1